◆　◆　◆

Max looked at him over the top of her glasses, "So now tell me why you think you get so indignant when someone else criticizes black people."

Mike thought a moment. He closed his eyes and pulled at his chin, carefully considering his response. The answer, he knew, was a simple one. To him it made perfect sense. But he also realized that the words he was about to say contradicted every other word that preceded them. "You've got to consider how bad an existence blacks have had in this country. I'm not talking about that 'my-great-great-grandaddy-was-a-slave-two-hundred-years-ago' bullshit either. I'm talking about as few as thirty years ago when fat, white racist motherfuckers turned fire hoses and police dogs loose on these people. All they were trying to do is vote or protest or ride the fuckin' bus for Christ's sake." He began turning red in the face as he sat up and gestured to make his point.

"We are a country of laws and the laws are supposed to protect people. But ever since Jim Crow the law has been against blacks. If a white guy shot a black man, he got an all white jury and he walked. The only justice black people got came at the end of a truncheon stick or a billy club. And nobody gave a shit."

◆　◆　◆

Sam Morton

DISAVOWED

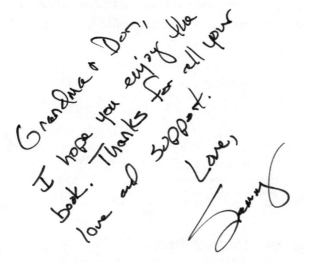

Grandma & Don,
I hope you enjoy the
book. Thanks for all your
love and support.
Love,

Copyright © 2005

Echelon Press
9735 Country Meadows Lane 1-D
Laurel, MD 20723
www.echelonpress.com

Copyright © 2005 by S. Morton
ISBN: 1-59080-445-7
Library of Congress Control Number: 2005935488

Cover Art © Nathalie Moore
2005 Arianna Best In Category Award
Editor: Kat Thompson

First Echelon Press paperback printing: April 2006

10 9 8 7 6 5 4 3 2 1

Printed in the United States of America

Dedication

Dedicated with love to Myra, Alexey, and Nikki.

Acknowledgements

To my creative family, The Inkplots Writers Group, who read and critiqued this manuscript several hundred times, I cannot thank you enough.

To my "test readers," Dave Wilson, Carla Damron, Bert Goolsby, and Kelly Hurley, thank you. I owe you each a box of red pens.

To all the strong female influences in my life from my wife and mother to my law enforcement partners and writing colleagues, thank you. To Dianne Norton for her innumerable suggestions and edits, I cherish your friendship and advice. The character of Max is dedicated in your honor and is a composite of the greatness you all possess and have shared with me.

To my editor, Kat Thompson, thank you for un-dangling my participles and for making this manuscript a more exciting read. To Karen Syed at Echelon, my heartfelt gratitude for taking a chance on *Disavowed* and on me.

To all my former colleagues at the Richland County Sheriff's Department, thank you for showing me, and daily living out, the meaning of sacrifice and dedication to justice and right.

To Mike and Cathy, all my love.

Lastly, to Mama. I wish you could have lived to see it.

Prologue

The maternity ward lies in gentle slumber, the soft breathing of newborn babies and the muted grunts of brand new tiny lives tucked and cradled and proudly displayed all in neat rows; brand new little people stretching their tiny limbs into an unexplored world. The ward is peaceful and calm. In the quiet of this night lay many families' hopes and dreams of birthdays and Christmases and graduations to come.

On one side in incubators are the preemies, those who came just a little too soon, illuminated by the soft green luminescent glow of the machinery that monitors the babies' vital signs. At the nurses' station, dressed in loose fitting, faded green scrubs and huddled over a stack of charts, the RN on duty speaks aloud, more to keep herself from drifting to sleep than for any other reason. Her elbow propped on the desk and running her hand mindlessly through her straight, shoulder-length auburn hair, her eyes drift from the nurse's notes she is transcribing onto the official chart record.

"Baby girl Seymour, jaundice treatment at 11:30... Little Mr. Barton, hemoglobin check, normal, 12:16..." on and on into the night, kept wired by two cups of hot, black coffee every hour.

She does not see him come in from the maintenance corridor, nor does she hear the quiet tread of his soft-soled shoes on the waxed tile floor as he makes his way methodically

1

into the ward. Were he to be detected, he is prepared with a story about checking a conduit for the heating and air system, but he creeps in unobserved. Sneaking past the preemies, he stops in front of baby boy Phillips, a small black child whose ebony ringlets of fine hair cling to the side of his head. His eyes shut, he looks like an angel at peace. The baby is one day from going home to an accountant father and a mother who teaches second grade. He was born into a family with an older brother, Allen, and a sister only twenty-six months older than he. He sleeps soundly having dreams that only babies have.

From beneath the zippered breast of his overalls, the intruder pulls a small white pillow purloined from an airline. Without thought or hesitation, he slips the pillow over the child's face. The baby gives a start, a small struggle as his brain becomes starved for oxygen. But the weight of the killer's hands holds him snugly in place without the slightest noise.

"The only good nigger is a dead nigger," he repeats to himself over and over in a silent mantra meant to inspire his deed. "And this is just one less we'll have to worry about later."

In less than three minutes it is over. The desires of a generation snuffed out in one senseless, violent act for the Brotherhood. White Power strikes again as it always does, under cloak of darkness, afraid to show its face, this time to steal the life of a child. Just as silently as he came, the intruder sneaks out through a back stairwell into the night. He lights a cigarette, flips the lid of the lighter closed with his thumb creating a loud, metal flicking noise that echoes down the alley. As he bounds toward his car, a sinister smile crosses his lips.

"Job well done," he says to himself out loud. "Job well done."

Chapter One

Columbia, South Carolina: alternately the hottest and the coldest place on earth. In the summer shimmering waves of heat rise up from the asphalt and concrete and reflect off the glass of the city's skyscrapers and government buildings to bake and blind commuters and pedestrians. It is a light, airy city and tucked among the skyscrapers and government buildings reside old churches and houses built from the rust-colored clay dredged from the banks of the Congaree River that defined the city's western boundary.

Just off of Gervais Street in the heart of the Congaree Vista sat a hot little joint called the Dixie Fish and Oyster Company, a fresh-fish market converted to a seafood restaurant. In the kitchen, popping grease and frying flounder intensified the god-awful July heat as Mike Chandler served up the daily special to the suits on lunch break from the houses of government. He wore the white apron that all short-order cooks wear, his T-shirt translucent with grease.

"Salt-and-pepper catfish with grits, and a flounder Po' boy, extra onions. Order up!" he shouted as he slapped the metal bell with the flat edge of a stainless steel spatula.

He sweated against the heat as the only ventilation, a huge exhaust fan near the stove, provided little comfort. He dropped another basket of hush puppies into a rectangular vat of roiling grease and rubbed his brow with the shoulder of his T-shirt.

His tender, white skin reddened against the friction drag of the fabric and the penetrating sting of perspiration. He often wondered to himself how he wound up here, a fry cook.

The one thing he wanted to be was the one thing he had always been–a cop. But he couldn't be one of those anymore.

Clint, the affable, large-bellied owner of the restaurant, poked his head around the corner of the kitchen, "Hey, Mike, some lawyer's out front wanting to talk to you. Why don't you go ahead and take your break. Try not to be too long, okay."

Mike nodded his head in acknowledgement, laid down the spatula, and wiped his hands on a grease-saturated rag tucked under his apron strings. He walked into the dining room to see Henry Stearns motioning him over to a table in a crowded corner of the smoking section. Mike let out a resigned sigh. *Great, what the hell does he want now?*

Stearns was a good lawyer. Like many he had begun his career in the local public defender's office, moving into private practice after a few years. Now he worked in one of the big, "chandelier" firms where lawyers are called attorneys and they don't go to court, they litigate.

"Mike, how's it goin' man? Have a seat," Stearns said extending his hand. "Can I buy you lunch?" As usual, Stearns was dressed impeccably. He sported a deep, seemingly perpetual tan, short salt-and-pepper hair and closely cropped beard and mustache. Perfect grooming was part of his calling card to his clients, but it had always seemed to Mike to be a bit overdone.

"You don't think I actually eat this stuff, do you?" Mike said waving the invitation off. "Besides, as you can see, it's rush hour for us and Clint said not to take too long, so you better tell me whatever you came to say."

"Okay. No problem. I have a business proposition for

you." Stearns stopped talking, waiting for Mike to take the bait, but he just stared and raised his eyebrows wanting Stearns to get on with it.

"Mike I've got a missing person I need you to look for. My clients don't think the police department is doing a very good job and they want someone to give it the attention it deserves."

"Look Henry, I appreciate the offer, but I told you last time, I'm not looking to do any detective work. I don't even have a PI's license. You and everybody else in town knows what happened and I just...to hell with it, you know," Mike said, his eyes cast down suddenly lost in thoughtful reflection. "Here I fry fish for a few hours. The worst that happens is somebody chokes on a bone or something. They bitch at Clint and get a free meal. I still get paid and go home at quitting time. No hassle, no worries, end of story." Mike lifted his hands and tilted his head with resignation. "If your client's sweet little girl has run away to be with her big burly boyfriend with the tattoos and Harley, I'm real sorry, but tell them to get on Lieutenant Rish's ass over in Missing Persons. I'm not interested."

Mike started to slide his chair out to get up, but Stearns, half out of his seat, reached across the table and grabbed him by the wrist. "Look, Mike. My clients aren't a couple of worried parents. They are a group of very wealthy investors who stand to lose a great deal of money if somebody doesn't find the guy who ran off with it. Now I know you think this pissed off, selfless martyr bullshit keeps you protected from the real world, but my clients want the best and I told them it was you. They will pay very well. So will you take the job or not?" Stearns' voice was strong and he held Mike's gaze a moment to instill in him just how resolute he was.

"Look, I've got to get back to work," Mike said after a long moment of silence. He glanced around the full dining room and saw the line of patrons waiting to be seated that had formed by the door. "How about if I meet you later this afternoon in your office?"

"Better yet, how about I buy you supper? Say Harrigan's around 7:00 o'clock."

"No promises, understand? I'm just saying I'll consider it, okay?"

"Good deal." Stearns looked relieved. "I'll see you tonight."

Harrigan's Bar and Grill was a popular restaurant among young, upwardly mobile Columbians. The tables and chairs were all made of heavy wood and were surrounded by brass railings. Reservations weren't necessary, but seats were hard to come by otherwise. Mike arrived about ten minutes early. Stearns was already there, sitting at the bar, engaged in conversation with one of the other patrons when Mike approached.

"Well, hey Mike, glad you came," Stearns said as he stood from his barstool, blowing a plume of smoke from pursed lips and crushing out the remainder of his cigarette. "Our table is ready, but do you want a drink first?"

"No, thanks. Let's just get started if it's alright with you."

Stearns paid his bar bill and motioned to the hostess who sat them in a large corner booth toward the back of the restaurant. Henry wasted no time in producing a file from his briefcase. He laid it on the table in front of him, pulled from it a newspaper article, and handed it to Mike. The headline read, "Archeology Professor Missing. Police Say Leads Sketchy."

"Did you see this in the paper the other day?" Henry asked.

Mike cocked his head to the side and squinted to see the clipping in the dim light of the restaurant. "Yeah. What about it?" Mike wasn't going to make this easy.

"Well, did you read it?"

"I glanced through it. I didn't commit it to memory if that's what you're asking," said Mike. "I take it that since you've gone to the trouble of pointing it out that this is the guy you want me to look for."

"Yes, for Christ's sake. Why do you want to make having this conversation like pulling teeth?" Stearns asked, a little irritated now.

Mike didn't reply. He looked down at the table and breathed a heavy sigh. "All right. I'm sorry, I guess it's just self-defense. After what happened I'm sort of afraid to let this stuff get too close. I guess I'm scared I'll start missing it too much and I'll want to do it full time and you and I both know that can't happen. Okay, start again. This is the man you need me to find...if I take the job?" he added, still with a cautious air.

"Yes. See my client is who actually filed the missing persons report, not the professor's family. They don't seem too concerned about him one way or the other, which is why we feel like if he's missing, it's purely by choice."

"Okay, you mentioned money, investors. What's your client's deal with this Professor, ah...Bennigan," Mike said casting a glance at the article.

"Parris Bennigan," said Stearns. "Mike, my client is an amateur historian, archeologist type. I wasn't aware of it but I think it's somewhat common knowledge for people who follow this sort of thing that just before the Civil War ended, the Confederate government tried to supplement its treasury with silver mined from the west. There's a story, which most people considered more or less a myth, that in late 1863 a load of silver left Douglas, Arizona and made it to Ware Shoals in Laurens County where a detachment of Union soldiers came across it. According to contemporary accounts, the soldiers killed the Confederate guards, stole the wagon, and buried the silver nearby, hoping to reclaim it after the war. Story goes that the Union soldiers were killed in battle a few months later, their entire regiment knocked out, and the secret of the lost silver died with them."

"I'm assuming this history lesson has something to do with your missing professor," Mike said, rolling his eyes and striking a mischievous smile.

"Yes it does, smart ass, just give me a minute," Stearns said, matching his smile. "Like I said, this story was considered pretty much a myth until last year when my client came into possession of some estate papers. Tucked in among them was a letter written in March 1864 by a Union soldier named Chapman. He wrote it from a field hospital, we assume shortly before he died of his wounds. In the letter he claims to have been one of the soldiers who hijacked the silver shipment. He asked his wife to pray for his forgiveness for killing the guards and, get this," Stearns said looking around the restaurant and lowering his voice, "he tells her the location where the silver is supposedly buried."

Mike's interest was piqued. "So, let me see if I can fill in from here. Your client contacted the professor to help him find the silver. Not wanting any interference, legal or otherwise, as to rightful ownership, your client contracts with Dr. Bennigan under the table offering him a substantial sum of money and maybe exclusive rights to publish articles in an academic journal or whatever," Mike counted the points off on his fingers as he recited them to Stearns. "Bennigan finds the silver, decides to be greedy, disappears, and now we have ourselves a little dilemma."

"They didn't make you a top grade detective for nothing did they, slick," Stearns said, laughing and reaching to slap Mike's shoulder.

"So now you want me to find your little professor and, you hope, the silver."

"You got it."

"Just out of interest, and to see if you can afford me," Mike said smiling, "how much silver are we talking about?"

Stearns considered the question for a moment and then said, "Today's market, I'd say about a million, maybe a million and a half."

Inwardly Mike was astonished, but he played his interest close to the vest, merely raising his eyebrows and giving his head a dubious toss to the side. He breathed a heavy, thoughtful breath and after a moment, said, "Alright let me see the whole file. I'll study it tonight and give you an answer tomorrow morning. Is that alright?"

"Sounds fair to me." Stearns smiled and tried to hide a self-satisfied expression by shuffling the remaining files in his briefcase.

Mike smirked and suspected that being picked for this case was not an act of benevolence, nor was it an accident. Once detective work was in your blood, you very rarely got it out and no detective, especially Mike Chandler, could turn down a case like this. Stearns knew what he was doing.

"Just out of curiosity," Mike said as he picked up his menu to examine the fare, "Why didn't Chapman's wife or any of his ancestors try to verify his story or claim the silver?"

"Good question. As near as my client can tell, the wife died pretty soon after receiving the letter and it just got lost among her personal belongings after the war. Funny, you know, it seems like everybody having anything to do with this silver has wound up dead somehow or another. Anyway," Stearns said unfolding his menu, "what are you having?"

After a heavy supper and some superficial conversation, Mike took the Bennigan file back to his apartment. He lived over a garage behind a large brick house on Saluda Street. It belonged to an elderly couple in one of Columbia's older, and well to do neighborhoods. The walk-up wasn't spacious, but Mike decided he didn't need a lot of room. He lived alone. Jenny left him shortly after what everyone, including Mike referred to euphemistically as 'The Incident'. Besides, it was about all he could afford on a fry cook's wages and what little savings he had been able to put away in the last few years

The memory of his last day at the office tortured him. Not a single day went by when he didn't relive it, changing it ever so slightly so that it came out all right. Regardless of how he ended it in his mind, reality never changed. It was almost a ritual now, all the scenes flying through his consciousness at once, no matter what he was trying to do, no matter how he tried to otherwise occupy his thoughts. The yelling, the prodding, hell bent for truth. The scream. The fall. The accusations. A career destroyed.

What took milliseconds in Mike's mind actually took place over a series of weeks. To him it seemed simultaneously to have been a lifetime ago, and yet all too recent and vivid. The thoughts nagged him, but he couldn't make them go away. He opened a beer and plopped onto the weary sagging springs of an old, overstuffed chair. He unfastened the ribbon binding Stearns' file and spread the pages out across his legs. He stared intently at the pages but he saw not a word. Mike shook his head, trying to exorcise his demons, but the nightmarish images flooded back. Had it really been that many months ago?

Chapter Two

"We gotta talk. You ain't gonna believe this," Ken McMaster, Mike's longtime partner and best friend said.

"Well good morning to you, too. What's up?"

"Jarrod Payne is what's up. This time I think we may have enough to nail his skinny little pedophile ass to the cross." Ken had a deviously sinister smile across his large, round charcoal-black face, a smile he earned the right to wear.

He and Mike had been after Payne for three long years. Payne was filthy rich and, therefore, felt privileged to exercise a strange sexual appetite for children. Boys or girls, he wasn't the least bit particular about the gender as long as he could penetrate them and sting their skin with a thin leather whip or pinch them until they screamed for death. Payne was intelligent in that he preyed on kids who were runaways, or throwaways whose families stopped caring for them long ago.

"Spill it, man. Spill it," Mike urged, taking his propped feet down from atop his desk and sliding to the edge of his chair as if the gesture would yield him this treasure of information a second faster than normal.

"Not here. Let's step into your office," Ken said referring, naturally, to the men's room.

A lot of police agencies had their detective divisions set up on the "FBI model" meaning that all the desks were arranged inside of one large room. Nobody but the captains and lieutenants had offices with doors. Mike never knew what set of large ears might be lurking around the coffeepot, so most confidential communications were conducted in the one place that resulted in the utmost privacy–the lavatory. A quick glance could tell him if someone was on the john and the resonance of low voices rolling off the tile prevented someone from easily eavesdropping outside the door.

"Remember Amber, the crack-whore from down in Springdale?" Ken asked.

"Yeah."

"It appears Mr. Payne's been supplying her for a few months. She's got about a $500-a-day habit now and she's been building up credits. She was into him for about twenty-five grand when he decided to collect. She ain't got nothing worth that much, but Jarrod was playing it pretty smart. Amber didn't know that a full-grown female coochy-pop wasn't exactly his cup of tea anyway. She found it out when Payne collected his due from the virgin anus of her five-year-old son."

"That's fucked up," Mike said, disgusted by the thought of that bastard even coming near the boy.

"I'm telling you, she's pissed and I think she'll give us his head on a platter on this *and* a dope charge if we need it."

"Okay," said Mike, looking around the room for eavesdroppers out of habit, even though he knew they were alone, "let's keep this just between us. No leaks. No advice. No coaching from the sidelines." The pace of his words accelerated. "We've done it somebody else's way the last few times and somehow it's always gotten screwed up. We won't tell anybody what's up until we go to pick him up. Agreed?"

"You got it, my friend."

Mike and Ken worked all day and through the night. Ken took down written statements from Amber and he tried as best he could to get something from TJ, the little boy. Ken, tough-looking and large, was great with kids. He was single and had no children of his own. Whenever Mike and Ken spoke to school groups or scout troops, the children seemed fascinated by the gleaming gold badges and big guns, but when the presentations were over, it was Ken they flocked to as the pair made their way to the door.

"How do you do it, man?" Mike often teased him after a speaking date.

"Do what?" said Ken

"You know what. The kids. They love you, big guy. What do you do, put off some kind of kiddie pheromone?"

"Oh." Ken laughed a big chuckle that shook his whole frame, "I guess I do. Kids aren't so bad until you get 'em in a restaurant or an airplane. Then something genetic kicks in and they have to scream as loud as they can for as long as you're near them."

Mike knew Ken should take the lead when they went to interview TJ. When Amber motioned them into the apartment, she moved her arms almost in slow motion, her demeanor mirroring what Mike assumed was her inner despair. Mike took his place out of the way in a corner. Ken took off his shoes and shifted his body onto the floor off the tattered, burnt-orange fabric of an ancient couch, which seemed as broken and hopeless as Amber.

Ken had to corral the toddler to sit close to him and hopefully keep his attention. As Mike watched the rambunctious blue-eyed child rumble about the house in his tiny blue jean overalls and striped shirt, he thought it both remarkable and sickening that someone would want to sodomize a little boy as precious as this.

This kid doesn't need this on top of everything else in his life. Mike eyed the rat-trap, subsidized apartment. The den doubled for a dirty clothes bin, at least it seemed that way to Mike who saw pants and shirts and underwear strewn from corner to corner. Grimy drinking glasses sat on either side of the couch, some empty and all having a cloudy haze on them, which meant they hadn't seen detergent or hot water in a while.

The kitchen sink overflowed with dirty plates and utensils and on the stove remained a large aluminum frying pan, caked with cold, white, gelatinous grease from hamburgers which could have been made last night or last week. A musky smell, an earthy combination of mildew and a half-dozen other odors borne of the poor and unwashed, assailed the detective's olfactory senses. It was the stench of a thousand bad memories and destitution, trapped and swirling in this tiny apartment, holding its occupants hostage with the centrifugal force of hopelessness and despair.

In the middle of it all sat Amber, a twenty-three-year-old with auburn hair. She was a girl who, had it not been for seven years of drug abuse, would have been quite attractive. Her skin had grown translucent from malnutrition and months of alternating bingeing and withdrawal. Her eyes were sunken in and while they always seemed to reflect a soul that had given up, they looked all the more hopeless now.

Maybe this will finally shake some sense into her. Then he immediately dismissed the idea as too much to wish for. *This girl's had it and the kid is probably doomed, too.*

The doctor's written report mentioned anal tearing and stretching, trauma this and hematoma that. Mike and Ken asked him to lay it out in English and he told them that, basically, TJ's anus looked like it had been through a meat grinder. This interview, they both decided, was critical.

14

Ken brought with him a pack of colored markers and some paper. He let the boy choose a color and both of them whirled away on the paper. TJ, like most five-year-olds, rambled. He talked one minute about comic books and his friends at school, and the next he spoke haltingly about the bad man who hurt his "tutu."

It was a difficult interview. Ken appeared to fight frustration at trying to keep TJ on one topic. Amber was silent except for a few muted sobs, less at what her son said than at the thought that someone could hurt her little boy.

"TJ," Ken said softly, "the man who hurt you, what was he wearing?" The child kept drawing never looking up from the paper. Ken gently placed his thumb and forefinger on TJ's chin and lifted the little boy's face to try to make eye contact. "TJ, it's important to tell me. Do you remember what the man had on?"

TJ looked at Ken as if he were the stupidest grown man in the world, accenting his glance by rolling his eyes and shrugging his shoulders. "Birfday suit," he said in a matter-of-fact tone and went back to his drawing.

"Birthday suit," Ken repeated slowly. The look on Ken's face made Mike believe he might be ruminating over something, but for the life of him, Mike couldn't imagine what. *Great. You got the kid to tell you that Payne is naked when he has sex just like 99.9% of the rest of the world. That'll stand up great in court.*

He was concentrating hard on what else Ken might ask, so hard that he almost missed TJ's soft, barely perceptible voice as he spoke without looking up from the paper, "And Mama's necklace."

Mike did a mental double take, almost having to rewind his brain the few seconds back to the boy's words. His heart stopped and his muscles tensed. The two detectives eyed each other knowingly.

"What did he just say?" Ken asked looking at Amber.

Their eyes locked and Amber didn't seem to quite know what to make of Ken McMaster at the moment. He looked as if he was ready to pounce. She appeared still locked deep into her introspective review of how she had destroyed her life and now her son's. Slowly coming out of her thoughts, she looked confused by the detective's intensity.

"What did he just say about a necklace?" Ken pressed.

Amber ran a hand through her hair and raised an eyebrow, "He said Payne had on my necklace."

Ken fired the questions. "What kind of necklace? Was it distinctive? Could you identify it?"

"Yeah. It was an engraved St. Christopher my parents gave me when I was 12. It was the only thing of theirs I didn't steal or sell before they kicked me out. I used to let TJ play with it a lot. Why? Is it important?"

Ken had already slid his massive frame back onto the couch and was tying his shoes. He was rushing as if he had slept through his alarm. "Important?" he shouted, "Fuckin' A' right it's important. Sorry kid, you didn't hear that," Ken said looking down at TJ who, still drawing, paid him no attention. Mike knew Ken was experiencing a sensation in police work that was as close to sexual arousal as anything could come–that moment when you know you have just gotten the one key piece of information that will bring down the most elusive of criminals. Mike felt the sensation coursing through his veins as well.

"Amber, my dear, TJ has just given us something to look for in a search warrant at Payne's estate. He has also just boosted his own five-year-old credibility because he's going to be able to ID that necklace in court. With that and the doctor's report, I think Mr. Jarrod Payne will be experiencing some rectal trauma of his own for the next several years."

It didn't seem to all sink in. Amber asked, "TJ will have to go to court?"

"Don't worry. We'll videotape him or something. We'll worry about that later. Just sit tight and be somewhere I can find you. Mike and I will work fast on this, okay?"

Amber nodded her head and looked at the floor, lost once again in thought.

"Take care of the little one. He can keep the markers," Ken said. Mike and his partner slipped out the door of the apartment and got into their unmarked car.

Mike and Ken called together four other detectives telling them only that they had a search warrant to execute. They wanted everything to seem completely routine. The group gathered in the parking lot of a pancake house about three miles from Payne's home at 6:15 on a Wednesday morning. The predawn sky was cluttered with cumulus clouds tinted deep purple and reddish-orange in the early morning sun. Mike went in the pancake house and bought everybody coffee as the troops rolled in.

"There's cream, sugar, and Sweet-n-Low, in the bag if anybody wants it," Mike said. "Who else we got coming?"

"Here comes Hoffman pulling in now. That's everybody," said Ken.

"Jeez, would you look at those antennas on that thing," Mike said noting the two five-foot whips attached to the bumper of David Hoffman's unmarked cruiser. "Hey Hoffman, you look like a tuna boat riding down the road with those things," Mike called out as the detective slowed to a stop and lowered the driver's window.

"Hey pal, I'm a middle-aged, balding white guy driving a solid black Crown Victoria. That ain't exactly what you call undercover now is it? This thing has police written all over it so I might as well have a great radio system in case my ass gets in a sling."

Hoffman got out of his car and began doctoring the coffee Ken handed him as the rest of the detectives gathered around the hood of Mike's car. Mike began passing out copies of the search warrant to each of the team members.

"Okay guys. On its face this looks pretty ordinary, but if you'll notice the name on this 'S and W' you will see we're going after Jarrod Payne," Mike explained.

"You guys got a pretty good case on him this time?" asked Trey Caldwell one of the younger, but extremely competent detectives.

"You bet," said Ken jumping in, "but it's crucial we find something on this search to corroborate the victim's statement. If we don't, all we got is the rambling story of a five-year-old with a short attention span."

Mike continued, " Ken's right. Look for anything of a sexual nature. I don't care if it's perverted or not. Videos, magazines, sex toys, restraints, anything. We're also looking for a St. Christopher necklace engraved with the letters 'AVD'." Mike puffed his chest and said in a mock smug tone, " I hope you guys appreciate the fact that Ken and I have given you an item to search for which can easily be stored in a very small container. That, of course, makes everything fair territory—drawers, closets, brief cases, gym bags–anything."

"All right," Mike said, the caffeine boosting his already surging adrenaline into overdrive, "let's do it. Ken and I will go to the front. Drew, you and Eric take the back door. David, why don't you and Ed stay out in the tuna boat on the perimeter until we're inside just in case sweet britches decides to make a run for it. We'll radio you once we're in and you can come join the fun."

"Sounds good to me," Hoffman said. "Can I ram the SOB if he tries to run?"

"Suits us fine," said Ken, "Just make sure one of those antennas doesn't sling forward and whip him to death before we're able to get a statement from him. Let's go."

The six detectives piled into three cars and drove off in single file to the Payne estate. Mike looked back at the parade of cars. He smiled to himself, thinking that police cruisers, their trunks loaded down with every conceivable kind of emergency equipment, made an unmistakable undulating motion. They threw up a distinctive dust pattern as they trudged down dusty, rural Southern roads. The profile of an unmarked police car heading to a call in the glare of the sun created an ambience all its own. Mike knew it and so did all the other Southern boy cops along for the ride that day. It was all part and parcel of what made this job better than any other in the world.

No matter how many times Mike did this sort of thing, the power of the badge never ceased to amaze him. Jarrod Payne certainly deserved what he was about to get, yet he, like the hundreds of other people who lived in the houses Mike had searched, had no idea what was about to happen to him, how his life was about to change. Payne's house was about to be invaded by an armed force. He, most likely at this hour, was still asleep. Most definitely he hadn't a single clue how his life was about to change. Mike Chandler and Ken McMaster had known for hours.

It was 6:42 A.M. Hoffman and Ed Livingston pulled off

the road beside the mailbox while the other two cars turned onto the winding, pebble drive. A granite colored French provincial house stood a half-mile off the highway. As the cars rolled to a stop, Starnes and Caldwell ran for the back lawn. Mike and Ken walked hurriedly up the front steps.

"You ready, partner?" Ken asked looking intently at his friend.

"Let me answer that question with a question, sir. Shall we knock, ring the bell, or just kick the fuckin' door in?"

"Oh, door kicking is awfully gauche in this neighborhood. Let's ring up the butler and be announced, shall we?" said Ken, answering Mike's playful tone.

"Oh, let's do!" With that Mike balled his fist, reached back as far as he could, and pounded on the door four times, nearly splintering the wood. "POLICE! SEARCH WARRANT. OPEN THE DOOR NOW!"

He could hear dogs begin to bark, but he heard no movement nor saw any light come from the inside of the house. Mike then repeatedly rang the doorbell and then he heard heavy footsteps coming down the hall.

Payne opened the door slowly and deliberately. He eyed the two cops and dragged his hand from his forehead down and across the stubble on his unshaven face. A small medallion hung from a thick, gold herringbone chain that was entangled in the dense tufts of black chest hair visible in the "V" of a plush light blue bathrobe.

"For Christ's sake Chandler, it's barely sunrise. What the hell do you two want?"

"We've got a search warrant for your house, Payne," Mike said as he and Ken pushed their way inside before he had a chance to close the door on them. "You better tell us now if anyone else is here, house guests, maids, butlers, people who wipe your butt for you, whoever."

"Fuck you, asshole. You ain't looking for shit till I call my lawyer."

"Wrong again, pal," McMaster chimed in, waving the warrant inches from Payne's face, "This piece of paper gives us complete control of the house and everything in it including the phones. You're not gonna call anybody. Besides, you're not entitled to a lawyer until we interrogate you and that, my friend won't be until we get downtown. Now answer my partner's question. Is there anyone else here?"

"No," Payne said, breathing a resigned sigh, "Just me."

McMaster accompanied Payne into the living room of the opulent house while Mike radioed for the other detectives to join them inside.

"All right, Mr. Payne. We obtained a warrant based on a complaint that we received that you've had sexual intercourse with a child," McMaster began to explain.

"What the hell are you talking about?" Payne exploded, rising from the couch, outstretching his arms. "This is bullshit and you know it!"

"Look," Mike shouted, pointing his finger in Payne's face, "if you want to know why we're here and what we're looking for, you better sit down and shut up. Now as my partner here was saying, we've got a complaint and we're here to look for any evidence of the crime. So, this is your chance, pal. If you got any kinky little sex toys, whips, chains, videos, kiddie porn, or whatever, you can tell us where it is and we'll simply go get it. Otherwise, we'll tear this fuckin' house apart brick by brick."

"You can't do that," Payne shouted.

Every detective in the room turned toward each other, chins tilted down, gazes to the ceiling in the same, and "Oh you just watch me" expression. McMaster turned back to Payne and said, "Mr. Payne, we're going to begin our search now. You can either stay here with a detective or you can accompany us through each room, but we're going to execute this warrant."

"Oh, you can bet I'm going with you. Me, a pen, and a piece of paper so I can write down everything you touch. I'm telling you, you motherfuckers even look too hard at something in this house and I think it's damaged, I'm gonna sue. You'll be working the rest of your redneck, cornball lives to pay it off."

The detectives started in the most obvious places. Each team of two began searching the bedrooms. They pulled out drawers, looked through closets, and rummaged through dirty clothesbaskets. For two hours they searched. David Hoffman began recording the items they seized on the return of the warrant.

As the search concluded, Hoffman approached Mike, "Hey, Mike. There's not a whole lot here. I mean, a couple of X-rated videos and some magazines. Damn, half the guys at the office have this kind of stuff laying around the house."

"Yeah, this isn't good. He's got to have it somewhere. Maybe it's just not at this house. I don't know. Anyway, you guys wrap it up here. Kenny and I will take him downtown. Given what we didn't find, I'd say this interview is crucial."

"Good luck, man," Hoffman replied. "If we find the mother lode of pervert porn I'll let you know."

During the ride down to the police station, neither McMaster, who was driving, nor Mike said a word to Payne who was cuffed and stuffed into the rear seat of the smallish Ford Taurus. The bumpy road jolted the car's worn shocks, but at last, McMaster made a right hand turn into the parking lot of the John Thornton Law Enforcement Complex. He pulled around back to the detectives' entrance.

Mike opened the back door and put his hand around Payne's right bicep, resisting the urge to jerk him out of the back of the car. He uttered the obligatory, "Watch your head," and walked Payne through the back door while Ken parked the car.

The hallway, already narrow, was constricted further by shelves on one side holding the leaves of paper that eventually became the mountains of documentation associated with a detective's final product, the case file. The pair barely drew a glance from the others in the large squad room at the end of the hallway. Detectives scurried about, phones rang noisily, the administrative staff clacked away at their keyboards, and a chorus of voices blended somewhere near the ceiling to form an unintelligible rumble.

Mike led Payne to an empty conference room. He flicked on the lights, moved behind Payne, and stooped slightly to unlock and remove the handcuffs. Payne rubbed the circulation back into his wrists and Mike motioned for him to sit down on one side of the table.

"Mr. Payne, it's my duty to inform you at this time that you are under arrest for Criminal Sexual Conduct with a Minor. Before we proceed with any interview, I'm obligated to advise you of your constitutional rights," Mike said mechanically.

"I know what my rights are, asshole," Payne replied. As he uttered the words, Ken McMaster slipped though the conference room door and quietly closed it behind him.

"I have to read them to you anyway," Mike said in a raised voice. "You have the right to remain silent. Anything you say can be used against you in court. You have the right to speak with a lawyer and to have a lawyer with you during any questioning. If you cannot afford a lawyer, one will be appointed for you, if you wish. If you give up the right to remain silent, you may stop talking at any time. Do you understand these rights as I have explained them to you?"

Payne said nothing.

"Mr. Payne," McMaster said, "Chandler asked if you understood your rights."

Payne shot a sideways glance at the detective. "I ain't saying shit till I get my attorney."

"Well that's just fine, Payne," Mike said, bending down within inches of the suspect's face, "You want an attorney, I guess you'll get an attorney, but let me tell you something, Ace. You're looking at thirty years on this one charge and if we walk out this room right now, with nothing resolved, then I'm gonna look for more kids and more charges."

"We might even be able to find the two kids from last time you were in here to see if they still want to recant their stories in light of your current situation." Mike stood up straight, looked him up and down, and spat out his words. "We'll pack it so far up your ass you won't see daylight again for the rest of your life. What do you think of that?"

Payne's face reddened. He sat stiffly in the chair, resting on the first inch of the cushion. He looked at the detective with disgust and said, "Fuck you, Chandler. You know I don't like kids. I prefer paying for sex from ugly fat women, like your mother! What do *you* think of that, motherfucker?"

Mike leaned over the table. He was on his tiptoes and his nose was a fraction of an inch from Payne's face, "I think if I'm a motherfucker, I've just found my long lost brother."

McMaster placed his hand on Mike's shoulder. He leaned toward his ear and whispered, "Why don't you go get us all some coffee and let me take a shot at him?"

Mike neither replied nor looked at his partner. He straightened up, stared at Payne, and then turned toward the door. As he walked out of the conference room, a host of detectives stood nearby, all having had their ears pressed to the door. As Caldwell and Starnes returned from the search warrant, word had spread quickly about who was being interviewed behind the closed door.

"Don't you guys have work to do," Mike asked, walking past them as they parted to let him through.

"Sounds pretty intense in there, Mikey," said one of the listeners.

"Phil," Mike said with an incredulous expression as he stopped and spun on his heel to address the young detective, "You've been doing this, what, two years?"

"Yeah, about."

"Well, maybe it's over your–ah hell, it's definitely over your head–but once upon a time there was a guy named Pavlov whose whole life's work was on something called conditioned response. See, you can't beg a guy like Payne to give himself up. You've got to prod him a little, make him angry enough so that he just spits it out, 'Yeah I'm a piece of shit and I fuck little kids.' It's an act, get it?" Mike said, his arms spread welcoming a response.

"Sure, Mike. Thanks for the psychology lesson, too," the detective said with mock adoration.

"Hey, kid, you're sitting at the feet of the master." Mike winked as he walked toward the coffeepot.

After filling a Styrofoam cup with strong, but tepid, black coffee that had been sitting in the pot far too long, Mike walked over to the two-way mirror and observed Ken back in the conference room taking his soothing, nice guy approach with their suspect. With his arms folded, Ken sat on one end of the table directly over Jarrod Payne.

"Look Mr. Payne, I know you don't particularly like my partner, or me for that matter, but he's straight up about this warrant. Right now we've got you charged with one count of CSC with a Minor. One count. And this is your chance to tell us your side of the story. See, an attorney will come in here and he'll advise you not to make any statement whatsoever. Now this kid may be lying. His mother might be some pissed off hooker who you stiffed out of her blowjob money one night and she sees a chance to get even with your rich ass. But if you don't give us some kind of statement, then we only have the kid's side of the story. If that's all we've got to go on, then we have no choice but to lodge you in the jail and ask for a high bond."

"Who is this kid?" Payne asked.

"I'm afraid I can't tell you that right now," McMaster said.

"Oh, so you want me to sit here and say I did something I didn't do, but you aren't even going to tell me who's making the accusation. Your asshole partner rattled off those constitutional rights. How about the one where I get to face my accuser?"

"You'll get to do that in court, Payne. Right now you're in a police station not a courtroom and this is an investigation, not a trial. All Chandler and I are doing is giving you a chance to set the record straight."

Mike eased back into the room. McMaster glanced around at him and continued his sentence, "If you're not guilty, we'll work just as hard to prove that as we will if you are."

"And you know you're guilty, Payne," Mike interjected. "And this moment, we're your father confessors. You're bought and paid for and there's nobody within a hundred miles who can help you right now except for my partner and me."

"And we won't be able to do that if you don't help us by giving us your side of the story," McMaster added.

Payne fell silent. He put his hands together as if he were saying a prayer. He stared straight ahead, thoughtful. Then suddenly, he cut a hateful, contemptuous glance at both the detectives.

"Fuck you," he shouted.

Both detectives stared at him. Payne stood from the chair, put his hands on his waist, and paced.

"Sit down," Mike yelled.

"I'll sit down when I'm good and fucking ready! But first let me tell you and your stupid nigger partner here that I'm not falling for that 'good-cop-bad-cop-TV' horseshit. You don't have anything on me or you wouldn't be trying so hard, so get this through your thick fucking skulls, I ain't *done* shit, you ain't *got* shit, and I ain't *saying* shit. So take me to jail, if that's what you're going to do." With that he did sit. He crossed his arms and put his feet up on the table, looking at the detectives with righteous indignation.

Mike shoved his feet off the table. "It's your choice, Payne. But you know what? We *are* going to put you in jail. As a matter of fact, I know some people down at the lock-up pretty well. I might see if I can't arrange to have you put in a cell with some big fucker who's got a dick three times bigger than my arm. Word about you ought to spread quick. Poor, little rich white boy. You know, even killers don't like child molesters, unless they have them bent over the bottom rail of their bunk!"

Payne's eyes widened. Mike surmised he was feeling both anger and dread. His entire body language suggested he wanted to reach out and strangle Mike. He could almost see Payne's fingers tense and curl as if he were actually clamping

27

his hands around the detective's windpipe.

But Mike knew who was in control. He and Ken had booked Payne once before on drunk driving charges, the only thing they could make stick after one of their disastrous attempts to prove he was a drug distributor and child molester. On purpose, Payne had been placed in a holding tank that was damp and cold. Its gray cinder block walls were slimy and the place smelled of cigarette smoke, sweat, and urine. He shared the room with sixteen other men who had been detained on everything from drunk and disorderly to armed robbery. The men were nasty and the guttural sounds of their snoring reverberated off the tile floor and concrete walls. He only stayed there for eight hours before his father's lawyer bailed him out, but from the vociferous and numerous complaints Payne made, Mike knew he hated the entire experience and the memory of it probably now made him want to throw up.

"Look, Chandler. I know you want to get your rocks off by putting me in a cell with one of your old lovers." A stuttering, nervous laughter followed his words. "But if you'll let me have the phone call I'm entitled to, I think my attorney can arrange to have me released from here," he said trying to regain his composure and a little leverage.

Mike and McMaster looked at each other shaking their heads bemusedly, "There you go again, with that TV cop show crap. Payne, maybe you didn't understand me the first time, but I'll explain it again just for you because we're so close. You have exactly two rights–the right to remain silent and the right to have an attorney. Everything else is a privilege. Maybe if you'd paid a little more attention in civics class you'd realize that you get to make phone calls, and you get as many as you want by the way, *after* you're booked in the pokey. Now, step this way so we can go downstairs to have your fingerprints and photo done."

Payne stood at the detectives' direction, turned with his hands behind his back as he was handcuffed. Again he was wordless. Mike smiled to himself. Payne's outward silence probably meant that on the inside he was churning. He decided to stir the pot a little more. As he led Payne toward the stairwell to the basement, Mike leaned toward his ear, sneered, and said, "Those guys in jail will tear you apart, literally. You'll be lucky to get out alive." He felt Payne's posture stiffen and saw his eyes shift from right to left. He wondered what sorts of horrors were invading the pervert's brain now. McMaster shot Mike an annoyed glance as if to say, "Don't push it."

They were three steps away from the top of the stairs. A secretary called to Ken McMaster. He had a call waiting. It sounded important, she said, so he broke away toward the phone.

As they approached the first step, Mike looked around at his prisoner, smiled his trademark smart-assed grin, and said, "Tell me, Payne, have you ever put your dick in a full grown woman you didn't have to blow up?"

The man's eyes narrowed and he glared at Mike with all the hatred he seemed capable of mustering. "I might be going to hell," he said in a low growl, "but I'm taking you with me." With that, Payne lowered his head and charged the detective like a bull. He left his feet and his forehead hit Mike, a glancing blow off of the detective's left shoulder. Mike's knees buckled, but the angle of the strike pushed his body against the wall of the stairwell, the rail pressed against his sternum.

Payne's momentum pushed him forward out of Mike's reach. He tumbled down the twenty-one concrete steps, rolling backward like a gymnast, except that his cuffed hands prevented him from controlling the fall. The back of his head smashed against the leading edge of each of the steps. He screamed in pain, as his skull fractured more and more with each blow.

Mike tried to reach out but Payne was falling too fast. Everything seemed like it moved in slow motion. He yelled for help. "He's falling! He's falling!" was all he could say. The thick case file fell from his hand and scattered when Payne's head hit him. Leaves of loose paper floated in the air like feathers, coming to rest on the treads of the stairs. Then everything stopped.

Payne's body lay on a landing just three steps from the basement. He was face down, his hands abraded, purple, and stiffened, were still clamped behind him. His face and neck were cocked at a painfully odd angle and a rivulet of blood trickled from the corner of his lips. His eyes were wide open. The hair on the back of his head was saturated with dark red, oxygenated blood. High impact, red spatters marked the direction and velocity of his fall.

Detectives rushed from both the basement and the first floor. A couple stopped to help Mike, but he broke free and hastened down the steps. The command to call an ambulance was yelled repeatedly the first few seconds.

Sergeant Richard Brennan from the forensics lab was the first one to get to Payne. "Get those cuffs off of him," he yelled to the detective on the landing directly above.

"Sir, can you speak? Can you tell me what happened," Brennan asked trying to get some response.

Payne slowly moved his eyes to lock his death stare onto the sergeant. In a voice rasping with air and gurgling with blood and spit, he whispered, "Chandler pushed me."

He closed his eyes.

A lab detective behind Brennan yelled into an office, "Is the ambulance on its way?"

Brennan had his fingers on Payne's carotid artery. He didn't wait for a response. He gave Mike a look both intense and accusatory as he began tearing Payne's blood soaked shirt away from his chest. "Call 'em back and tell them to step on it. This guy's going fast," he shouted as he began CPR.

Sam Morton

Chapter Three

Payne was dead before he reached the emergency room. Mike had wanted to accompany him in the ambulance, but a horde of hands and more reasonable heads dissuaded him. Now it seemed all the better.

His captain's words plowed and ripped their way through Mike's head like a migraine. "Payne's dead." As the captain looked at Mike, rivers of disappointment flowed behind his eyes.

Mike sat on the top of a conference table, his feet in a chair. He sat motionless with his head in his hands, the tips of his fingers massaging each temple. He had rolled up the sleeves of his blue oxford button-down shirt, loosened his tie, and unbuttoned his collar. Every moment or so he would inhale deeply and think to himself, "Jesus Christ what did I do wrong? What did I do?"

Ken sat in a chair close to his partner, looking up at him sympathetically. He felt like he should say something, but he didn't. He and Mike had known each other long enough to communicate without words. When Ken heard the screams, he dropped the phone and came running. He assisted in getting Payne into the ambulance. When things calmed down a bit, his eyes met Mike's for the briefest of instants. Ken knew at once his partner was in great pain and Mike knew in the same moment that his friend would do anything in the world Mike asked of him, but Ken was powerless to help.

Captain Dave Perotti paced angrily in front of the two detectives. He, too, had his shirtsleeves rolled up and his brown polyester pants swished with each stride. He placed the thumb and forefinger of his right hand on his forehead while he walked as if the action might make this disastrous scenario somehow plausible.

"All right, suppose one of you tell me why one of the richest guys in the whole city was in this police station being interrogated without my knowledge in the first place," the captain demanded.

"We thought we had enough to nail him this time. Given our past experience, we just didn't want to take the chance of any leaks, Captain," McMaster said. Mike realized his partner was trying to give him some breathing room and enough time to compose himself.

"*Thought* you had enough to nail him? *Thought* you had enough? You don't bring somebody like Payne in here because you *think* you've got enough. You better damn well know it. In this kind of case, if you can't sink the ship with the first shot, you better not fire the torpedo. Am I making sense to you? And this leak crap, that just plain pisses me off! It's bullshit. You guys didn't have a case so you decided to be cowboys and circumvent the whole system so somebody with some sense around this place wouldn't have the chance to tell you to slow down. Thanks for your confidence in my leadership ability, boys," the captain said venomously.

"It was my call Captain," Mike said defensively without breaking his straight-ahead stare. "Every time in the past three years we've gotten anywhere close to making a case on Payne, he's either bought off the witnesses, or the evidence our informants describe in such great detail somehow seems to disappear before we get there. We didn't want that to happen this time."

"Okay, smart guy, tell me what fabulously incriminating things you found at his estate today," Perotti said, his chest bowed out and his hands on his hips.

"Nothing," came the muted reply.

"Right, not a goddamn thing! And now the Chief has to explain to our many friends in the press how Jarrod Payne ended up dead at the bottom of a flight of stairs in our office while in our custody," Perotti said.

Mike winced and grew faint. His face flushed and he had no answers to give his captain.

"I'm sorry, Mike, but I don't have any choice right now, but to place you on administrative suspension until Internal Affairs does its thing. I'm afraid I have to ask you for your gun and credentials."

Mike slowly pulled the gun and holster from his waistband. The badge holder clicked as he snapped it off of his belt. Defeated, he handed the symbols of his authority over to his boss. To most people on the force, the badge and gun were just decorative accouterments to their wardrobe. They gave as much thought to wearing them as they did to wearing their watches and rings.

But Mike Chandler was not like most cops. His dressing was a sacred, daily ritual to him. First he tied his necktie to make himself look like a professional. Then he slipped the lip of the black leather holster over his belt and adjusted it to his hip. The gun represented the awesome power he, as a law enforcement officer, wielded–the power, if absolutely necessary, to deny life. Finally, he clipped on his badge, the instrument that gave him the jurisdiction to exercise that power. Behind this thin, gold piece of metal was the consent of three hundred thousand people, who each day gave their tacit approval for Mike Chandler to enforce the law. He never forgot that. He wore that badge reverently, vowing never to dishonor it or the people it represented. Yet at this moment, he felt too unworthy to even look at it as he passed it to his captain.

McMaster started removing his badge as well, but Perotti stopped him. "You were on the phone when this happened, so I can salvage you for some work. Look, I know it's difficult right now, but before you leave, I want detailed written statements from you both, from the time you got the tip on this guy up through today. And for appearances sake, McMaster, why don't you go to another room to write yours. Both of you know I'll stand behind you. And you know if I think you screwed up, I'll tell you that, too. Right now it doesn't look good, but give me the straight poop in those statements and I'll do what I can." Perotti left the room and closed the door behind him.

"You gonna be okay, partner?" McMaster asked.

"Yeah, I guess so. The guy did it to himself, Kenny. I didn't push him…"

"I know you didn't, Mike."

"…he even tried to take me with him. Surely IA will see that, won't they?"

"Let's hope so, partner. Let's hope so," McMaster said as he picked up a statement form and headed for the door.

For three weeks, each time he dreamed it, the nightmare was the same. The judge was a craggy old Englishman with a white powdered wig and flowing, black satin robe, a hooknose and crooked, accusatory finger. The judge's voice reverberated the litany of punishment in a cavernous courtroom, lined in foreboding mahogany.

Sometimes Jennifer shook him awake. He would be soaked through with sweat and nearly hyperventilating, his hands clawing at his neck to remove the ghostly hangman's noose, which a second earlier had seemed absolute.

"For God's sake, Mike, you've got to get over this. You're going to drive yourself crazy and me along with you if you don't get some sleep," she'd say.

She didn't seem to mind the attention it drew, the sympathetic nods, the offers to do whatever people could, the "how are you two holding up" inquiries. Jennifer played well the martyred girlfriend of the misunderstood, persecuted public servant, but she did appear to mind having to put up with the realities of the invasive public scrutiny.

Mike would roll over and try to close his eyes, but his waking moments were consumed with the real vision of Payne's deadly tumble down the stairs. He found no solace in the night, only the horrible specter of what was and what might result from it.

Days were no better. In his view, the sun merely cast a light of exposure on him. In the mall, at the grocery, on the street, he felt watched and stared at. He felt tainted and impure. Time had lost its meaning to him as a unit of measure. It served only to denote what periods were more torturous on his psyche than others.

It was, therefore, as if the gods had decided to smile on him when he got the call from Sgt. Larry Davis, Internal Affairs.

"Mike, we've completed our investigation. I'd like to lay it out for you. Can we meet say, tomorrow at 11:00 on the third floor conference room at the courthouse."

"Sure, Larry. You want to do it at the courthouse? Not your office?"

"Yeah. Fewer interruptions that way. We can talk as long as we want without any distractions."

"I don't suppose you can give me a heads up, huh?" Mike asked.

"No, not really. I've just got one more thing to clarify with you. Basically, depending on how you want to approach this thing, I think you'll be satisfied with the outcome, but I'd really like to wait till tomorrow."

"Okay. See you at 11:00 sharp." Mike hung up the phone. He went into his garage, removed a pair of pruning shears, and set off for Jennifer's rose garden. He whistled as he clipped the extended rogue canes and inspected the underside of the leaves for aphids and spots. He worked in the yard for hours and that evening, for the first night in the last eighteen, he slept soundly.

Mike was waiting at the door of the darkened conference room by 10:35. Davis walked up precisely at 11:00, a Styrofoam cup of coffee and car keys in his left hand and an armload of thick accordion binders tucked under his right armpit. He set the files down in a chair, then unlocked the conference room and switched on fluorescent lights that flickered to life on the ceiling. He shook Mike's hand and motioned for him to sit. Davis removed the navy pin stripe suit jacket and draped it across the back of the chair opposite Mike.

What a prick. He knows this is killing me and he's making me wait–an exercise in control.

Davis checked the hallway and shut the door, twisting the cylinder into the locked position. "Well, let's get down to business," he said as he pulled separate but identical folders from one of the binders.

"Mike, here's the bottom line. Each of these case files has the exact same factual information in them. The only difference between the two is the recommendation page in the back which suggests which, if any, disciplinary actions Internal Affairs feels is necessary."

Mike felt as if he were being reeled in. "I see," he said, trying not to reveal any emotion.

Davis continued, "Let's just cut to the chase. You screwed up. You brought in a prominent citizen on flimsy charges, a guy who had slipped through the system before. To the public it appears that you had some sort of vendetta, and to make things worse, Payne winds up dead while you're processing him. This is bad press that the chief doesn't need, so we're going to minimize the damage to him and the department as much as possible."

Mike felt the hammer begin to fall. "So just how does Internal Affairs plan to, ah...minimize this alleged damage?"

"As I told you over the phone, depending on how you wish to approach this...here's the deal," Davis said holding up one of the files. "You sign this form taking full responsibility and resign. On the form you agree never to pursue another job in law enforcement anywhere. The recommendation page reveals that you are guilty basically of extremely bad judgment, that you're a 'rogue' cop who can't be trusted anymore. A statement will be issued to the press to that effect. We'll make some administrative or policy changes to ensure nothing like this ever happens again, you know, for show essentially. You walk out the door, no criminal charges and that's that."

"That's that, my ass!" Mike said. "My career is over, my reputation is destroyed. Uh-uh, no way, pal."

"Or," Davis continued, nonplused, "you don't sign the form and we send up this folder," he said holding up the second file. "This one holds you criminally negligent. We'll recommend that McMaster gets fired, and Captain Perotti demoted and transferred. All the detectives who were involved in that search warrant at Payne's house will be suspended for two weeks without pay, and you, my friend...this file will be forwarded to the Grand Jury and we recommend that you be indicted for manslaughter."

"Are you deaf, asshole?" Mike was screaming now, "I said no fucking way! McMaster's informant will back us up. Payne was dirty and I ain't giving up twelve years for a piece of filth like him."

"You'll never find...or should I say, the informant appears to have left town. IA couldn't find her. Her apartment has been abandoned and no one knows where she is."

"And I suppose all her statements she gave us have just vanished from the case file," Mike yelled red-faced and trembling.

Davis sat back and intertwined his fingers in his lap, a Cheshire-like grin blossoming on his face. "Every one of her statements was lost. Must've happened during all the confusion after the fall. You and McMaster really ought to have kept a neater case file, Mike."

Mike felt the hammer strike home, right between his eyes. Every muscle and organ in his body felt weighted by lead. "How did you guys get her to disappear?"

"Watch your mouth, Chandler." Davis leaned forward, blustered, and hostile, "you're in no position to accuse or to negotiate. So tell me right now what you want to do."

"Let me think about it. I'll have to get back to you," Mike said softly, defeated.

"Bullshit, you'll get back to me on it. Do I look stupid enough to let you walk out of here knowing the next time I see you you'll have a microphone on every part of your body that'll hold tape? You tell me right now, or we go with the indictment file."

Mike tried to think for a moment, but he felt dizzy, like he could throw up. He was backed into a corner and could think of no way out.

"If I sign this, you'll leave Ken and the others alone right?" he asked, almost begging.

"Guaranteed," Davis said, relaxing his posture. "And, by the way, if you change your mind, remember the indictment file will always be close by."

Mike's hands shook as he picked up Davis's pen from the conference table. He studied the form, staring through it mostly, letting the thoughts whirl through his brain. He sighed heavily and asked, not looking at Davis, "Where do I sign?"

For many, those who have enough money or those who are too young to care, the therapy for suffering a crushing defeat is a journey, both spiritual and geographic, to "find" oneself. For Mike Chandler, this voyage turned out to be purely introspective. The paper and television stations treated his dismissal with appropriate flair.

"A spokesperson for the police department described the incident as isolated, the actions of one overzealous officer who was terminated this morning. A lawyer for the Payne family refused comment," droned a local news anchor.

An editorial in *The State* simultaneously congratulated the police chief for his decisive action, while questioning the selection process for officers. Mike's defense to the fray was isolation.

He didn't tell Jennifer about the details of his meeting with Davis. Jennifer was most certainly not the type of woman to take things quietly, particularly what he felt to be extortion. Had she known, she would have raised hell all the way from the chief to the mayor and Mike couldn't risk that.

"It was just the honorable thing to do, Jen. I was in charge. Payne was in my custody. Ultimately I was responsible."

"But you could have *fought,* Michael, for God's sake. We could've hired a lawyer. We could have done a hundred things but you just rolled over and played dead. Dammit, I don't understand you sometimes." Jennifer's words came out almost breathlessly she was so angry.

He couldn't remember how many times they had had this conversation. Each time Jennifer tried to get answers from him, he withdrew further. Mike felt like she thought he was a coward.

"I really am trying to understand, Michael, but how can I if you won't talk to me?"

"I'm sorry if I'm not giving you the answers you want to hear, but I don't have anything left to say that I haven't said already."

"We don't do anything anymore. You've become a recluse from the world by hiding out in this house and you've become a recluse from me by being in every room in this house except the one I'm in," Jennifer said.

"That's because every time I come into the room, you start in on me about what's wrong. You're like a freakin' reporter without a camera and a bright light. You want to know what's wrong? Okay, for the millionth goddamn time, I lost my job, my career, and all my credibility. I was the good guy and I got screwed. I'm embarrassed to go out in public. I'm too ashamed to be around our friends. Bottom line. End of story."

"Well you shouldn't be," Jennifer intoned with a beleaguered smile that Mike took to be patronizing.

"Thank you very much, Doctor Sunshine. Why is it when you have problems, I walk around here on eggshells? You can scream, yell, slam doors, and break all kinds of things and I'm just supposed to let it go. I'm depressed. I'm moping. Yeah, because of me we've canceled out on a cookout or two, I'll grant you that. If I'm putting a dent in your social calendar, excuse the fuck out of me, but I think I'm entitled, so just leave me alone," Mike fumed.

"That's it then?" Jennifer asked.

"That's it." He looked away, lifting his foot and reaching down to brush imaginary dirt and dust off his shoe. "Just let me get back on my feet somehow. I'll be okay," Mike said.

Over the next few weeks, they rarely spoke at all. Idle conversation ceased, lovemaking was nonexistent. The more each of them drew inwardly, the more they grew apart as a couple.

Jennifer spent more time at her office, coming home just in time to go to bed and get up again for work. Mike spent endless hours working around the house. Sporadically, he made discreet inquiries about jobs. "Something without a lot of contact with the public," he would insist. There were no takers.

Every once in a while, neighbors would bump into Jennifer in the market or out shopping. "We're holding up okay," was her reply to the obvious questions as the tears welled up in her eyes. Mike concluded she, in her mind, became as much a victim as he was.

Mike knew she opened up to her closest friends. He had overheard a telephone conversation when he came in from the garage early one evening before supper. "Mike just pisses me off. I'm doing everything I can to keep our relationship together and he's doing all he can to drag it down. I'm paying all the bills, taking all the phone calls, and making excuses to everybody who wants to see him or talk to him. It was just a job for Christ's sake. I don't understand why he doesn't go to a smaller department or something, but every time I bring it up, or even try to be supportive, he takes my head off. Well I got news for him. If he doesn't get his butt off his shoulders pretty soon, I'm out of there. Life's too short to spend it with someone pathetic and pitiful." He was crushed at her words. But he could offer no defense.

The break-up wasn't without pain or without thought; it was simply without expressed emotion. After weeks of silence and isolation, neither Mike nor Jennifer thought it was necessary.

"Mike," Jennifer said unceremoniously, "this obviously isn't working. I can't take it anymore. You're moping around, not even trying to get work and you either can't or won't let me help. I can't carry this alone, so if you're not going to let me in... I'm going to leave. I just don't feel like I have a choice." She looked sad, but she wasn't crying.

Mike stared at her in silence. He wished he could care, but he couldn't. *She can't carry the load. She can't bear the burden. When the hell could she carry a burden of any kind? Go ahead. Get out. I don't need you. Never have.*

"I'll be at O'Kelly's," Mike said, reaching for his windbreaker. "Take whatever you want out of here. Shit, if you want to come back tomorrow with a truck and your brother, you can unload the whole freakin' place. I don't care. Just lock the door when you leave and have a nice life," Mike said as he slammed the door on his way out.

Jennifer snatched the door open and pleaded, "If you'll just talk to me... Mike...godammit. Mike!"

Mike didn't turn to look at her. He merely put his hand up to indicate he wasn't going to listen. Then he turned the corner toward O'Kelly's pub and walked out of sight.

The memory pricked at his heart and made his stomach feel as if a boxer had punched him. That was the last thought he had of Jennifer, of anything resembling a normal life, though it was plagued with frustration.

Mike rubbed his temples and shook his head to rid his mind of the thoughts as he opened for the third time that night the file Stearns had given him on the missing professor Bennigan.

Sam Morton

Chapter Four

"Henry," Mike said into the telephone receiver, "this is Chandler. I'll take the case. I'll need $5,000 plus expenses."

"Great, Mike. What changed your mind? The thrill of the hunt, perhaps?" asked Stearns.

"Henry, you read too much. What changed my mind is knowing that this was important enough for you to pay $5,000 plus expenses. How's that?" Mike gave a throaty laugh.

Actually, Mike had already partially solved the case. He knew that people tend to stick with old habits. He called the university posing as a reporter and told them he was working on an article on the professor's disappearance. He spent several minutes on the phone with Bennigan's colleagues who never once questioned his credentials.

"Does Dr. Bennigan have any relatives whom I might contact?" he asked the secretary in the College of Archeology.

"Why, yes. He has a sister in Groton, Connecticut. Would you like me to give you that number?" was the reply.

"That would be nice," Mike said. "It'll add a little more human interest angle to the story," he added carrying on with his ruse.

With the sister's phone number in hand, Mike called a contact at the phone company, an executive he'd helped avoid a drunk driving ticket after an office party four Christmases ago…

"How many kids you got?"

"Three." The driver's answer was punctuated with the sprightly odor of gin.

"Well nothing sucks worse than having to shell out money to the city at Christmastime, pal. Pull your car over to the side of the road and get in. I'll take you home. I'll have to tow your car, but a tow bill sure beats the hell out of going to jail, eh?"

Ever since, the executive gave Mike any information he wanted, proprietary or not. Mike knew enough not to wear out his welcome, so he called only sparingly.

"Frank, I know this is a little above the call of duty, but I really need this one," Mike said.

"Look, Mike, if you say you need the information, that's good enough for me," the executive replied.

"Thanks, man. I owe you."

"Forget it. Okay... yeah, Sis's long distance activity sure picked up about the time her brother disappeared. Let's see." Mike could hear papers shuffling over the receiver. "Here's a collect call from Atlanta, then later the same day from Miami. It would take me while to check, but I bet they're coin phones from the airport or bus station. Looks like there's about one every two weeks from Nassau down in the Bahamas. It's the same number each time. You got a pen?"

Mike copied down the information his friend gave him. As soon as he had the numbers, he hung up and immediately dialed the number in the Bahamas.

"Prince George's Inn. How may I direct your call?"

"I'm sorry," Mike said, "Wrong number."

"I think our missing professor might be vacationing with your assets in the sunny Caribbean," Mike told Stearns by phone.

"How's that?"

"I've tracked Bennigan to a hotel in Nassau. Now it's up to you whether you want to try to have him arrested and brought back to the states, or go confront him and get your money, or have me do it," Mike said.

"He knows my clients and me. I don't want to risk him seeing us and running again. I'd rather not have to lose any more money by having to pay off a bunch of corrupt government officials just so they'll do what's right," Stearns said, as if thinking out loud. "He doesn't know you, Mike. How about if I have a ticket waiting for you at the airport? Could you go?"

"My straw hat and swim trunks are already packed, 'mahn'."

"Yeah, right. When you get there, just make visual contact with him, and call me. Whatever you do, don't approach him. This is way too important. Got it?" Stearns asked.

"You're the boss," Mike said.

"Call me. If you need additional troops, I'll send some people down."

"For Christ's sake, Henry, this isn't some CIA operation. I think I can handle it without having the Green Berets drop in from above," Mike said.

"Let me and the guys who stand to lose a million bucks be the judge of that. Now promise me you'll call."

"Okay, Okay. I'll call."

"My secretary will contact you with your flight time and number," Stearns said.

"Roger-wilco, commander. I'll be standing by," Mike said in a mocking, officious voice.

"Mike."

"Yes, Henry."

"You're a better smart-ass than you are a martyr any day." Stearns hung up the phone.

Stearns buzzed his secretary on the intercom. "Jeanine, call over to Metro Travel. I need two tickets to Nassau for this afternoon. One as early as you can get, and the other later in the day."

He then pulled out a Rolodex from a locked desk drawer. These cards were kept separate from the ones he used in his law practice. These were numbers he didn't want anyone in his office to know he had. They were the numbers for "other" associates and a few girlfriends he kept secret from his wife.

He flipped to the card he was looking for and dialed the number. "Jacob, this is Henry. I need you to fly down to the Bahamas today. Chandler thinks he's found our man. What? No, I said I could trust him to do a good job, but I don't want him getting righteous on us. If he winds up helping Bennigan run, we'll never find that silver. Yeah, look, I'll e-mail you a picture of Chandler and flight arrangements for both of you. You just get to the Nassau airport and keep an eye out for our little detective. Oh no, he'll never know what hit him when it's all over."

As Mike's flight to Grand Bahamas Island approached the Nassau airport, he could see through crystal blue water the coral reefs outlining the island. Thin lines of breakers lapped at the white sand beach and as the plane descended through pockets of warm, turbulent air, Mike observed small brownish dots transform into glistening, oiled tourists soaking up the sun's tanning rays. Bright sunlight added sharper definition and vibrant color to the shoreline, the water, and the waves.

The resonant sound of steel drum Calypso greeted Mike and his fellow passengers. In threadbare, cut-off khaki shorts, white pullover Polo shirt, Bass moccasins, and sunglasses, he looked no more or less a tourist than anyone else in baggage claim.

After he retrieved his one overnight bag, he began searching for a sign for ground transportation. Through the surrounding plate glass of the airport's main level he saw dozens of taxis and hotel limousines speeding down a palm lined avenue. A Bahamian policeman directed traffic, the blackness of his skin accentuated by his starched white imperial jacket and pith helmet.

When the policeman stopped the oncoming cars, Mike crossed the street to a taxi stand. Third in line, he breathed in warm tropical air and listened to the wind hissing through and rattling palm fronds overhead. When he got into the back seat of a waiting cab, he couldn't help but notice the Mercedes emblem on the hood.

"I'm trying to get to the Prince George's Inn," Mike said.

"All right, sir," was the driver's clipped reply. He pulled down the lever activating the meter, cut a glance into the rearview mirror and asked, "This your first time in Nassau?"

"No, but it's been years," Mike said. He was always taken aback, mesmerized by the melodious voices of the sea island blacks, a perceived incongruity in what his eyes saw versus what his ears expected to hear. The speech of the Bahamians, like the Gullah of blacks from the coast of South Carolina, is a Creole blend of French, English, Dutch, and African. The resulting rhythm of the spoken word laid in harmony upon the ear. If speech alone conveyed dignity, Mike thought, then the men and women who spoke these arias of prose were royalty indeed.

In less than twenty minutes, the driver pulled to the door of the Prince George's Inn. Mike tipped him generously from the advance money Stearns left with his ticket. He thought the hotel looked several years old. The orange-pastel tinted stucco on the outside showed signs of age and wear, black swirls of dirt swept up by untold seasons of rain and hurricanes staining the bottom of the walls. The top of the building was streaked with faint lines of tar washed from the roof.

Mike entered the foyer that displayed an elegance belied by the building's rough exterior. The floor was polished teak and the desk clerk stood behind a mahogany counter surrounded by the warmth of dark paneling.

"May I help you, sir?"

"Single room, please."

"Certainly. And how long shall you be staying?"

"A week," Mike replied handing over his American Express card. He thought about paying cash and using an alias, but he figured that even if Bennigan recognized him or his name, he wouldn't know why Mike was here. He also considered showing the clerk Bennigan's photo, but he thought better of it and decided to see if he could spot the professor without arousing anyone's curiosity.

Mike took the stairs to his third floor room. The rust brown carpet was compacted and worn thin. The mattress seemed spongy and well used and the stucco walls were finished with a high gloss paint giving them a slippery feel in the condensation that formed with the mingling of air conditioning and the humidity of the noonday sun.

His window arched in a Moorish style lending a Spanish flair to his corner of the Caribbean paradise. He peered out, his view overlooking a street market. Large jewel-tone umbrellas shaded vendors hawking straw hats and colorful island shirts.

On every corner small, thin black children peddling seashell necklaces and bracelets assailed tourists. And everywhere the streets teemed with people. Americans, Europeans, Canadians, Japanese–relaxed, carefree, unshaven, and irrepressibly casual. Sometimes the only noticeable difference between the islanders and the tourists were the telltale cameras and gleaming white, brand new tennis shoes.

Mike let the privacy sheer fall back into place. As much as is sounded like a scene from a B-grade 1940s detective movie, he felt his best plan at the moment was to take a newspaper into the lobby and wait on Bennigan to make an appearance.

By four o'clock that afternoon, he had twice read every line of his paper and two others he found in the lobby. At 4:10, even Mike thought he looked a bit foolish sitting for hours inside an empty hotel lobby when outside the streets buzzed activity. He stood and stretched, tossing the newspaper behind him onto his chair.

He walked to the back entrance of Prince George's Inn and squinted against the sunlight shimmering off the cool blue ripples of the swimming pool. Mike shaded his eyes with the palm of his hand. The pool was empty. It was the time of day when folks were coming in off the beach. Parents were putting little ones down for naps before dinner and sun worshipers were bidding their god a pleasant journey into the western sky.

A few people were lying out by the poolside. An attractive girl lay on her stomach, the strings of her bikini top untied and hanging on each side of her lounger. An older lady, bronzed and wrinkled, pushed up her sunglasses, adjusted her floppy hat, and then changed position in her chair as she turned the page of her novel.

And then Mike's gaze froze. He halted his breathing for a

second and raised one eyebrow in that expression of self-satisfaction he had known so many times before. There, sunning himself in a chaise was a golden-tanned Professor Bennigan.

I'll bet the son-of-a-bitch has been there the last three hours. Mike stepped back into the lobby to a pay phone. He pulled a slip of paper from his breast pocket and dialed the calling card number Stearns had included in his travel packet.

"Henry. Good news. I've found the professor. He's busy catching skin cancer at the moment, but he is at the hotel my source told me about."

"That's great, Mike. What about the silver?"

"Hey, I just found the guy. It's not like he's got his feet propped up on it by the pool. Besides, he's probably converted it to cash by now, anyway. I mean how useful is a brick of silver when you go to pay your bar bill?"

"You're down there to find my client's silver."

"I know. Just let me tail this guy for a few days and see what his spending habits are. If he's buying up half of Nassau, then he's cashed in. If not, maybe it's still hidden away somewhere. I'll keep you posted every day and you can let me know when and if you want me to make contact."

"I want you to keep me posted several *times* a day. Other than that it sounds like a plan," Stearns said.

"That's why I'm the detective and you're the over-paid stuffed shirt."

"Stick to him closely. I'll expect a call first thing in the morning," Stearns said, ignoring Mike's remark.

"Hey, Henry? What do you call a hundred lawyers at the bottom of the ocean?"

"I give."

"A good start."

"Goodbye, Mike." Henry hung up.

As Mike replaced the receiver on the pay phone, he nodded to another tourist who squeezed past him in the narrow passageway that led to the elevator. He pressed against the phone booth to let the man pass.

Business is picking up, Mike thought. He reveled in the thought that two hunches had played out so well. He loved this work. And the five grand would see him through for a while. *Maybe if this turns out I could do some other private work. Another city, another state, even. You can't be a fry cook forever.*

Mike decided to return to his room. At the proper angle, he could see about three-quarters of the pool area. He could spy on the professor from there without looking suspicious. Mike didn't have long to wait. By a quarter to five, Bennigan rose from his lounge chair and began gathering his wares. Mike raced to the end of the hall and down the stairs, a shopping bag in hand to make it look as if he'd just come in from town. He and Bennigan approached the elevator together.

The professor pushed the button for the second floor. Mike pushed the one for the third. Neither man spoke. And as the doors opened at the second level, Bennigan exited without acknowledging Mike.

Mike quickly changed into a pair of long pants and a different shirt. He wet his hair and combed it into place. Then he hurried back to the lobby. His stomach began to growl and he hoped Bennigan planned to go out for dinner soon.

Following the professor turned out to be easier than Mike thought. Nassau, at least this part of it, was a pedestrian town. Although the old guy moved along at a brisk pace, Mike kept his distance and managed to keep his target in sight.

Parris Bennigan stopped outside of Mistress Quigley's, a place that appeared to Mike to be a quaint bistro on a main street. Each table had a small candle and a linen tablecloth. The professor went in and took a table near the back. Mike sat at the bar. He purposely sat perpendicular to Bennigan. He didn't want to face him directly and chance making eye contact and perhaps arousing suspicion. And he could keep the professor in sight using his peripheral vision.

Mike took a menu. *Sandwiches. Salads. Roasted pork for $12.95. That's the most expensive thing on here. Maybe he hasn't cashed in after all.*

Mike ordered a fried conch sandwich and a beer. It looked like Bennigan ordered a salad of some kind. Mike ate his meal slowly but he concentrated on the professor and his movements so he didn't really taste the fried shellfish or the smooth, ice-cold beer as it rolled down his throat.

Bennigan took his time. He was a slightly built man with bony arms and an angular face. He had a beard with flecks of salt and pepper gray that matched the color of his wispy hair. He took a bite of his salad and then put his fork down to turn the page of the island weekly tourist paper he picked up when he walked into Mistress Quigley's. He seemed oblivious to Mike's occasional glance.

Try as he might, Mike couldn't shake the odd sensation that he was being watched. His skin prickled and he felt some sixth-sense pressure at the base of his brain. Several times during the meal he took a fleeting look around the restaurant, even tried to see past the reflection of the plate glass windows into the street. Nothing. Only people smiling and laughing, eating and drinking–tanned tourists and even tanner natives soaking up the atmosphere and fine food of Mistress Quigley's.

He shrugged and tipped his ice cold drink to his lips, cautious, but unaware that out of all the eyes that looked upon him that night, one pair was sinister and deadly.

The next morning, Mike woke early. He phoned Stearns with a quick report, relating the previous night's meal and short stroll before returning to the Prince George's Inn. After the call, Mike went to the lobby to wait for Bennigan, but by 11:00 o'clock, he hadn't seen him. He checked the pool, walked the halls, and returned to the lobby, a procedure he repeated several times. But still no professor.

There's got to be a better way, Mike thought. He couldn't stand guard outside of Bennigan's room and he had neither surveillance equipment nor anyone to help him. Although it was risky, he decided to approach someone at the hotel to assist in keeping tabs on the professor. For the next few hours, Mike took to clandestinely assessing the hotel staff to select just the right person to help him.

Mike quickly narrowed his sights on Hetty Chambleau, a domestic at the Prince George's Inn. Heavyset and wearing a light blue housekeeper's uniform, Hetty possessed a round, cherubic face and what appeared to be a pleasant, if not naïve, demeanor.

Mike noticed she took her time examining notes and letters, almost anything written, as she emptied waste bins from the guestrooms. On her break, she absentmindedly nibbled a chocolate bar, chewing slowly as she concentrated on a tabloid newspaper article about a miracle diet. Mike thought she'd be perfect.

Hetty was midway through her second floor rounds when Mike made his approach. She walked away from her roll cart, leaned over the railing, and called down to a co-worker.

"Trina... Toss me up a can of dat air freshna'. De' lettle boy in 212 left his shells behind and de' whole room smell like fush."

Trina, unseen, lobbed a perfect throw over the rail. Hetty caught it with ease and when she turned around, there stood Mike with a nervous grin on his face.

"Uh...excuse me ma'am. Uh..." He stumbled over his words.

"Well, what is it? If you jus' gone stand in my way, you gone have to pick up a mop, young fella'. I got fufteen mo' rooms to clean before de' end of my shift."

"I'm sorry. Can I talk to you while you clean?"

"If you intending on talkin' to me boy, that's about de' only way you gonna be able to," Hetty said as she brushed past Mike spraying "tropical breeze" scent into the fishy air of room 212.

He followed her in. "I need your help. Do you know Professor Bennigan down in room 226?"

Her face widened into a broad, toothy smile. "Yes. Professor Ben an' Jerry we call him. You know dat man eats ice cream like dey ain't makin no mo'. He's down here on extended research, he say. He's a nice man. I hate to see him go."

Mike's heart jumped. "Go! Where's he going?"

"He tol' me he's lookin for a small apartment to rent for a year or so, so he can work on his book or paper or some such like dat."

Mike rubbed his chin considering his newfound information.

Hetty narrowed her eyes. "Why? Who is you to be askin' about Professor Ben an' Jerry?"

Mike recovered quickly. He shot a glance in either

direction for effect. "Can you keep a secret, Hetty?"

She leaned closer and whispered, "I's de best secret keeper around dis hotel. What you got to tell me, boy?"

"I've been hired by Professor Bennigan's daughter. He really is a professor, an anthropologist who knows all about strange cultures, but he's retired. He spent six months around his house, kind of went stir crazy, and started reading up on voodoo."

Mike saw he had her hooked so far. Her breathing was controlled and she hadn't blinked her eyes in the last thirty seconds. He continued, "Anyway he hooked up with some old root doctor down in Beaufort, in the lower part of the state we're from, and this root doctor told him all about a voodoo healer down here in Nassau. So Professor Bennigan thought he would come down here to seek him out. This witch doctor is supposed to have some kind of potion to make you live longer. Some people say up to a hundred and twenty years old. The professor thinks he can make history, and lots of money, if he finds this guy and his potion."

Hetty pursed her lips and nodded as if this all made perfect sense.

Mike again looked around to see if anyone else could be lurking about. Hetty's mop hadn't moved in five minutes.

"Funny thing is, "Mike said, "about three weeks after this all started, the root doctor turned up dead."

Hetty dropped the handle to her mop and swallowed hard. "Dead?! I ain't wantin' to hear no mo' a dis here," she said waving both hands in the air.

"No, no, no...listen to me. It was probably natural, but that's not why I'm here anyway. The professor's daughter hired me to come down here and keep an eye on him. She doesn't believe in this voodoo stuff. She just wants me to make sure her dad doesn't spend up all his retirement money on some crazy idea. And not knowing how folks down here might treat an American who's not really a tourist, she doesn't want to see him hurt either. My problem is I can't just camp outside his door. You have a reason to be here a lot. I just need you to let me know when he's leaving the hotel so I can follow him at a safe distance. I'll be glad to pay you out of my salary."

"I don't know. The hotel got rules."

"Look it's for his own good. I can give you his daughter's phone number if you want to call," Mike said taking a big chance.

"Well he sho' is a nice man. I guess dey ain't no harm in it. But don't you let de' hotel manager know what's goin' on or I'm fired for sho'."

"Whew. Great. It's a deal. I mean it's for his safety and everything. I don't believe in all that voodoo stuff anyway," Mike said, vigorously shaking hands with Hetty.

She released a non-committal "*humph*," bending down to pick up the mop handle. As she dunked in into a bucket of sudsy water, Mike began to walk out of room 212. He took a few slow steps and, when he felt he had timed his pause long enough, he turned back to Hetty.

"I want you to understand how important this is, Hetty," he said, arching his brow to signal the seriousness of his request. "I just said I don't believe in voodoo but plenty of people do. If the professor finds this witch doctor and he does have this potion, it could be big."

"A very powerful mojo," she said as she mopped the floor with long strokes.

"Right. And if this is all true, we all could be very rich, very soon, and live a very long time to enjoy it. So be sure you call me any time you see him leave his room. And don't you tell anyone either. It's extremely important. I really am concerned for his safety, too. They say that root doctor had the death stare. Looked like he fought the devil himself."

She continued to clean the floor. Hetty appeared calm though Mike was certain her heart felt like it might explode right through her chest. She never looked up at Mike as he left the room. He knew she understood.

Chapter Five

Mike glared at the clock, it's numbers glowing red in the predawn light of his fifth day in Nassau. He was caught in a panicky half sleep, ripped into semi-consciousness by the blaring ring of the telephone.

"Hello..." Mike stammered, still not quite sure of his surroundings.

"Da' bird has lef' de nest."

"What?"

"Da' bird has done lef' de nest, I said." She added emphasis to her voice.

"Hetty, is this you?"

"Of course it me. Unless you got a whole mess of people watchin' yo' professor for you." She sounded indignant.

"What the hell are you talking about...birds and nests?"

She giggled. "I saw dat in a spy picture once." Her tone turned sour, "And don't go cussin' me at 5:30 in de mornin'. Anyway, yo' professor is waiting outside de hotel for a taxi. He say he going to the north side of the island an' catch some 'scursion boat for a day trip. So if you want to go wid' him, you better roll yo' ass out de bed."

"Thanks, Hetty. I owe you," Mike said.

"I'm keepin' de tab," was the reply.

Mike slid out of bed in a hurry and pulled on a pair of rumpled jeans from beside the nightstand. He pressed his feet into a pair of Docksiders, clenched the brim of his baseball cap between his teeth, and buttoned his shirt as he trotted down the hall, toward the elevator.

As Mike swept through the lobby, he picked up a morning paper. He stopped short of the exit door and craned his neck around the doorframe for Bennigan. The professor stood at the taxi stand conversing with the concierge. Bennigan had on a pair of sandals, tattered white shorts, and a straw hat like the islanders sold in the market. Mike figured the professor was definitely out for a day of leisure.

Mike returned to the lobby just long enough to pour a steaming cup of coffee. He walked outside the hotel and sat on a bench he hoped would be within earshot of the taxi stand. He wanted to be as inconspicuous as possible so he took a sip from his cup, set it down beside him, and nonchalantly opened the paper.

"How far, Miguel, did you say it was to the marina," Bennigan asked the concierge.

"Farraday's is only about a twenty-five minute drive. You plan on fishing all day?"

"Only if they bite early. Otherwise I might tour the coastline. I'm thinking about buying some property down here."

Mike could have swallowed his cup of coffee whole and never felt the burn. *That's it. He's cashed in. I better go call Henry.*

Mike waited on the bench until the professor's taxi drove away, and then ran into the lobby and dialed Stern's home number. Sterns, like Mike, was groggy this early in the morning, but he perked up quickly enough upon Mike's report.

"Great work, Mike. Now get to that marina and somehow follow him. He might be going fishing and, then again, he might lead you to his little island banker."

"You got it, Henry. I'll give you a report when I get back."

Mike arrived at Farraday's Marina only fifteen minutes after Professor Bennigan. He stayed in the parking lot and watched the professor from a distance. He didn't want to risk being seen. As soon as Bennigan and his pilot pulled away from the dock, Mike charged into the office.

"Hey. That old guy who just chartered a boat, uh...he's my dad. Only, he doesn't think he's my dad..." Mike was improvising as hard and as fast as the thoughts came to him.

The harbormaster, a portly, gray-haired older black gentleman, stared silently, looking at Mike over the tops of his glasses. He was propped back in a rickety, wooden chair on wheels behind a large steel desk littered with charts, maps, and papers. The chair creaked with each movement and it sounded to Mike as if it might splinter at any moment.

"Look, he has a mental disorder, okay. The guy thinks he's Redbeard's nephew and he's out looking for sunken treasure. I'm sure your guide is perfectly capable, it's just, I don't want the old man to go bonkers and go pearl diving or something."

"Won't do him no good. Oysters are out of season," the harbormaster said, laughing with a wide, toothy white smile.

"No, that's not what I mean." Mike shook his head, the urgency coming through in his voice. "I don't want him to do anything to get hurt. I'd like to charter a boat and a guide to stay within sight of him. I need to hurry. He's been gone almost five minutes already," Mike said gazing at the maritime clock on the wall behind the harbormaster.

"De boat's forty-five dollars an hour wid a tree hour

minimum. Don't care what you do as long as you return de boat in good shape."

Mike tossed the American Express Card Sterns got in his name on the counter. "I'll pick it up when I get back."

"Santiago will be your pilot. I'll send him to the dock. You can call him Ti," the harbormaster said, his voice rising as Mike's pace quickened toward the exit. "He doesn't speak good Eng..."

"I don't care what he does," Mike yelled, running out the doorway onto the dock. "Just get him here in a hurry."

Five minutes later, Ti and Mike shoved off from the dock. "Follow that other boat, but don't get too close."

Ti gunned the outboard and headed away from Bennigan's boat.

"No. No. That way," Mike screamed over the roar of the engine.

Santiago stayed his course.

Mike tapped his arm and pointed in the direction of the other boat. "That way."

"Ah..si," Ti acknowledged, shaking his head with vigor and easing the craft to port.

Mike realized at that moment that his guide, Santiago Umberto Castileogne not only did not speak good English, he spoke not one word of it. "Geez, this is gonna be fun," Mike said as he shook his head.

Jacob Lynch arrived at Farraday's Marina less than five minutes after Bennigan pulled away from the dock with Mike in pursuit. Like Chandler he dashed into the harbormaster's office, breathless.

"I need a launch. And make it quick. I need to follow the last two guys who were just in here."

"And jus' what kind of mental health specialist is you?" the harbormaster asked.

"I ain't no mental health specialist, Ahab, I'm a private detective. I need to catch up with those guys before they make off with my client's kid."

"What you' talkin' bout making off with a kid?" The harbormaster's voice dropped an octave and he furrowed his brow. "That's Redbeard's nephew and his boy out dere lookin' for pirate treasure."

"Look, I don't have the slightest idea in hell what you're blabbing about. All I know is that the younger guy ran off with his ex-wife's kid and the older guy is some kind of sex pervert who wants to buy him. The longer you keep me here with this Jamaican jack-jaw horseshit, the closer they get to makin' the exchange and the less likely mama's ever gonna see her kid again."

"I ain't no fuckin' Jamaican," the harbormaster said incensed.

"I need a goddamn boat!"

"Apologize for callin' me a Jamaican, or elsewise we ain't got no mo' boat."

Lynch fumed. He wanted to take out his knife and gut his nemesis right there on the desk. Through clenched teeth he forced out, "I'm sorry for callin' you a Jamaican. Now can I *please* have a boat and a pilot?"

"But of course. *Bahamians* are always glad to oblige our American friends. Dat will be $150 per hour wid' a tree hour minimum. Will that be a cash deposit or credit card?"

Lynch tossed him plastic. "While we've been here, ah... discussing, the availability of a boat, those two guys have already reached open water. By chance does my boat have a marine radio in it?"

"Why, yes it does," the harbormaster said smiling.

"Great," Lynch said. "Can we radio one of the other guides and find out their location without making the other two guys suspicious?"

"Oh, no. Sorry. We can't do that."

"Why the hell not?" Lynch said animated again.

"Because yours is de' only boat wid' d e radio. You'd be talkin' to yo'self or to me, which somehow you don't seem to be enjoyin' all that much." The harbormaster gave another wide smile, his teeth pearly white against the contrast of his deep black face.

Lynch was beside himself. "Look you bluegum piece of shit. My ass and a whole shitload of money are riding on me following those two idiots. You've got my deposit and my credit card number. I'll buy the fuckin' boat if I have to but get me the fuckin' launch and one of your fuckin' mushmouth Jamaican, Bahamian what-ever-the hell you black ass sons-a-bitches are pilots so I can get into the water and find them!"

"Findin' them won't be no problem," the harbormaster said calmly. "The older man told me where he was goin' on his charter. I know exactly where that launch is headed." He put his hands behind his head and leaned back in his chair as if he enjoyed this immensely.

Lynch was homicidally bewildered. "Where is he headed?" he asked with measured calmness.

"Normally that information is confidential, but seeing that this is The Bahamas, things are a little more relaxed down here..."

"How much," asked Lynch, his voice stern.

"Seventy-five dollars."

"Here," Lynch said retrieving his cash and throwing it on the counter.

"The older man is headin' to an out island twelve nautical miles north by northwest from here. Yo' pilot knows de' way. If dat young man can keep up, dat's where he headin', too."

From about a quarter mile out, Mike saw the professor's launch beached on the shore of the out island. He couldn't see either Bennigan or the pilot, but, drawing his thumb across his throat, he motioned for Santiago to cut the motor for a silent approach.

Vibrant surf caught Mike's boat and drew it in closer to the shoreline. When it reached the breakers, Santiago jumped in the knee-deep water and guided it onto the beach. He and Mike tied the boat to an outcropping of brush and driftwood just out of view of the professor's launch.

"You stay here and wait for me," Mike said.

"*Que?*" Santiago looked puzzled.

Mike forgot his guide's English handicap. "Stay. Wait," he said holding his hands out like he was training a puppy.

"*Si.*" Santiago nodded and plopped back against the launch, his hands knotted behind his head.

Mike felt his way through the thick undergrowth of scrub. The beach sand, both cool and uncomfortably intrusive, filtered into the bottom of his shoes. On any other day, the sound of the surf and warmth of the noonday sun would have been relaxing and hypnotic. But today, in pursuit of Professor Bennigan, the heat made sweat blur Mike's sunglasses and sting his eyes. And the pounding of the waves made it impossible for him to listen for any movement around him.

Mike stopped and leaned against a boulder in the shade. He took off his sunshades and wiped his brow against his shoulder. He removed his right shoe to dump out shovels full of accumulated sand. He neither saw nor heard the professor's approach.

Bennigan poked Mike mid-ribs from the side with a brass-tipped walking cane. "Well young man, suppose you tell me why you're following me."

"Jesus H. Christ, " Mike yelled with a start, stomping his bare foot down onto a burr in the sand. "Ouch, God Almighty!"

"Appears you and the Lord have a fine rapport, but how about talking to me, perhaps answering my questions? *Hmm*?" Bennigan spoke quickly, his voice high pitched but strong apparently from years of speaking in expansive and crowded lecture halls. He was a slight man with a thin, ferret-like face and pointed nose, but Mike felt like he bore a powerful presence.

"I don't know what you're talking about, old man. I wanted some peace and quiet so I came out to this island. I'm not following you and I certainly didn't expect to get mugged and assaulted in the middle of the Caribbean."

"Nonsense, boy. You've been tailing me for nearly a week. I may be old, but I'm not stupid. Every time I go through the lobby there you are clutching onto a paper, peering at me over the top. It's a wonder your fingers aren't permanently stained with newsprint," Bennigan said.

Mike didn't reply.

The professor continued, "Of course you probably don't let ink stay on your fingers too long. It is, after all black, and I assume even that doesn't sit well with you or your enlightened Klan brothers."

"Klan?" Mike yelled, his voice cracking. He opened his arms in a helpless gesture and took a step toward Bennigan.

The professor brought the tip of the cane up to Mike's chest and rested it convincingly on his sternum. "Another foot closer you cross-burning recalcitrant and I'll beat you to a bloody pulp. Enough of this. You want the silver back. You think because you paid me to find it, it's yours. Under ordinary circumstances I would agree," Bennigan accented each word by pressing the tip of the cane harder into Mike's chest. "But you want to finance your hate war. You want to burn and bomb and rape and torture. And you want to use the silver I found to do it. Well, too bad. It's gone and you'll never find it. So crawl back under your white little robe and slink back under whatever rock you came from."

"Hold on a fuckin' minute there, Pops," Mike said, brushing the tips of the cane aside, away from his vital organs. "First off, you need to take a breath before you have a stroke. Second, okay, I'll come clean. I'm after the silver, but I don't have a clue about this Klan stuff. I'm a detective working for a group of private investors who claim you made off with this treasure they hired you to find."

"And I suppose your 'private investors' didn't mention their plans to use the silver to rid the United States of blacks, Jews, folks like that," Bennigan asked, contempt dripping from each word.

"Actually, no," Mike answered matching his tone, "so why don't you be a good little professor and tell me where the silver is? You can go about your business and I'll go about mine."

Bennigan studied the young man. "You really don't get it do you?"

"Get what?"

"These men who hired you. They are dangerous and demented. Do you think I would have left a home and a career over such a small amount of silver if I thought otherwise?"

Mike reflected for a moment. The professor's question made sense. Still a million bucks was a million bucks, a hell of a lot more than an academic's regular salary. "Look, I'm only going to say this one more time. I'm a detective. A lawyer hired me to find you. Now tell me where the silver is."

"And a heck of detective you are, son. Tell me. Why do you think your client felt it necessary to have you followed?" Bennigan asked pointing over Mike's shoulder.

Mike turned and on the beach he saw a third launch grounded on the shore.

"How do you know that whoever came ashore is following me?"

"Because I saw him land and it's the same man who has been tailing you all week," Bennigan said.

Mike winced and shook his head in disbelief, "Damn, I've had this strange sensation ever since I got off the plane. I should've known..." His words trailed off. Mike was at a loss for anything to say.

"Yes," Bennigan said with a strong and forthright tone, "You *should* have."

"Look Dr. Bennigan. Since you are so perceptive, it's probably obvious that I'm real confused at this point. So why don't you explain to me what's going on?"

Bennigan hesitated for a moment, glancing around the clearing as if to check for intruders and then turned his eyes back toward Mike. He studied the detective from the ground up and stared into his eyes for any hint of deception. "All right boy. But not here. Follow me." He crooked a finger, already hook-like from arthritis, and ordered Mike to follow.

Bennigan led him from the clearing, stopping every few seconds to listen for footsteps or moving brush. Mike followed him about a hundred yards deeper into the island's interior, away from the sound of the waves. Using his cane for balance, Bennigan scaled a small hill and motioned for Mike to do the same. The hill was prickly with scrub brush on the sides, but at the apex, it plateaued and sheered off like a table.

"This will afford us the luxury of being able to hear anyone who approaches," Bennigan said.

Bewildered and hot, Mike didn't respond. He wanted to hear the professor's explanation.

"Okay," Bennigan began, "I'm not going to pretty this up any. I don't know what lawyer hired you. You're probably not going to tell me, but I'll tell you that his clients are indeed members of the Ku Klux Klan."

"Oh, come on," Mike said, exasperated. He shook his head and flung off puddled droplets of sweat from his forehead with the back of his hand.

"It's true. Ku Kluxers, White Knights, Aryan Nations, whatever you want to call them, they're a bunch of white supremacist militants who believe that if you're not a white Protestant, you're not worth spitting on."

"If you knew this, why did you agree to find the silver for them?" Mike asked.

"They approached me like they approached you. Sent a front man pretending to represent the interests of wealthy investors searching for historical artifacts. He showed me the original letter from the Union soldier named Chapman. I studied old maps of Ware Shoals and located where I thought the silver might be. There was about a month delay before the investors obtained permission from the property owner to dig. Then I went to work, found the shipment, and put it in private storage."

"So, what are you saying? It's in some Store-N-Lock somewhere?"

"No, you dolt. Archeological finds have to be cleaned and preserved. It's in a lab facility out of state."

"Okay, you still haven't gotten to the part about the

flaming crosses," Mike prodded.

"Patience, boy. You've been trailing me for a week. A few minutes more of conversation won't hurt you. Besides, you assume that the people I'm talking about parade around in sheets and pointy hats. If it were that simple, I wouldn't have taken the extraordinary measures I have to keep the silver out of their hands."

"Now, after I had completed everything except the delivery, I met with your employer, and mine, to collect my earnings. This time there were two men who came to my office. One said his name was Frank Murphy, the other Starks. I noticed Murphy wore a lapel pin, a white rose bounded by a cross on the left and a sword on the right. That in itself wasn't so alarming, but what nearly made me fall off my chair was when Murphy asked if I knew a Mr. Ayak?"

"I'll bite. Who is Ayak?"

Bennigan shook his head in exasperation. "Don't you know anything of history or political science?"

"Obviously not the particular period you're rambling on about. Just spit it out, for Christ's sake. It's a hundred degrees out here." Mike swiped the sweat off his forehead with the back of his hand a second time.

Bennigan swept his open palm the length of his face, back up again, and rubbed his temples as if he were suddenly stricken with a headache. "'AYAK' is not a who. It's an acronym. It's a traditional Klan greeting to see whether or not you're talking to a brother knight. It stands for, 'Are You A Klansman.' The proper reply is, 'No, but I know Mr. Akia,' which means, 'A Klansman I Am.'"

"Was that your reply?"

"I asked him if Mr. Ayak was in the Asian Studies department," Bennigan said laughing. "Anyway, I collected my check and rather than tell them where the silver was, I told them I was conducting some tests on it and that it would be returned to them within two weeks. They seemed satisfied and told me to call them when it was ready for delivery. In the meantime, I staged my disappearance, made arrangements with some trusted friends and jetted here to Nassau." Bennigan patted his knee in apparent self-satisfaction.

"Let me guess. No extradition treaty. Even for a million dollars worth of silver."

"Precisely. And it's $1.78 million to be exact, Mr. ah..."

"Chandler...Mike Chandler. Now back to the Klan thing. You want me to believe that based on a white lapel pin and one question which you may have misunderstood or could have misheard, you concluded these people are white supremacists?" Mike asked.

"No, son. I'm an academician, a researcher. I write papers and teach for a living. I know how to investigate and that's just what I did. I contacted a friend at Klanwatch. The pin is definitely a Klux symbol. The AYAK question is coming back into vogue with the resurgence of the different empires and their efforts to resurrect their traditional violence."

"Suspicious, I'll grant you, but..."

"I saved the best for last. There is a Frank Murphy from South Carolina on the Klanwatch rolls. I know, I know, Murphy is a common name. But just on a hunch I checked the deed office in Ware Shoals. Eight weeks before I began excavation, the parcel of land I found the silver on was reclassified as a sewer easement by someone in the county clerk's office–a county clerk named Rudolph Murphy, husband of Janice, and father of James and Franklin Murphy."

"Jesus, God Almighty." Mike's mouth dropped open.

"*Shhh*," Bennigan said with his finger over his lips. "I hear someone coming."

* * *

Mike and Bennigan decided not to wait to see who, if anyone, was slipping up on them through the island underbrush. Instead, they whispered a hasty agreement to meet back at the hotel in the professor's room. They sneaked off in opposite directions from the hilltop and somehow Mike stumbled his way back to Santiago and his launch.

Wordlessly the two men sped back toward Farraday's Marina. As he squinted against the rushing wind and the sea spray pelted his face, a million thoughts swirled through Mike's head. *Can this guy be telling the truth? The Klan, for God's sake. I've known Stearns for a long time. He can be a real SOB in court, but the Klan. But what about the third launch on the island?*

They neared the marina and Santiago cut the engine several feet from the dock. He steadied the boat against the pier as Mike gingerly stepped out. He walked into the harbormaster's office and leaned against the weathered wooden countertop.

"I need to settle up my account for the launch," Mike said.

"Total come to $225.00," the harbormaster intoned as he swiped an imprint of Mike's card. "I take it your 'daddy' is safe?" he said, raising his eyebrows.

Mike detected the sarcasm in the older man's voice and decided to play a hunch. "Yeah, ah, 'Dad' is going to be just fine. And I appreciate you stalling the other guy long enough for us to get away from him. You can charge a little extra on the card if you'd like."

"Oh no, young mahn. We settled on de' price before you scorched off outta here," the harbormaster said as he slid the charge slip gently across the countertop for Mike to sign. "An' I don't know what you talkin' 'bout no other mahn."

Mike smiled at the cagey old guy. "Yeah, right. Thanks anyway. 'Dad' and I needed to get a few things straight and the extra time helped."

"As I said, I don't know nothin' 'bout no other guy. But I'm glad he didn't catch up wid you, too." The harbormaster's smile matched his own as Mike made for the door.

Mike knew he had to check in with Henry Stearns since he had not called him since just before following Bennigan to the marina. That was nearly five hours ago. He would be expecting a report. *But what do I tell him.* "Gee, Henry I have an idea where your silver went. Say, how many crosses and lighter fluid can you buy with a million bucks, anyway?" *No, better keep it middle of the road. Tell him only as much as he needs to know until I know more myself.*

The telephone rang only once. "Stearns here."

"Henry, it's Mike. Look, I lost the old guy after he left the marina. I checked an out-island that I thought was his destination, but if he went there I didn't find him."

"Godammit, Mike! I'm paying you good money to stay on this guy. My client wants his silver not excuses. Do you understand? Now I don't want to lean on the old man, but if push comes to shove, we can take more drastic action."

Mike suddenly felt ill to his stomach. "I'm not sure I'm the right man for that kind of assignment."

"Rest assured I wouldn't waste good money asking you," was Stearns' acidic reply.

Mike started thinking it might be wise to hedge a few bets for the professor. He couldn't tell Stearns about their impending meeting, but he might toss him a bone just to take the heat off a little. "Henry, blowing off all of this steam you haven't let me get to the one good piece of news I do have."

"Well you better tell me what it is. You need all the help you can get."

"About an hour ago I did catch up with Bennigan back here at the hotel. He was on a pay phone in the lobby. I got close enough to hear part of his conversation. He was saying something about a find being sent to a private lab out of state. Now assuming he was talking about the silver, how many private labs in the country are equipped to handle that kind of job? Maybe a few discreet, well placed phone calls might help."

"It's a thought," Stearns said slowly. Mike could almost envision the gears turning in Henry's head as he mulled over the suggestion.

Maybe I've just bought the professor a little time. And while he had Stearns dangling off guard a bit, he decided to take another chance. "By the way, Henry, do you have someone else down here on this case?"

"Ah, no. Hell no! What are you talking about? Do you think I've got enough cash to support two indigent private dicks? Ridiculous," Henry stuttered.

"Okay, okay. Don't have a coronary. I'm just asking. There's some suspicious looking guy who keeps showing up every time I tail the professor. If he is a PI, he's a damn poor one. I spotted him three days ago. Figured I give him enough rope before I went over and busted his chops."

"Oh no! Don't do that, Mike. If he is, ah...some sort of detective, he must have some reason for, ah trailing you. Try, if you can, to turn the tables on him. Observe him, but by no means approach him. Whoever he is, he could, ah, blow this, you know, blow this thing out of the water. Just keep a low profile and wait for me to call you back."

"I'm sure you know best, Henry."

* * *

Mike was exhausted and decided, more than anything else, he needed sleep. He had begun his day before dawn. He had raced furiously through the surf with a Hispanic daredevil of the seas and found out he just might unwittingly, be working for the Ku Klux Klan. It was only one o'clock. He and the professor agreed to meet late in the evening, around midnight. He turned on the ceiling fan overhead and drifted into unconsciousness.

Mike rose about 8:30 PM still groggy from a fitful sleep. He had drifted in and out of semi-consciousness, wrestling with demons that invaded his slumber. He wanted to go straight to the professor's room, but he figured he might be seen. He thought about calling, but he assumed the telephone line might be tapped. The hours passed slowly until finally the clock reached 11:55 PM.

Mike opened his door and checked both ends of the hallway. He tiptoed to the stairwell and made his way silently to Professor Bennigan's suite, continuing to look over his shoulder to be sure he wasn't followed.

Mike brought his knuckles up and rapped gently on the door. He whispered, "Professor?"

The door fell open about an inch, creaking on its old hinges. "Professor? Are you here?"

Mike pushed the door open. He grinned to himself. In the soft amber light of the bedside lamp, he could see Bennigan napping on the huge king-sized bed, his head resting on a red silk pillow. Mike suddenly felt a strangely familiar sensation wash over him. He inhaled a pungent, burnt aroma that left a metallic taste in his mouth and he noticed a blue haze hovering near the ceiling. Then he saw that the professor's chest wasn't moving.

"My God," Mike said aloud as he drew closer to Bennigan's body. The pillow was not silk. It was a regular white pillow that glistened with the professor's freshly spilled blood. Mike placed his forefinger and thumb on either side of Bennigan's jaw and turned his head to one side. In the crown of his skull, a bullet left a jagged and large exit wound. Blood matted the professor's hair.

Mike examined the back of the headboard to the bed and saw splintered wood in straight alignment with the exit wound. Lodged in the wall inches from the headboard was a bloody, flattened bullet. Mike took out his pocketknife and dug it out. He wasn't a private eye now. He was thinking like the cop he used to be. He didn't trust the Bahamian authorities to do the job right. Besides he thought he had a good idea who might be responsible for this.

I led them to him. They flash a little bit of money under my nose and I lead them right here to kill this guy. Mike's heart throbbed thunderous beats. He held the bullet up to the light and examined it closely. He shook his head and stared at the lifeless Parris Bennigan. "Henry, my friend, get ready. Payback's a motherfucker."

Chapter Six

Mike's phone was ringing as he entered his own hotel room. It was 12:45 in the morning and Stearns was on the other end of the line.

"Mike, we need you on a return flight to the States first thing this morning. Your tip on calling the private labs to find the silver panned out. Found it in a facility in Boston. We won't need to bother with the professor any longer. Come on home. Your check is waiting."

"Henry, you know good and damn well the professor's dead," Mike said with a flat, almost defeated tone.

"I see," Henry said, a lead-weighted momentary silence bridging the miles between them. "And you think I, or should I say we, had something to do with this?"

Mike didn't answer.

"Mike. Your assignment's over. You have a certified check for $5,OOO waiting for you at my office. I highly suggest you get on a plane, collect your money, and get on with whatever it is you want to do. And just some friendly advice, I don't know what kind of ghosts you think you've been seeing down there in the Bahamas, but given your history, I strongly recommend you steer clear of any wild, unfounded accusations. Am I clear on that point?"

Mike was silent, only the sound of his heavy, infuriated breathing came across the telephone line. He hung up the phone. Once again he found himself an unwitting victim of his own good intentions. He had to do something. He had to make this screwed up situation right. But he had to move slowly. *Engage your brain before you move, buddy. It's the only way. I've got to bring these people down, but I've got to do it right.*

Mike didn't sleep. He didn't have the time. He wrote a note to Hetty, the hotel maid. He said in it he'd found the professor dead and he feared the same men might kill him. He wrote down Bennigan's sister's name and phone number and asked Hetty to notify her of her brother's death. He put five crisp hundred-dollar bills in the envelope, licked the flap, and sealed it.

He walked lightly down the stairwell to the first floor utility closet where Hetty would report to work in a few hours. He slid the envelope under the door. On the way back up to his room, Mike stopped by the professor's quarters and hung a "Do Not Disturb" sign on the outer knob, hoping that no one would find the body until after Hetty had read the note. He used his shirtsleeve to wipe the metal knob clean of his fingerprints.

Mike returned to his suite and hurriedly packed. Thinking that Stearns' man or men might have been trying to observe his activities, he fought the urge to leave right away. He forced himself to turn out his light and sit there in the dark for another hour. Even the most dedicated investigator, he thought, will give in to fatigue in the early morning hours if nothing happens for a while.

At 3:26 AM, Mike lifted himself from his bedside chair. Grabbing his tote bag, he opened the door to his room slightly. Seeing no one in the hallway, he crept noiselessly into the back stairwell, down the steps, and into the humid Bahamian night air. After he walked what he figured to be about a mile, he turned and headed for the beach, finding a dark, isolated palm grove about a hundred yards from a resort hotel. Mike took from his bag a sheet and blanket he purloined from the Prince Georges' Inn. Laying them on the carpet of sand and fronds, he curled up at the base of one of the larger trees. His mind racing, he listened to the soothing breeze through the palms and the hypnotic whoosh of the waves. Slowly, grudgingly, his thoughts slowed and gave way to sleep.

Mike was awakened from his deep, stress-induced slumber by the tickling of a sand crab as it crawled over his knuckles.

He rose and hurriedly brushed sand off his clothes. His watch read 9:37. *I've got plenty of time.* He slipped off his trousers, his bathing suit underneath, and pulled on a pair of flip-flop sandals and sunglasses retrieved from his bag. He repacked his pants and the sheet and blanket and made off toward the resort going in through the pool entrance as if he were a guest returning from a stroll.

Mike went directly to the shower room adjacent to the hotel's sauna. He quickly bathed, freshened up, and put on a fresh change of clothes. He opened the door a narrow crack, again checking for someone lurking about, though it struck him that he knew neither who the someone was nor what he looked like.

Seeing only an early risen hotel guest or two, he strode out, through the hotel lobby to the taxi stand. A bellman blew a whistle summoning the lead cab, in a line of ten, waiting to ferry resort guests about the island. Mike slipped him a dollar bill and hopped in the back seat.

"D'ya have a destination sir?" the driver asked, looking in the rear view mirror.

"Yeah, I need any bank that'll do me a cash advance on American Express."

"I believe most any of them will. But Grand Bahama National on Trafalgar is closest."

"Fine. Take me to the back entrance if it has one," said Mike.

"Very good, sir."

They rode in silence for the seven-minute trip to the bank. The driver seemed acutely aware that his passenger was in no mood for conversation. He first drove past the front of the bank, turning onto a side street. He pointed out the rear entrance for Mike, who asked him to leave the meter running and to wait.

Mike approached the only open teller window. Any other time he would have noticed the statuesque young woman behind the counter, a woman of exquisite beauty and angular features, whose deep black skin was accentuated by a yellow sundress and saffron colored flower over her ear. Today, though, the worried detective simply produced the American Express card he had been using.

"Can you tell me how much of a cash advance I can get on this?"

The teller took the card, swiped it through a magnetic reader and turned her computer screen so Mike could see it. "I can advance you $1500.00."

"Great," he said. "I'll take it."

She again swiped the card and punched in the code for a cash advance. While the reader was dialing for an approval code, she made an imprint of the card and had Mike sign it. The reader beeped and his heart stopped. He looked over the young woman's shoulder to see a digital LED readout which said 'APPROVED–372091002'.

"Would you like large or small bills?" she asked.

"How about eight one-hundred dollar bills and the rest in

fifties and twenties, US currency please."

She checked her drawer and said, "I'll need to get some of the smaller denominations from the vault. One moment, please."

As she walked around the corner, the magnetic reader began beeping and flashing. In large green letters it read, '<CALL CUSTOMER SERVICE> <LAST TRANSACTION VOIDED>'. The machine repeated the message with each insistent intonation of the beep. Mike's chest pounded with anxiety. Without thinking, he bolted through the swinging door separating the counter from the lobby. He reached for the gray telephone cord connecting the machine with the mainland and he ripped the line from the wall and the reader. The noise ceased. Quickly stepping back through the door, he balled the line up into his pants pocket as the teller returned with his money.

She had counted to thirteen hundred eighty dollars when the bank phone began ringing. Sweat beaded on Mike's brow. It trickled down his neck as his eyes darted between the ringing telephone and the cash in his palm.

"And fifteen hundred," the lovely teller said, laying the last bill of currency in his hand as the bank manager peaked his head out from his office, waiting to ask the teller something. Mike stepped lively through the door and broke into a near run as he neared the taxi. He nearly pulled the door through onto his lap in shutting it, he was so nervous.

"Take me to the main port where all the cruise ships come in."

With a silent nod, the driver checked his lane and pulled into traffic. Mike slid down as they passed the front of the bank again. The manager was on the stoop, holding open the door and looking in both directions, presumably for him.

Twenty minutes later, at the Port of Nassau, he paid the taxi fare and generously tipped the driver. He almost offered him another twenty bucks to keep quiet about his destination if anybody came asking, but decided against it. *He doesn't know what happened at the bank. And if they track me this far, Stearns will have to decide between forty different cruise lines to chase me any further.*

Mike entered the port's main lounge housing the ticketing and embarkation counters. He selected the closest cruise line. "I need a one-way ticket to Miami, please. Your lowest fare."

"Certainly, sir," said the attendant who appeared to be of some Mediterranean descent, Mike thought. "You are traveling alone?"

"Yes."

"I'll still have to charge you the double-occupancy rate. To Miami...let's see, that is sixteen hundred thirteen dollars, excluding gratuities, port taxes and customs fees."

"Holy shit! For a one-way ticket? For God's sake. I can get a plane ticket back for two hundred bucks," Mike said, more to himself than the ticket agent. He knew he couldn't go to the airport because it would be crawling with Stearns' people waiting for him.

"Do you necessarily have to go to Miami?" the agent asked.

Mike, chewing on his thumbnail absorbed in his dilemma almost missed the question. "What's that?"

"I'm asking you, sir, if you have to disembark in Miami. We have other fares to Galveston, Texas; Wilmington, North Carolina; and Boston. No, I'm sorry, Boston is preparing for departure now. The other two, I could book you at our lowest rate of around $650.00."

"Do it, man. Get me on the boat to Galveston."

"Yes, sir. It departs this afternoon at four, but check-in begins at noon. May I have your name?"

"Sherman," Mike said with twisted little ironic grin. "Bill Sherman. I'll be paying cash. That okay?"

"Certainly, Mr. Sherman. Now please place this orange identification tag on your luggage, you have only one bag? Alright, next you need to read...."

Mike completed the ticketing procedure and went to the Lido Lounge to await boarding. Realizing he hadn't eaten in nearly thirty-six hours, he bought a greasy and over-priced burger, fries, and coke. But he ate it as if it were worth every cent of the $11.50 he paid for it.

When first call came for boarding, he stood up, but then hesitated. He was still paranoid about being too noticeable. He waited about ten minutes and then ambled into line behind a weary and sunburned group of fraternity boys wearing Greek letter shirts with "Texas A&M" emblazoned on the back.

Once aboard, he completed the lifeboat drill and drifted anonymously back to his cramped cabin below decks. He ventured out only in search of the ship's gift shop where he stocked up on junk food to hold him over to the evening meal. Back in his stateroom, Mike stowed his luggage and crawled onto the bottom bunk. His adrenaline high was beginning to ebb. Against the mesmerizing monotone of the churning engines just feet away from his bed, he slipped into a deep, restful sleep.

Mike kept to himself for most of the day-and-a-half cruise back to the mainland. The first evening he took the early dinner sitting in hopes that fewer people would be there. He was right and wound up getting a small table for two to himself. He came out on deck the morning of the second day just to get some sun and fresh air. The ship was due to dock at 2:00 PM so the cruise line served only sandwiches and snacks on its Holiday deck.

With the sandwiches, the pursers also handed out U.S. Customs claims forms for re-entry into the States. Mike filled out only the portion with name and address, and that with his bogus identity. He had nothing but a carry-on bag and nothing to claim.

The ship docked at the Port of Galveston promptly at 2:12 with, Mike thought, noticeably less flourish than when the big boats take off for the islands. He stood in line to disembark. The process was slow as each passenger walked through a Customs checkpoint where agents looked at the claim forms and asked inane questions.

Every now and then they tricked a naive or hung-over tourist into an unintentional admission that the claim form really didn't tell the whole truth, but most people had either been warned by friends or were savvy enough to recognize the trap. As Mike drew closer to the counter, he squinted at a wanted flyer partially obscured behind one of the agent's heads. The photo on it looked familiar.

As he took a step nearer, his eyes locked on the picture, an old police department file photo of himself. The header above it said, 'WANTED BY THE FBI FOR WIRE FRAUD'. Below the picture was his name, Michael Edward Chandler.

"Holy shit," he muttered under his breath. His eyes grew wide and he felt all the blood rush to his head. He looked around quickly in all directions, but everyone seemed oblivious to his newfound nervousness and were preoccupied with getting through the counters. Mike took a second and tried to slow his breathing. *I've got to remain calm. Don't draw attention. Just get out of here and find a place to lay low. Then figure it out.*

He closed his eyes and opened them slowly. He was second in line to the counter. The lady in front of him cleared and he handed his claim form to the uniformed agent.

"Nothing to claim, sir?"

"No."

"You didn't make any purchases in the islands?"

"No, sir."

"Traveling alone?"

"That's right." As Mike made his answers, his eyes dashed anxiously back and forth between the poster and the agent, though he tried to force them to stop.

"Would you please step over to Agent Wilkins to my left?"

Mike's heart dropped through his chest. *Busted! Shit!* He briefly contemplated making a run for it, but Agent Wilkins looked to be about 6'5, perhaps 245 pounds. He was blond haired and blue eyed and looked like an ex-college football poster boy who would run Mike down, tackle him, and drag him back screaming. It would all make nice footage for the six o'clock news—home video shot from any one of the nine or ten camcorders being operated by irritating people who had no idea when to end their vacations. Mike walked over, sheepishly.

"May I inspect your bag, Mr. ah...Sherman," Wilkins asked examining the claim form.

Without speaking Mike handed over his tote. He didn't know what to expect, but whatever it was it wasn't going to be good. The agent slipped on a pair of surgical gloves and unzipped the bag. Gingerly, he felt along the inside lining and moved aside the packed away jeans and shorts. Satisfied, Agent Wilkins zipped up the bag, stamped the claim form, and, with a slight, have-a-nice-day-smile, pushed them back across the counter.

"Thank you."

"That's it?" Mike asked, amazed.

"Yes, sir. We apologize for the inconvenience but..." Wilkins leaned closer and lowered his voice as if to let Mike in on a secret, "you know, you're a white guy, traveling alone with a one-way ticket back from the Caribbean. You've only got the one bag and the cruise line's record shows you paid for your ticket with cash. I mean, it's a classic drug profile. Oh, but not to imply..."

"No, I know exactly what you mean," Mike said shaking his head and feeling a bit cheeky. "Don't you worry about it. You're right on the ball and I appreciate the job you're doing. Good work." Leaving Agent Wilkins smiling and proud, Mike decided not to press his luck. He headed for the door and the nearest taxi.

The Comfort Plaza Hotel certainly wasn't the Hilton, but it offered a bed, a bath, air conditioning and a phone, an amenity Mike felt increasingly in need of. It was 3:55 PM Galveston time, an hour later back in South Carolina. He hurriedly dialed the number to the Columbia FBI office hoping to catch one of his few friends at the Bureau before quitting time.

"Agent Meredith, please."

"One moment while I see if he's in," came the reply.

Breathing heavily, Mike drummed his fingers on the telephone stand and bounced his leg on the ball of his foot against the carpet. The wait seemed endless.

"Meredith here."

"Chuck, this is Mike Chandler. I'm in big trouble and I need your help."

"Mike? No kidding you're in trouble. What the devil is going on?" Meredith lowered his voice when he learned his caller's identity.

"Henry Stearns hired me to go to the Bahamas to look for somebody he said stole something from one of his clients. I find the guy and he tells me Stearns is in the front pocket of the Ku Klux Klan. Naturally I think he's blowin' smoke, but the next thing I know, the guy's dead and my picture's up in every post office in the United States."

"Look," Meredith said, "the Miami field office has a guy on a plane up here to get some background on you. They've called us for assistance figuring that some of us know you through the police connection. Since we do know you, we've been nosing around pretty hard just to try to figure out what's going on. My understanding is they also sent a couple of agents to Nassau. I hear they've been talking about you to some hotel maid for the better part of the day. They've got a note you wrote and all of your hotel and meal charges."

"So the wire fraud thing is just a cover to get me in custody, right. They really think I killed Bennigan?" Mike felt suddenly faint.

"You did this kind of work long enough to know how it works, Mike."

"I know, I know, but for God's sake, Chuck, I'm being set up. You've got to help me."

"Okay, I'll do what I can. Give me some facts to check out," Meredith said.

Mike quickly recited his meetings with Stearns and outlined in detail the entire story from his meeting with Bennigan on the island to acquiring the cash advance at the bank.

"I'll have to run this by some of the intel folks in D.C. Let me call you back in a couple of hours, where can I reach you."

Mike paused, in silence, for a long moment. "Chuck, I

swear I hope this comes off sounding paranoid rather than ungrateful because you don't have to help me at all, but... could I call you back instead?"

"I understand, Mike. Yeah, you can call me. But promise me that no matter what I turn up, you'll come in. Either you come in or let me come to you. I'm putting it on the line keeping quiet until we talk again. You at least gotta give me your word you won't run."

"You've got my word. I'll call you in two hours."

Mike waited one hour and then caught a taxi. He headed for the opposite side of town to use a payphone. *I bet they already know I'm in Galveston, but there's no use in giving them an address.*

He nervously counted the seconds as they ticked by and, at the exact moment that the two hours had elapsed, Mike fed the coin phone with quarters, and called Meredith.

"Mike, is this you?" It was 7:00 p.m. in Columbia.

"Yeah. It's me."

"Okay. Here's the scoop. The boys in Miami know you didn't commit the murder because they printed everything in the room. They found some old smudges and some fresh latent prints. Fortunately for you, your prints weren't among them."

Sensing a hint of resignation in Meredith's voice Mike asked, "Alright, what's the bad news?"

"The bad news is that they matched the prints up to a three-strikes loser who jumped bail on his last offense a year ago. His real name is Jonathan Bent, but among his twenty-three aliases is Jacob Lynch. He was staying at the hotel with you and Bennigan."

"I'd bet my next paycheck, if I ever get one, that he was the SOB following me around the island," Mike said.

"Probably so, but here's the kicker, Lynch is a card carrying member of a violent white supremacist organization based in the Midwest. Sounds to me like your professor was onto something. Now, my boss has authorized me to tell you that if you come in, and I mean right this minute, and agree to act as an informant or maybe even go undercover, no charges will be brought in connection with this case."

"Well, Chuck, I hate to play semantics games with you old pal, but I really don't expect that any charges could stick from this case, or since you've been so specific, any other case. So I think I'd rather just take some time to figure this one out." Mike burned with embarrassment as the words left his mouth. *Chuck was only trying to help. No use in being an asshole.*

"Mike. We, all the guys up here in the Columbia office, want to see you come in and help us. As a field office we don't have very much influence in D.C., but I'm telling you, for the last two hours every agent in the place has called everybody they know in Washington to stick up for you. Frankly, you're being framed for a murder you didn't commit, you're wanted for a wire fraud that you did commit, and the Attorney General would love to hold a press conference to tell the country to what lengths racist ex-cops go to commit genocide against blacks. With your past, you'd be fodder for the electric chair, or at least life in prison. So, I'm telling you, you don't have a choice."

Mike sighed, bowed his head in defeat, and stood silent for several moments.

"Mike are you still with me?" Meredith asked.

"Yeah, I'm here." He sighed again and said, more to himself than to Meredith, "You know, just when I think I'm getting everything worked out with my life, something bites me in the ass."

"Life's that way, buddy. But right now it's up to you to make the right decision. We know you didn't kill anyone or help get anyone killed. What you can do is come in and be a resource for us to break up this group before they advance to mass killings and fire bombings. I'm not doing a snow job just to get you to come in. I could get you if I wanted and you know that. We *need* your help and I'm asking you for it man to man," Meredith said.

"Sure you could find me," Mike was smiling a bit now. "Everybody knows you federal boys got your heads so far up your asses, you have to fart 'em out to see sunshine." Realizing what he had to do, his tone turned serious. "Okay, I'm coming in. How do I get to the branch office in Houston?"

Meredith had been waiting for this opportunity for the past ten minutes. "Just turn around. At the corner behind you is a black Crown Victoria with tinted windows. There should be two agents inside. If they can get their heads out of their asses long enough, they will escort you to the airport. A government plane will take you to Washington."

Mike felt his face flush. He whirled around and two junior agents, both wearing Raybans, radio earpieces, and shoulder holsters, waived a friendly hello.

Meredith said, "I'll meet you tomorrow morning in D.C."

Mike heard him laughing as he hung up the phone.

Chapter Seven

Two agents ushered Mike into the conference room at FBI headquarters, Langley, Virginia. The air smelled stale. A long mahogany table divided the room in half and chairs covered in a dark blue tartan pattern surrounded the table. Not a spec of dust appeared on the furniture and rich, dark paneling covered the walls. To Mike everything in the room seemed foreboding.

He sat alone in the room for several long, silent minutes. *I wonder where the two-way mirror is in here.* Mike casually glanced to each of the four walls. *They're probably waiting to see if I'll start talking to myself.*

Mike spotted a coffee urn in a corner of the room and decided to help himself. As he was mixing in the sugar and powdered creamer, the door opened and in marched four crisply dressed agents and Chuck Meredith from the branch office in Columbia. Chuck was the only one smiling.

"Well, if it isn't Chucky Mac and the G-Men," Mike said. "You guys could be a rock band. Hell, you're all dressed alike. Do y'all get a discount on those white shirts or what?"

Meredith chuckled and thrust his hand out to greet Mike. The other agents took their seats at the table, opened their portfolios, and laid down their Palm Pilots.

"Mike, this is Agent Donnelly, Agent Wilson, Agent Tucker, and Deputy Director James Lewis," Meredith said.

"Geez Louise, Deputy Director? Am I in that much hot

water that I've drawn the attention of the FBI higher echelons?"

"Mr. Chandler," said Lewis, "Agent Meredith here has spoken of your good character even in the face of what we know about Jarrod Payne."

Mike winced as Lewis continued. "He vouches for your credibility. We have enough circumstantial evidence to have the US Attorney's Office prosecute you. But these three agents have been working on breaking into the white supremacist organization for nearly two years. I am a busy man, so I'd appreciate it if you were a little less flippant about this."

"I'm sorry, I guess I'm just a little nervous." Mike looked down into his coffee.

"That's quite understandable." Lewis's tone eased a bit. He laced his fingers and put his elbows on the top of the table, leaning in Mike's direction. "Why don't you start with your involvement thus far. Then we'll bring you up to speed on what we know and tell you how we think you can help *us*." He leaned back in his chair to listen.

Mike began his story, telling the collected agents about the day Henry Stearns approached him in Dixie Seafood. He told them how he tracked Bennigan through the phone company and about flying to the Bahamas. He related his conversation with Bennigan on the atoll and the professor's suspicion. And then he told them about finding Bennigan dead from the gunshot wound.

Mike produced the flattened bullet he had dug out of Bennigan's hotel room wall. He had preserved it in a plastic baggie. Each agent examined it carefully before passing it along to the next. Agent Donnelly made a note of what Mike said and recorded the time he turned the evidence over to the FBI.

The agents listened intently for forty-five minutes,

interjecting a few questions for clarification. When he finished, Mike turned his palms upward, saying, "And that's how I wound up in this room."

All of the men in the room were quiet for a few moments, Donnelly making notes furiously, while the others stared up blankly at the ceiling. No one looked directly at Mike. He thought either they were letting all of this unbelievable information sink in, or they were formulating questions to see if he was telling the truth.

Finally, Agent Donnelly spoke up. "Mr. Chandler, I wish I could say that what you've just told us is too incredible to believe, but trust me, it's not. Wilson, Tucker, and I have tracked this organization since shortly after its founding. It's an offshoot of an Alabama Klan organization called the Knights of Purity. The brains behind this group is called the Board of Directors."

Donnelly got up as he spoke, and pressed a remote control unit. A slide projector rose from one end of the table and a screen slowly descended from the ceiling. He clicked to the first slide.

"This is Truman Wise, age sixty-seven, retired farmer, and former one-term Virginia state legislator. Over the past twenty-some-odd years he's held various leadership positions in the Klan.

"He was never that impressive at the state house, but what little political clout he did have he used to advance supremacist causes."

Donnelly continued to the next slide, a surveillance photo of Truman entering a bank. "About four years ago he began organizing the Board of Directors. He felt that any group, no matter what their purpose, could run successfully and efficiently if its leaders took a business approach. It's the same sort of business model that turned the Hell's Angels into an organized and extremely profitable group."

"If it's run like a business, then why doesn't the Civil Rights Division just go after their assets and put them under?" Mike asked.

Agent Donnelly spoke up, "We looked into that, but they're smarter than to claim anything on their books except dues. On paper it looks like the Board is worth $5,000 at the very most."

Donnelly advanced the slides one by one showing more surveillance photographs of Truman and other men at rallies; rural paramilitary encampments with men and women dressed as commandos; and children dressed in miniature Klan regalia.

"The next series of slides is whom we believe to be members of the Board," said Donnelly. "This is Byron Hempstead, a vascular surgeon at Keene Hospital in Detroit."

He advanced to the next slide. "Timothy J. Bressler, former Green Beret and Vietnam veteran. He's been a commercial and investment banker for more than twenty-five years, associated with the Knights of Purity since 1972. Currently he's in the running to be Kentucky's commerce secretary."

He clicked to the next picture. "F. Randall Morris, former prosecutor from South Carolina, now in private practice."

"I know that guy," said Mike. "He's infamous back home. He got more death penalty convictions than any prosecutor in the history of the state. I remember some flack a few years ago when somebody accused him of being too tough on blacks, but he had some figures that showed he convicted more white people than black people."

"We've done some checking into that also, "Agent Tucker

piped in. "He, like all politicians, manipulated the numbers, put a 'spin' on it. It's true he got more death penalty convictions on whites, but he *sought* it on blacks nearly sixty percent more often."

Donnelly turned off the slide projector's bulb, and raised the lights in the room. Every man in the room blinked his eyes to adjust to the brightness as Donnelly continued his presentation over the whir or the projector's fan.

"Unfortunately, that's all the photos we have available. But we know the names of the remaining three: Drucker Sligh, admissions dean of Duvall College in Pennsylvania. By the way, we also suspect he has networked his way into other state colleges to deny financial aid to minority students. Secondly is Christopher Bartles, a pharmacist who invested well and now owns a chain of drugstores. And lastly, there's Joseph Striper of our own Drug Enforcement Administration, the Board's most recent addition."

"A cop?" exclaimed Mike.

"Yes," Donnelly said pausing momentarily, "a cop. Do you notice a string of continuity among these men, Mr. Chandler?"

"Well...all of them have high-paying jobs or are well-connected."

"Precisely," said Tucker. "And that's why they are so dangerous.   The   doctor   and   pharmacist   taint   drugs   or misdiagnose minority patients to make them sicker.   The banker and the college guy deny money, even to those who qualify, by manipulating the paperwork. And our friendly DEA agent is there to allow cocaine, crack, heroine–you name it–to remain on the street or to be redistributed, especially in urban neighborhoods."

"The most dangerous trend we've seen recently is the

Board's policy of disavowal," Donnelly said.

"Run that by me again." Mike crinkled his brow in confusion.

"Disavowal. Over the last several years there have been a series of shootings, bombings and other crimes where perpetrators with supremacist connections get caught, turn themselves in, or commit suicide. In each of the cases, just prior to the crime, the perp will resign his membership, disavowing any tie between his group, their beliefs, and his crime.

"That kid, Benjamin Smith, in Los Angeles in 1999 is a classic case. He was an avid follower of the World Church of the Creator." Donnelly flipped through a large brown accordion file and produced a photocopied newspaper article from the *L.A. Times*.

"On July 3, he resigns from the church. On July 4, he goes on a killing spree murdering blacks and Asians. Even kills Orthodox Jews on their way to synagogue. Everybody and his brother at the Bureau know the World Church sanctioned his activities. Shit, they probably had hard-ons for days after the killings, but we can't prove it. We can't substantiate criminal conspiracy, we can't bring them up on RICO charges. Hell, we can't even go after their assets. It's like they're coated with Teflon."

"That's B.S.," Mike said.

"And everybody knows it," Agent Tucker said, "but it's still pretty effective. Legally we can't make more than a circumstantial case. Even the press, without a direct relationship, will only report an "alleged" tie to the organizations. They generally take the attitude of 'no direct connection, no story.'"

"Can't you turn some people? Maybe get some of the

organizations' ex-members to give these guys up and testify about their connections?" Mike asked.

"We've tried," Donnelly said, angrily crushing his empty white Styrofoam cup and tossing it in a wastebasket. "We had three people tell us that Timothy McVeigh was at a white supremacist ranch in Idaho just days prior to the Oklahoma City bombing. But then the group produced four times as many people to say our witnesses were mistaken, it was only someone who resembled him."

"McVeigh didn't say shit and we've shot our own credibility to accurately identify people by publishing composite sketches of John Doe four, five, and six–chasing ghosts," Donnelly added with a disgusted tone. "The people we can make cases on are just foot soldiers, and we can't touch the people who are the brains of the operation."

Mike shuffled through the paperwork in front of him, glancing at headlines and field notes. "How does it work? Does the Board order these incidents, or does someone like a McVeigh just listen to all the rhetoric and figure out who to target? What?"

"As best as we can tell, the Board votes on what group or individual to target. They also tend to select a symbolic day, like July 4 or April 19th, the day of the government raid on the Branch Davidian sect in Waco," Donnelly explained.

Mike pursed his lips, letting all this information sink in. None of this felt real. It was too unbelievable to imagine that people actually felt this way and acted on their impulses. Raising his brows and shaking his head to come back to the moment, he asked, "How does the Board recruit the people to carry out these missions? They can't choose just anybody."

Donnelly snickered, "Actually they do. Believe it or not, they take volunteers."

"You're shittin' me," Mike said incredulous.

"No. Hate crimes are on the rise, but still, when you're talking about bombing a building full of people during working hours or killing a bunch of kids, there aren't too many people seriously psychopathic enough to do it. So when a volunteer comes along who seems determined to follow through, the Board usually jumps all over 'em."

"Do you know how high up this thing reaches, with all these powerful people, I mean?" Mike asked.

"We think we have a handle on that," Donnelly said as he reached under the lip of the table and pressed a hidden button, opening a side door concealed among the paneling. "We've got somebody we want you to meet. Mr. Chandler, this is Mr. Jason Dilworth, retired geneticist."

Mike rose and shook his hand. "Dr. Dilworth is formerly the seventh member of the Board of Directors. His departure created the space that Striper filled."

Mike dropped his hand as if it suddenly became made of lead. His expression turned sour and he asked, "What the hell is he doing here, then?"

Dilworth, bedecked in a business suit, bowed his head. He was tanned and wore a colored watch on his wrist, and a college ring on his finger. He had the salt and pepper hair, not of one aging gracefully, but of a man burdened with a heavy heart.

"Mr. Dilworth has turned into an excellent resource for us in the battle against the Board," said Donnelly. "If you're willing to work with him, and us, I think we can have a tremendous impact."

Mike glared at the new arrival. He detested anyone or anything that displayed prejudice, but he would never in his entire life understand why anyone would murder over the color of another person's skin. It was a line of moral commitment that obviously Dilworth had crossed. Mike was neither prepared nor willing to grant him any quarter.

"So what? Did you get tired of roasting little black babies over a spit? Or were you about to get your ass busted and rather than rot in prison you found Jesus and a whole bunch of friends at the FBI?"

"Neither," came the soft-spoken reply as Dilworth continued to stare at the floor.

"What then. I'm interested in what makes a learned gene-splicing race baiter turn his other Ph.D. cheek for the good of God, country, and fellow man."

Dilworth looked up from the floor, color rising in his face. "Do you know what a cleft pallet is, Mr. Chandler?"

"Yeah, it's a hairlip. What's that got to do with anything?"

"My grandson was born with one. Mr. Truman and the Board voted, and ordered me to 'dispose' of him, kill my own grandson because he was 'different' and an embarrassment to the dawning age of the Aryan paradise," Dilworth said, his breathing heavy and labored, tears beginning to pool in his eyes. "That's why I'm here, sir. I'm prepared to fight the Board with the last breath in my body. Are you going to fight with me, or are you a coward?"

Chandler seethed. The men were nearly chest-to-chest, eyes locked onto each other like two boxers waiting for the bell. The air between them thickened with tension. The agents listened to their exchange without a word, calculating it seemed to Mike, how the men would interact and whether they would be able to work together at all.

After what seemed like several minutes, Donnelly spoke up, "Well. Why don't we all break for lunch?"

Meredith suggested he and Mike grab a sandwich at a little shop a few blocks from the Bureau.

* * *

As they ordered and sat down to eat, Mike asked, "So are you here because the food's good or just to keep an eye on me?"

"Well actually the food is decent, but you know how the game is played. How would it look if the FBI allowed an international wire fraud and murder suspect to leave for lunch unescorted? The next thing you know we'd start building federal pens on golf courses in Florida and letting inmates watch TV."

Mike bobbed his head a little, laughing as he bit into a dripping Rueben sandwich.

"Seriously, Mike. What do you think you're going to do?"

"Are you asking me as my friend or are you asking as Agent Meredith, FBI? By the way, are you wired?"

"For Christ's sake Chandler." Meredith threw his sandwich down on his plate. "We've got a fuckin' serious problem on our hands and we're this close to breaking it wide open," Meredith said holding his fingers a half inch apart. "Do you realize how much time and work Donnelly and those guys put into cultivating an informant like Dilworth? He didn't just fall into their laps, you know. And now you hold an important key. We can't send Dilworth back in, but we can send you if you're willing."

Mike put his sandwich down. He'd looked away during Meredith's admonition. He tried several times to look his friend in the eyes, but he never quite made it past his own trembling hands.

"Mike, you were a cop and these guys know it. They know you were framed, but I guess in some sense they feel like you got yourself mixed up in a real fucked-up situation and they want you to somehow make it right. They expect it of you. I think if you back out now, they'll probably want to prosecute you less for whatever you may have done than for what you're afraid to do."

Mike's blood rose and then he did look Meredith in the eyes. "Look at my history, pal. I tried to take down a child molester. He's dead." Mike drew in a sharp breath and let it out slowly, suddenly aware that his voice had grown loud and was drawing attention.

When he turned back to Meredith, he lowered his volume, but kept his words just as intense. "I tried to find a silver shipment whisked away by a kindly old college professor. He's dead, too. What if something goes wrong here, Chuck? What if I screw this up? Who's gonna die next?"

Meredith sat thoughtfully for a moment. Finally he spoke, "I can't answer that, Mike. But I know one thing for damn sure. If you don't do this, more than two people will die and before it's over, we'll all pay because right now you're ready to wash your hands of it." He threw his napkin on the table after having taken two bites of his sandwich. "I'll be outside."

Mike ate his meal, but he didn't taste it. His stomach was tense and every potential excuse swirled through his brain. He knew what the right answer was, but he felt obligated to consider all the wrong ones, too. If nothing else, he wanted to eliminate every hesitation he might have.

His decision made, he sat at the table for a few minutes composing himself. He tried to control his breathing and let out several heavy sighs as if to prod himself out his chair. When he walked out of the bistro, Meredith was leaning against the building, one foot cocked behind him on the brick. He glanced at Mike, one eye closed, squinting into a bright midday sun.

"Well..."

"Well?" echoed Meredith.

Mike slipped on his sunglasses and looked away, facing the capitol building. "Enough of these two-hour federal government lunches. Is this how you people spend our hard earned tax dollars? C'mon, man, we got us some Kluxers to bust up."

Meredith clapped his hands together prayer-like and mouthed a silent "thank you" to the sky. He put his arm around his friend's shoulder and together they walked back to the FBI.

Meredith flashed his clearance badge as the two men strode through a metal detector at the front entrance of the building. He said nothing, but Mike noticed on the elevator ride up to the 12th floor, that Meredith displayed a satisfied grin and occasionally nodded his head.

When they reached their floor, Meredith escorted Mike back to the same conference room. "You wait here while I go tell Donnelly the good news. You're gonna make their day, man. You're doing the right thing, Mike."

Again Mike was left alone in the official looking room. How, he wondered, could so many decisions that affect so many lives, be made in a place so far removed from the street and the battles fought on them?

Mike felt alone in his thoughts. He had not seen Jennifer in six months. He hadn't spoken to McMaster or anyone at the department in eight. *I can't even call for anyone to give me advice, not even to say hello*. He started to feel depressed.

He was jolted out of his self-pity by the turning of the heavy brass cylinders in the conference room door. Donnelly entered quickly with Wilson and Tucker on his heels. "Chuck just gave us the news, Mr. Chandler. That's great." They each began pumping his hand like businessmen who just closed a multimillion-dollar deal.

"When do you anticipate I'll infiltrate this group?"

"Not for at least three months. We talked about it while you went to lunch. You're probably familiar enough with the Klan, but you need to be fully briefed by Dilworth on this organization."

"Yeah," said Mike, "I guess I need to apologize to the guy for what I said. I mean, his grandkid and all. That's a tough break."

"You do need to work with him. Until we get you inside, he's our most valuable resource," Wilson said.

"I know. If you're gonna try the Devil, you got to go to hell to get your witnesses," Mike said, repeating an oft quoted remark from prosecutors' closing arguments in the hundreds of criminal trials he had participated in.

Wilson continued, "You don't have to like him or what he stood for. You don't even have to believe he's sincere about bringing the Board down. But you do have to believe he's telling you the truth from an operational standpoint. Without that kind of logistical information, you're a dead man from the start."

"Gee thanks."

Donnelly jumped in, "That's the other thing we talked about–having you work with a psychologist from our behavioral science unit to fine tune your, ah...reactions."

"How about giving me that again in English, there chief," Mike replied.

Wilson, slightly embarrassed, explained, "All of us took notice that when you get nervous or under pressure, you respond with a sharp tongue. We're afraid your wit might give you away."

"What he's trying to say, Mike, and please don't take

offense," Donnelly said, "is that you're a smart-ass. The guys on the Board are serious, deadly serious, about their mission. If one of them orders you to do something you're uncomfortable with, you've got to learn to deal with it. You're probably gonna encounter a lot of that. This is a racist organization, after all. You can't go cracking on these guys or pretty soon, you'll draw so much attention, you'll be branded a troublemaker. You need to fit in, not stand out in a good way or bad. We want you to be a good little soldier and at least pretend to do everything those fucks tell you to."

"And your shrink can transform me into this charming racist killer?" Mike asked.

Both Wilson and Donnelly ignored the remark. "We want you to work with Dr. Max Sheldon. Dr. Sheldon is one of the premier authorities in the country on behavior modification. If we can't change you from being a smart-ass, maybe the good doctor can get you to quit eating pork rinds and chicken and all that other fried shit you Southern boys eat. Hell, right now Meredith is about to go into shock because he can't get a glass of sweet tea in this town." Donnelly grinned.

"Now who's the smart-ass?" Mike smiled.

"Look," Donnelly said, "It's been a long, strenuous day. Why don't you get Meredith to take you back to your hotel and we'll get a fresh start in the morning, say 9:30, with Dr. Sheldon?"

Each of the men pushed his chair back from the conference table. The agents shook hands with Mike and thanked him again for his decision.

By half past nine the next morning, Chuck Meredith and Mike Chandler sipped coffee in the lobby of the behavioral science unit on the tenth floor of the Bureau building. Blue carpet covered the floor and in a blue and gray cubicle sat the unit's receptionist with a telephone earpiece attached to her head.

The girl was pretty enough, Mike thought. She looked to be about twenty or so with blond hair, brown eyes, and a delightful lilt in her voice as she answered each call, "Behavioral Science Lab, may I help you?"

Probably some senior agent's daughter.

After waiting about five minutes, the cheerful young lady said, "Agent Meredith. Mr. Chandler, Dr. Sheldon will see you now. I'll buzz you in. Walk through to the back of the lab. Dr. Sheldon's office will be the third door you come to."

The door groaned a tired buzz and the lock clicked granting them entry. Mike had no idea what a behavioral lab looked like, but this certainly would not have been his first thought. He expected gurneys with straps and machines with probes and electrodes. This place didn't even look clinical. It reminded him of an office in downtown D.C.–interview rooms, couches, chairs, muted pastel colors. *Not a shock treatment switch anywhere.*

"Do you know this Dr. Sheldon, Chuck?"

"By reputation only."

"Is he some old Dr. Frankenstein whose gonna tie me down and drip water on my forehead till I say nice things? I'm really having second thoughts about some craggy old bastard screwing with my head."

As they approached Sheldon's office, a young woman in a white lab coat turned the corner nearly bumping into Mike. He immediately took notice of her beautiful, piercing grayish-green eyes and thick brown hair that cascaded past her shoulders. Her lips were full, the deep color of deep ripe berries. The fragrance of her hair wafted toward Mike and he drank in the aroma.

"Sorry ma'am. I almost knocked you over." Mike, instantly attracted, stood still, awestruck by this tall, beautiful woman.

"Quite alright Agent...?"

"*Mister* Chandler. Mike Chandler," he said extending his hand. "The guy behind me whose knuckles are dragging the ground is the agent," he said, his eyes meeting hers in unconscious flirtation.

"Well I see we have our work cut out for us," she replied.

"Excuse me?"

The beautiful young woman extended her hand. "I'm Dr. Maxine Sheldon. It appears that you and I will be working together for a while, Mr. Chandler, from what Agent Donnelly said. Come into my office and we'll see if we can't blame all your problems on your mother." Sheldon threw her head back and laughed as she led Mike out of the hall.

She brought Mike into a decorously appointed office. The top half of the walls were painted a subtle, soothing blue. The bottom half was wainscoting finished in glossy white. On Mike's left stood a bookcase extending the length of the wall. In it, he saw, rested everything from murder mystery novels to psychology texts, including the DSM IV–Diagnostic and Statistical Manual of Mental Disorders--Fourth Edition–and one title that stood out prominently from the rest, "The Brain Game: Changing Attitudes in Changing Times" by Dr. Maxine Sheldon.

He sat in a wingback chair facing the doctor's desk. In front of him arranged in a "T" shape were her three degrees– bachelor's, master's, and doctorate in psychology–and her state board certification. Doctor Sheldon decorated her office with Van Gogh prints and posters from the Museum of Modern Art, as well as charts and poster-sized magnetic resonant images of a human brain. Everything about the office seemed professional with a feminine touch.

"So, Mr. Chandler," Sheldon said smiling Cheshire-like, elbows on her desk, interlacing her fingers and placing her chin on her hands, "heard any good nigger jokes lately?"

Mike flushed. He pushed himself up in the chair, its leather creaking with his awkward and uncomfortable squirming. "I'm sorry. What did you say, doctor?"

"We're going to have to work on that. It's not impossible, but you're gonna have to make an extra effort." Dr. Sheldon studied Mike with an analytical gaze, appearing to make mental notes on his psyche like an appraiser sizing up a damaged car. "What about all the Jews in Hollywood? Doesn't it make you sick the way those kykes suck up every bit of money they get their hands on and you and I give half our paychecks to the government?" Her expression displayed a measured disgust, her upper lip turned up into a slight snarl. "Yep, niggers and Jews just running this country into the ground wouldn't you say?"

Mike felt his heart race. Something about this seemed all wrong. He stroked the sides of his neck with his thumb and forefinger, tugged at his chin, and simply looked at the doctor. He didn't reply.

"Do you always rub your neck when you get flustered?" she asked.

"I'm not flustered," Mike said, clearing his throat and moving again in his chair.

Sheldon again threw her head back in a loud guffaw. She smiled and her eyes twinkled a victory dance. "Mr. Chandler," she said holding her fingers an inch apart, "you're about this far from either running for the door or coming across this desk and punching me in the face."

He calmed a bit, the color in his face returning to normal. "I see. This was a test and I failed miserably, didn't I?" he groaned, a self-effacing grin settling on his lips.

"My five year old could read you like a book. But don't worry, that's why we're here."

"It's just that I'm not used to professional people like you using the 'N'-word," he offered by way of explanation.

"Well, you're going to have to get used to it," Sheldon said, her expression growing more serious. "And for the record, in your mission, we don't use the *'N'-word* in here. It's 'nigger', 'boy', 'coon', 'monkey', whatever else derogatory you want to come up with. The Board is not fond of the term 'African-American' and you're not fighting them from the outside. To be successful at infiltrating them, you've got to become one of them."

"Okay, I get it."

"Let's hope you do. I thought this would be easier. I mean you're white, you're from the South. Doesn't some of this just come natural?" the doctor asked slyly.

"Now wait a minute..."

"You've got to work on that defensiveness, too. The racist mind, no matter how well educated, is at least aggressive to the point of having a snappy, pointed retort. You sound like Lyndon Johnson getting up to debate civil rights. This is not an intellectual pursuit and you shouldn't try to make it one. This is a battle of the races not a battle of superior wit." The doctor rattled off her diagnostic advice still seated comfortably at her desk. She was all business.

"Gee, Dr. Freud, I'm sorry to disappoint you. Perhaps you could include me as a failed case study in your next book!"

"*Tsk, tsk*, Mr. Chandler, you're a racist, not a member of

the high school debate club," Sheldon replied, leaning forward into his comfort zone.

"Up yours, bitch, " Mike said as he flipped her the finger.

"Better," she said, settling back down into her chair. "Much better."

Sam Morton

Chapter Eight

For the next ten weeks, Mike's schedule was grueling–Monday and Wednesday with Max; Tuesday and Thursday with Jason Dilworth; and Friday spent debriefing with FBI agents or watching surveillance films, getting acquainted with the American white supremacist hierarchy.

The sessions with Dilworth proved difficult for Mike at first. Dilworth, though, seemed to relish them. It gave him an opportunity to ease his heart of the burdens of so many past wrongs. Mike could tell that to Dilworth, as to many whose advancing age brings them face to face with inevitable mortality, some iron clad truths had become mutable, among them the belief in the superiority of his race.

In their meetings, Mike liked to study the retired geneticist. He pondered his lean frame and gray hair, his tanned skin and the wrinkles around his eyes that gave him the look of an intellectual. He wondered what clues there might be in Dilworth's professorial voice, the dignified statesman-like accent that turned 'father' into 'fahtha' that might inform his listeners that before them sat a man once bent on destroying not a single black or Jew, but on their genocide.

Being born in the South in the 1960's Mike knew discrimination. It was hard not to. People just inherently knew black people were different. Mike grew up in a time when the "Colored Only" signs had long disappeared, a time when schools taught both black and white children in the same classroom, a time when people nodded politely at those of color, yet a time when insidiousness lurked behind their smiles.

Mike liked to think of himself as enlightened. He could work shoulder to shoulder with anyone. He had friends of all colors. Hell, his partner and his closest friend was a black man. Yet he knew racism. When a black driver cut him off in traffic, he uttered the vilest of racial epithets without the slightest hesitation. But the other driver never heard, never felt the stinging of the word, so it was okay. He shuddered in revulsion at any group of young black kids, wondering whom they were out to harass. He knew all the trigger words–nigger, spic, chink, gook, slope-head, spear chucker–all on automatic recall at the hint of a transgression. But the words, even when spoken aloud, were never heard and that made it all right. Mike settled on a sense of moral superiority by being less racist than those around him.

He and Jason Dilworth worked in the sterile atmosphere of the FBI conference room. Mike thought more than a few times that a better setting for the words and ideas they discussed might be a hole-in-the-wall bar with twangy honky-tonk music, but that implied a social intimacy with Dilworth he did not yet feel, and wasn't sure he wanted to. So the conference room it was.

"I can understand the Board's problems with the mud people," Mike said, his sessions with Max yielding its dividends, "but what's up with the Jews? I mean at least the ones in this country are white."

"Caucasian, yes, Aryan, no," said Dilworth. "Make no mistake, to the Board, to all supremacy groups, Jews are the spawn of Satan."

"Where do they get that?"

"The Bible," said Dilworth in a matter-of-fact tone.

"Run that by me again."

"John, chapter eight, verse forty-four. Jesus is speaking to a gathering of Jews. 'Ye are of your father the devil, and the lusts of your father ye will do.'" Dilworth reached into the breast pocket and removed a small, dog-eared New Testament. He began flipping through the pages creating breeze Mike felt on his cheek. "I'm never without this now," he said emphasizing the last word of his sentence. "Ah...you see here further down in verse forty-seven, 'He that is of God heareth God's words: ye therefore hear them not, because ye are not of God.' After Jesus told them that, they tried to stone him. He hid himself."

"I thought you were a geneticist, not a preacher," Mike said inquisitively.

"This isn't advanced theology, Mike. It's basic Klan dogma. Any aspiring member could recite this to you after two meetings. Here read this. It'll explain a lot about how racist hatred ties everything together."

Dilworth slid a sheet of paper across the conference table toward Mike. As he picked it up he saw that it was a transcript of an interview given to a newspaper reporter by Ennis Andrews, grand dragon of a local Klavern in Detroit. He began reading silently, awestruck by the pure venom spoken directly from the racist's lips.

It started back in WWI with Warburg and Rockefeller, the two biggest Jew boys in the United States at the time. It was their grand design to destroy white America and establish ZOG, the Zionist Organizational Government.

See Rockefeller paid for several nigger regiments to go fight in Europe. Fight my ass. Our own boys had to fire on 'em to keep 'em from running like cowards. But those two rich kykes got their wish. The niggers got to Europe and got a taste of that white meat. Then they came home and were determined to get more. That's why even today so many white women are raped by blacks.

That's why in 1919 when these uppity niggers returned from the European front, New York, Philadelphia, and Chicago almost burned to the ground. That's where these regiments came from. But hell, they don't teach that in the history books because the Jews have a monopoly on our schools and book publishers.

When Mike finished reading he looked up from the paper and heaved a sigh. Dilworth seemed to measure the silence for a moment and when he apparently felt the information had had time to sink in he said, "Many of what the Board refers to as radical factions, like the more violent Klan groups or the Skinheads, believe that all Negro and Jewish males should be castrated and the females sterilized. 'Chain them in the yard like dogs,' I believe was the conventional wisdom. Supremacists also hate Jews because they crucified Christ."

"But Jesus was King of the Jews, right?"

"Yes," said Dilworth, "but according to Klan leadership, he was a different breed of Jew than those practicing Judaism today. He was the Son of God. All other Jews are sons and daughters of the devil."

"This is a little bit confusing," Mike admitted.

"It's not so confusing once you realize that Klan beliefs are centered around what its members *want* to be true, not necessarily what is true. For example, some believe Lincoln freed the slaves merely to send them back to Africa. They are convinced that John Wilkes Booth was a Jew and that Lincoln's assassination was a Jewish conspiracy to keep blacks in this country."

Mike knew he was about to touch a nerve, but he especially wanted to get to the heart of Dilworth's motivation for becoming an FBI informant against his former colleagues. "Sort of like they wanted to believe your grandson was 'different' for having a cleft pallet?" Mike's anticipation hung in the air.

Jason Dilworth didn't flinch at the question. "Exactly," he said. "My grandson's condition is not even considered, well, a condition. It's a cosmetic defect correctable at birth." Dilworth grew animated, sliding his seat even closer to Mike's and leaning in toward him to make his point. "When they asked me to 'eliminate' him, to kill my own grandson, that's when I knew. That's when it finally hit me that I wasn't making a political statement or involved in a social cause. I was killing people— the Board, of which I was a member, was the jury, and I was just one of its many executioners."

Mike listened to him intently. He no longer had any doubt about Dilworth's conviction or sincerity. "How old is your grandson now, Jason?"

"He's six, and he's all boy." Dilworth beamed at the memory, but after a brief moment, his smile disappeared and he once again grew serious. "Mike, there's something else you need to know about a Klansman's view of the world, too. Most of them are comfortable with both the theories of creationism and evolution," Dilworth said.

"I'm afraid I don't follow. What's the significance of that?" Mike asked.

"They believe that God created Aryan people and that blacks descended from the apes."

"Oh, I get it. The flat noses, big ol' lips and all that, you can take the boy out of the jungle...right." Mike tossed his head back in mocking laughter and just as quickly plunged it down between his hands. He rubbed his face quickly and, looking beyond Dilworth as if he weren't in the room said, "God, this is so freakin' sick."

Dilworth placed his hand gently on Mike's shirt cuff and said softly, "Mike you have to remember something. I'm not justifying or rationalizing what the members of the Board think or do, but you have to take them seriously." He bent even closer to Mike apparently hoping to convey the gravitas of his words, "Always remember that every revolution begins with a reviled idea." He sank back into his chair. "But it's all right. God willing it will be over soon."

Brought back to the present, Mike withdrew his arm quickly from the doctor's touch and gave him an unintentional glare. A strained silence hung between them for a moment before Mike cleared his throat and said haltingly, "What exactly did you do for the Board? I mean, if they felt like blacks were just advanced monkeys, what was your value?"

"Oh, the Board knew better," Dilworth said, looking down. Shame covered him like a blanket, hanging heavy on his shoulders and he spoke with the clear voice of self-loathing. "I'd always felt blacks were socially inferior. I wouldn't even hire one to clean my office. My office and my house got broken into over a span of about three years. Both times the police caught them. Both times they were blacks. That just increased my disdain.

"Then twelve years ago a group of little thugs mugged my wife. They didn't hurt her...physically. Shoved her around a little, took her purse, scared her half to death, called her a white bitch and threatened to beat her up because she didn't have more cash. She never got comfortable going out alone after that. They stole more than her money. They took her peace of mind."

Mike remained silent, leaning on the table and listening. He saw Dilworth's anger rise with the retelling of the story and he found himself oddly empathetic.

"From that moment on, "Dilworth continued, his face red and jaw clenched, "I vowed I would get even with every one of them I could. It's not as if I had the strength to hunt them down like some vigilante, so I decided to use my work." He stared at the floor again. "For the last ten years I've been doing cancer research. I genetically manipulated certain forms of melanoma so that they target melanin."

"What's melanin?" asked Mike.

"It's the substance in people that gives them pigmentation. Black people have an abundance of it. Lighter races have less."

"Oh man." Mike's head began to swim with the implications of what he had just heard. "Did it work?"

"In the lab we had a seven percent mortality rate on mice injected with melanin and the cancer gene."

Mike waited for what seemed like several minutes before speaking again. Dilworth continued to stare down. "But you never tried it on humans, right?"

"No. I never did, but the Board kept my research and..." Dilworth swallowed hard.

"And what?"

"Well, seeing my drive and determination, the Board

began recruiting young med students a few years ago. Someone with some experience or a bright new doctor could easily follow my work." Dilworth closed his eyes. A tear rolled slowly down one cheek.

Mike wasn't sure what to do. He looked around the room and fidgeted in his chair. He still wanted to blame Dilworth for his racist attitudes. But he found himself increasingly unable to fault him in light of such obvious and sincere remorse. This time it was Mike who reached out a hand to Dilworth's arm. "Let's get back to it. We've got plenty of work to do."

Mike's sessions with Max were interesting. That's the only adjective he could come up with. The process of changing someone's behavior never proved to be easy. Max explained that it involved altering the way one thinks as well as the way one acts or reacts.

"It isn't really a new concept," Max explained. "During WWII, our government had to train men it sent in as spies not to jingle the change in their pockets. That's a distinctly American trait and a dead giveaway for someone trying to pass themselves off as European."

"I never even thought about that before, and even if I had, I never would have known people everywhere didn't do that," Mike said.

"Well, unfortunately a few of our spies had to find out the hard way," Max said. "Thankfully we learned from those lessons and during the Cold War when we trained females for espionage, we were better prepared."

"How do you mean?" Mike felt like he was in a one-on-one student lecture, but he was sincerely fascinated by the information. He was smart enough to realize that what the doctor was saying just might keep him alive.

"Well, we had, and have for that matter, some extremely dedicated covert operatives. But all the loyalty and the best Russian accent in the world couldn't keep these young ladies from smiling when they interacted with people."

"That was a problem?"

"Sure. Russians winters are harsh, the economy was terrible, food lines were long, and Communism was oppressive to everyone, especially women. Trust me, there wasn't a whole lot to smile about, so every time one of our female agents did, it raised a red flag if it didn't give her away altogether."

Mike appreciated the lesson. He now realized that split second actions he felt instinctually had to be reigned in. He felt like his whole life now operated on a two-second-tape delay. Think, breathe...then react.

Fortunately for him, Max had abundant patience. "All right, Mike. In the most honest terms you can, tell me what negative things you think about black people."

Mike had long ago abandoned his embarrassed resistance to such questions. He trusted Max beyond measure and he knew she received the things he said to her with the same honesty with which he spoke them. "Well, they're just different. They are loud. Young men, especially, group up in packs like they want to intimidate people. I think to some extent they purposely try to be different. Society sets up a norm, a set of standards, and they do whatever they can to violate them.

"A lot of them I come across want a handout to go buy a quart of malt liquor, but they wouldn't hit a lick at a snake to earn enough money to buy a meal. Most of them just want something for nothing while the rest of us bust our hump just to get by."

"Do you know," Mike continued leaning forward and

lightly striking the table with the heel of his hand for emphasis, "for the first three months of the year my paycheck goes to the federal government for entitlement programs that mostly benefit blacks. It pisses me off to know that and then turn around and see some seventeen-year-old black kid driving a Mercedes. It just isn't fair." He sat back in his chair, a look of exasperation on his face.

Max looked at him over the top of her glasses, "So now tell me why you think you get so indignant when someone else criticizes black people."

Mike thought a moment. He closed his eyes and pulled at his chin, carefully considering his response. The answer, he knew, was a simple one. To him it made perfect sense. But he also realized that the words he was about to say contradicted every other word that preceded them. "You've got to consider how bad an existence blacks have had in this country. I'm not talking about that 'my-great-great-grandaddy-was-a-slave-two-hundred-years-ago' bullshit either. I'm talking about as few as thirty years ago when fat, white racist motherfuckers turned fire hoses and police dogs loose on these people. All they were trying to do is vote or protest or ride the fuckin' bus for Christ's sake." He began turning red in the face as he sat up and gestured to make his point.

"We are a country of laws and the laws are supposed to protect people. But ever since Jim Crow the law has been against blacks. If a white guy shot a black man, he got an all white jury and he walked. The only justice black people got came at the end of a truncheon stick or a billy club. And nobody gave a shit."

Max made notes for the next few minutes after Mike finished his answer. She stopped writing and tapped her pencil on her steno pad. She looked through her notebook and pursed her lips as if formulating a strategy. "I want you to try something. Did you notice you used no profanity when you talked about your dislikes of blacks, but in their defense, you said a curse word almost every sentence?"

Mike's face turned crimson. "No, sorry about that," he said as if he had failed a test.

"No, don't be sorry. Turn it around. Don't change the idea, just transfer the emotion. I want to hear about the fuckin' seventeen-year-old black kid who's driving a damn Mercedes while I'm working my ass off to pay for his fuckin' welfare check."

"I get it. Yeah...fuck him and the slave ship he rode in on."

"Mike Chandler, you racist son-of-a-bitch!"

Three weeks later Max and Mike were in yet another session. Although he was growing fond of Max and genuinely enjoyed her company, to Mike the sessions were beginning to be all the same, each Monday and Wednesday running together.

"Okay, what's this?" asked Max as she sprinkled pepper randomly from a peppershaker onto a white sheet of paper.

"It's the Million Man March," Mike said without conviction, his head resting on his right palm while he twirled a pen on Max's desktop with his other hand.

"And this?" Max said as she folded the paper causing the pepper to accumulate in the crease.

"It's the niggers lining up outside Kentucky Fried Chicken after it was over," he sighed.

Max shot him a quizzical look. "Why do they think more than a million blacks came to the Million Man March?"

Mike, now flipping through the pages of a *Psychology*

Today didn't even look up in his reply. "Because Farrakan only counted the ones swinging from the trees."

"Mike, what's wrong with you?"

"Nothing," he said still glancing at the magazine.

She pulled it down from in front of his face. "Well, that wasn't a smart-aleck response so we're making progress, but it was a bullshit answer nonetheless."

"I'm just preoccupied, I guess. I mean it's 75 degrees outside. It's beautiful. The sun is shining, the birds are flitting all over town and I'm either stuck in a room with Dilworth telling me how to attach electrodes to colored genitalia for maximum pain or I'm in this lab with you trading stale nigger jokes."

Mike kept his face blank with difficulty. His boredom and frustration were building to a breaking point. These seemingly redundant and endless sessions seemed like so much wheel spinning, not getting him any closer to bringing down the Board. The training was rote and devoid of action. But then again, he reminded himself, people tended to wind up dead when he took action.

"Why is my progress so important to you anyway? I mean, it's like I'm in Catholic school and you're going to pop me with a ruler if I don't say 'Jewboy' with the proper inflection." A hint of disdain tinged Mike's voice.

"It's *important*," Max replied. "Because one slip up could cost us this case. It's *important* because the intensity of your performance, if you will, depends on the intensity of your rehearsal. It's *important* because so much is riding on this." Max's face flushed.

"Like your professional reputation maybe?" Mike's tone remained cool and disinterested.

"I meant *your* career, hell, maybe even your life, Mike!

Screw my professional reputation. What the hell kind of question is that, anyway?" She stood from her chair and crossed her arms. She leaned in toward Mike as if she were bracing for a fight.

"I'm just wondering what your motivation is?"

"What?" Max was practically breathless. "Where is this coming from?"

"Donnelly and the other agents have been working on this case forever, so they want to bust some ass. I get that. Jason wants to bring down the Board over his grandkid. I get that. I'm the tool to do it with and I have my own motivation, which I have bared to you, so I'm okay with that." Mike counted off his points on his fingertips as he spoke. "What I don't get is why you're so intense and compulsive about how I 'perform'."

"Let me see if I understand your question." Max's voice was measured, calm, but in its apparent tranquility, Mike could sense an approaching storm. He realized he pushed too far. "Because I'm not a field agent, because I wear a lab coat and don't go around flashing a badge and a 9mm, because I don't express an outward desire to 'bust ass,' as you say, my motivation for doing a good job is somehow devious to you?"

"No, it's not that..."

Max cut him off in mid-sentence. "Because, Mr. Chandler. I'm an agent doing my job. Any motivation beyond that is frankly none of your business." She remained standing behind her desk, rifling through papers and stacking books. Mike stared out her window over the skyline. Silence stood like a translucent barricade between them.

After several moments, Mike breathed in deeply and said. "I'm sorry. I was out of line."

Max did not look at him. She angrily picked at her cuticle and adjusted a ring on her right hand, twisting it with what

Mike thought was a disproportionate amount of tacit fury.

More minutes passed. "I respect you, Doc. I just don't trust myself to do what I need to do and antagonizing you about your approach was just a hell of a lot easier than admitting that about myself," Mike confessed.

This time she looked at him, a look of hurt and anger still apparent on her face. "Why don't we break for the day and pick up tomorrow?"

"You're not going to let me off the hook are you?" Mike felt disheartened and embarrassed that he had angered her so.

"I just need to be pissed right now. Tomorrow's another day, huh?"

He withdrew, embarrassed and his heart pounding with guilt, trying to think of a way to tidy the mess he had just made.

Mike left the FBI building and began walking back toward his hotel. It was early in the day, but he decided that he lacked the concentration he needed to make any further progress today. He hated personal conflict. He always thought that odd for a cop whose business it was to be confrontational. The argument with Max had thrown him out of his orbit and he thought it best simply to return to his room, cocoon for a bit, and lick his wounds. It would prove to be a painful decision.

When Mike entered his room, he noticed the message light flashing on his telephone. "You have three new messages," intoned the flat, mechanical female voice of the in-room voice messaging system. He listened to all three, and all were hang up calls. No words, no breathing, no noise. Just silence and then the abrupt, violent termination of the call as the phone on the other end slammed down.

He shrugged off the calls and pressed the remote button with his thumb to turn on the television. He clicked rapidly through the channels hoping to find something to capture his interest, to make his head quit throbbing, and to make him quit reliving his quarrel with Max that replayed over and over in his head.

He had not yet been in the room more than thirty minutes when his phone rang.

"Hello."

"Mike Chandler?" The voice belonged to a female. Mike sensed tension in her voice he didn't understand.

"Yes."

"My name is Katherine Engle." Again her words seemed clipped and edgy.

"How can I help you Ms. Engle?" Mike asked.

"I am Parris Bennigan's sister."

It all fell into place for him now. He felt the weight of those five words down to his toes. His conscience writhed under the mass of their accusation and the guilt it inspired in him.

"I see," he said. His voice was flat. "How...how did you find me?"

"Well, I'm certainly not quite the detective you are," she said, her voice quavering, "but one of the federal agents on Parris' case said you were now working with them to help catch the people who did this. So for the last two days I've been calling hotels within a few miles of the FBI office. It took me until today to find you."

"Ms. Engle," Mike began, his tone contrite and his words halting, "I'm not quite sure what to say. I feel like your brother helped save my life, and I helped cost him his."

She didn't respond, but he could hear her measured breathing as if she were trying to control her temper, or her tears.

"I'm very sorry," Mike added in soft words.

"I just," the woman began and then stopped monetarily. "I just wanted to hear you say that." Again she trailed off into hushed stillness.

Mike tried to get a mental picture of what Katherine Engle might look like. He desperately wanted to do something or say something that made a difference. But the only images coursing through his brain were those of meeting Bennigan on the atoll and of the final view of him lying lifeless on his bed. Even now the phantom acrid blue roil of gun smoke invaded Mike's nostrils.

"I know this sounds very trite," Mike said, "but is there anything at all I can do?"

"Parris had a quite a defined sense of principle and justice, Mr. Chandler. That's why he took those people's silver in the first place."

"Yes, I got the impression that he lived the virtues he believed in."

"Yes lived, past tense, Mr. Chandler," the woman said with a pointedness that made Mike wince. "You want to do something for me?"

This time Mike remained silent on the line.

"Don't allow his death to be in vain." She began to cry. "You finish the job you started and you get these people. Do you hear me?"

Mike choked up as well and his "yes" was cracked and nearly inaudible, so he repeated it into the phone with determination. "Yes. I will get them, Ms. Engle. I promise you that. I will get them, or I will give my life trying. I promise."

Katherine Engle hung up the phone without another word, her frustrations apparently vented, her demons exorcised with a simple but firm exhortation to Mike Chandler. Get them. Mike's concentration suddenly returned. Anger overwhelmed self-doubt. Grit and resolve overtook self-pity and through the narrow aperture of conviction, vengeance transformed itself to justice. Mike realized what he must do.

At ten o'clock the next morning, Mike leaned his head in Max's door concealing his body, his arms behind his back, outside her office.

"Knock, knock."

"Morning, Mike." Her voice possessed a light air to it, with no trace of animosity.

"I brought a little peace offering." Mike brought his arms from around his back, producing a large spring arrangement of roses, irises, carnations, baby's breath, and greenery. He stepped forward into her office, proffering his gift and another apology.

Max's face broadened into a smile. Her eyes lit up with genuine appreciation. "You didn't have to do that. They're beautiful." She took them from his hands.

"So, friends again?"

"We never weren't friends, Mike. People disagree. I just need longer to process than some. You could've come in here without those flowers and everything would've been fine."

"Well, shitfire, there, Doc. Give 'em here and I'll go get my money back." He reached for the bouquet and began laughing.

She slapped his hands away playfully. "Leave them alone!" She reached into the bottom of her credenza and extracted a clear, quart-sized vase with a red floral ribbon on it.

"I see I'm not the first person to bring you flowers to the office," Mike said, raising his eyebrows in mock inquisition.

She wouldn't be thrown today. "And you won't be the last, I'm sure. I'm charming like that," Max replied as she arranged the flowers in the container.

"Well!" Mike began laughing again.

"Actually detective, if you notice the algae ring and haze fogging up my vase and the faded ribbon, you would deduce that I don't often get flowers at all."

"*Actually,* Doctor, if there weren't something infinitely more interesting to look at in the room, I might have noticed the vase." As soon as the words left his lips, he cringed. He knew he had gone too far yesterday. Had he just pushed the pendulum to the other extreme? He inhaled and held his breath.

Max's hands stopped in midair, ceasing to tug and fluff the bouquet. She tilted her head in his direction and looked him squarely in the eye. "Very good answer," she intoned in a voice lower and huskier than Mike had ever heard before. He exhaled and silently thanked God.

"Look, Doc. I'm raring to go today, but still I'm feeling a little boxed in. I think that's maybe what led to my less-than-charitable attitude yesterday."

"Shitty attitude, you mean."

"Okay, well, yes, to use the proper psychological vernacular, um, shitty attitude."

Max laughed. "I see what you mean," she said pursing her lips and tilting her head in agreement. "Why don't you plan a little outing. Take a day and see Washington. Go to the Smithsonian, the monuments. Get some fresh air."

"I got a better idea," Mike said leaning forward onto her desk with a glimmer in his eyes. "Why don't *we* take an outing. You live here. You could show me around. Take me for some good Italian. You drive, I'll treat."

He seemed to catch Max off guard. She hesitated, started to respond, and then stopped again. "Mike, as much as I think you are a likable person, I don't make it a habit of seeing people I work with." Nervous laughter penetrated her words. "Especially someone whose name technically follows the label 'Subject' in my professional files."

He remained silent, hoping the doctor would talk herself into the idea.

"Mike...I, uh. No, I couldn't. It wouldn't be right."

"I'm not asking for a date, Doc. I'm asking you as a board certified psychologist to help me keep my sanity by getting me out of this prison, at least for a little while." Mike looked at her sideways and poked out his bottom lip.

"Well, I guess..." she smiled at the thought, then caught herself. "No, absolutely not! What would the agents think or my section head? No," she said, shaking her head with a disappointed finality more to convince herself than Mike.

"Okay," he taunted, "but I'll go ahead and warn you. If you don't change your mind, I'll take the outing you suggest, only I'll march right down to ACLU headquarters and fill out an application. Then I'll make out a new will leaving everything I own to the United Negro College Fund. When all these agents freak out around here, I'll tell them it was your idea from the start."

She again laughed her infectious, throaty laugh raising her chin. How could she resist? "Alright, I'll go. But just for a few hours. And if we're going out for dinner I'll have to get a sitter to pick my daughter up from school," she said flipping through the pages of her Daytimer.

"Why? I mean bring your daughter along. We could even spring her from kindergarten early. It'll be our own little Bastille Day for Mike Chandler and..."

"Amanda."

"...and Amanda Sheldon."

"Are you sure?" she asked crinkling her nose, unconvinced.

"Yeah, I love kids. Besides she will keep us from talking shop and that in itself will keep me from feeling like I need a shower after every sentence that comes out of my mouth." Then his expression grew somber as he said, "Unless having her around me will make you uncomfortable."

"Oh, no. Not at all. It's just most of the men I know don't enjoy spending their free time around a five-year-old."

"I'm not like most men you know," Mike said locking onto her eyes with a gaze that could melt steel.

"Okay, it's a date," Max said immediately taking on a surprised look.

"Hey, you're the one who said it Doc, not me."

They agreed to meet in front of the Forensics Science building at 1:00. Max said they needed to be at Amanda's school in Falls Church by 3:30. They would have enough time to grab a quick lunch and drive to the Washington suburb just west of Arlington.

Mike returned to the place he had called home since his ignominious return from Nassau, ten weeks ago. He freshened and stopped by the automatic teller for a withdrawal, to live up to his part of the negotiated outing. He was waiting for Max as she wheeled her glimmering black Ford Expedition next to the curb by the building.

"Hey, this is a mighty big vehicle for such a small woman," he ribbed.

"I like it. It puts me up above the other cars on the road so I can see what's going on. Besides it's big and powerful and nobody gets in my way, not even in this D.C. traffic."

"Just as I thought...penis envy," Mike said, settling into the leather passenger seat.

"Oh puhhhlease," Max said laughing. "I thought you weren't going to talk like a sailor today."

"That would be a *racist* sailor thank you very much and my promise doesn't take effect until the little one is present."

Max rolled her eyes in mock exasperation and drove to a sandwich shop on Virginia Avenue. They ate a light lunch and made general plans for the sightseeing tour. Mike made it a point to discuss dinner in particular.

"Mike, we're eating now and you want to talk about where we're going to eat later?" Max asked, amused.

"Of course, it's the mark of a seasoned police officer. Half the town could be dead and all the buildings looted, but before we ever ended a morning squad meeting, everybody knew where we were going for lunch that day. It's a rule."

Max smiled. "Don't tell me I've spent weeks trying to break you of all your bad habits and it's all been for nothing," she teased.

Mike pointed his index finger upward indicating he had a response, but first he had to finish chewing and swallowing the huge bite of sandwich he had just stuffed into his mouth. "Now," he said, his words muffled as he continued to chew, "is not the time for psychoanalysis. We're talking about food, a subject quite near and dear to my heart."

He took a sip of his tea before continuing. "Besides, I've noticed you've got a few idiosyncrasies of your own, there, Doc."

Max laid her sandwich down on its wax wrapper. She raised her eyebrows in an exaggerated "Oh, really?" expression, cleared her throat, then crossed her legs and playfully interlaced her hands on the tabletop. Leaning forward a bit to adopt her classic psychiatrist pose she asked, "And what might those be, Mr. Chandler?" She batted her eyes as if to further tantalize a response.

Mike mimicked her motions. Leaning toward her, "Well, Dr. Sheldon, I've observed that frequently during our sessions, you take your left hand and wipe your lips, particularly after you've used some nasty racial epithet. It's kind of like you're trying to wipe out what you just said."

"Go on," she said softly not breaking the stare she had locked onto his eyes.

"Then there's that odd way you put on your lipstick." Max held his gaze, but she furrowed her brow as if she were confused.

"You put the stick to your lips," Mike said. "But then you wipe the lipstick on with the fourth finger of your right hand," he said gently taking the three middle fingers on her left hand into his. He noticed they were as damp as his palm. "Then you rub your lips together and smack them gently."

Max's face eased into an expression of recognition, and slight embarrassment. Their faces were mere inches apart. Still looking at him intently she said softly, "So...why do you think you have taken notice of these very personal things about me, Mike?" She almost purred the words.

For a moment, he said nothing. He consciously controlled his breathing, which was beginning to become audible and match the pace of his racing heartbeat. The tension was palpable. At that moment, he ached to kiss her, but he knew what was at stake. He knew that even if she were thinking the same thing, one false, hasty move could cost him dearly. So he fell back on his trusty lifeline of smart-aleck humor. "I suppose it's just my keen powers of observation as a trained law enforcement professional. Another quirk, for instance, is the way you wrap a napkin around your drink–can, glass, bottle–always a napkin. You fold it in half lengthwise and then wrap it around the base of your drink. You don't have shades of obsessive/compulsive do you?" he asked smiling.

Max let go a loud, half-laugh-half-sigh. She seemed disappointed and relieved at the same time. Finally breaking his gaze and pulling her hand from his, she looked down, her cheeks flushed a delicate rose. "I just don't like to touch sweaty glasses," she said smiling and bringing her face back up to look at him.

After a brief strained moment she said, "Well, back to dinner plans. If you want Italian, there's the Olive Garden or Spaghetti Wonderland or..."

Mike cut her off, "Or I could open a can of Chef Boyardee in my room if I wanted. No, I want to go to a place whose name ends in a vowel and the cooks are 300-pound women who don't speak English and post their green cards by the register."

"Well, there's Fabrini's. It meets all of your criteria, except the cook may be bilingual," she said biting into the last piece of sub sandwich that dripped oil and vinegar onto its wrapping.

"Bueno!" he said thrusting his hands upward in approval.

"I think you mean 'bella' Don Chandler," Max said chuckling. "Bueno is Spanish."

"Yeah, yeah, whatever. I'm hungry, not fluent."

The ride to Amanda Sheldon's kindergarten took just thirty minutes using the beltway. During the drive over, Mike told many of the inane jokes he was famous for among his friends. Max tousled her brown hair, laughing along graciously at the lame jokes, and nearly crashing into the guardrail when Mike hit upon an occasional hilarious bon mot.

To Mike, Max appeared more relaxed. He felt his own synapses uncoil and sensed a refreshing comfort being in her presence. His idea had its desired effect. Away from the office, they were having normal conversations about movies, the weather, and the terrible D.C. traffic.

Trying not to be obvious, Mike studied the doctor out of the corner of his eye. From the very first time he'd literally bumped into her, he thought she was attractive. But without the lab coat and her professorial glasses, he thought she may be the most beautiful woman he had even seen. She wore only a scant trace of perfume. Her makeup and lipstick only highlighted and enhanced her natural beauty. And her choice of cars excited him even more. *Something about a woman in a four-wheel drive...mmm, mmm.*

Max drove with the expert skill of a seasoned D.C. commuter. She changed lanes and hit the gas pedal with the appropriate frequency to deter other drivers from cutting her off, except for the occasional jerk.

"Hey, asshole," she screamed, throwing up her hands. "What the hell do you think you're doing?"

"Whoa, who's talking like a sailor now?" Mike asked.

"Hey, buddy, you said the rules didn't take effect until my precious child is in the car. I'm just following your lead, besides if I'm going to shout out cusswords I have to do it now. I don't speak that way in front of Amanda."

Max pulled into the semi-circular drive at Forest Glenn School. She queued up with other parents picking up kindergartners. They spied Amanda by the curb, obediently waiting for her mother. Mike immediately knew to whom the child with the blue knapsack-style book bag belonged. She had the same facial features, only softer. And her hair was a bit darker than her mother's. As Amanda spoke to one of her little friends, she smiled a full smile, laughing and tossing back her head. *I know where she gets that.*

Max parked the Expedition by the curb. She and Mike got out the car and Amanda eyed him suspiciously.

"Hey, good lookin', how was school today?" Max asked her daughter.

She shrugged indifferently.

"How would you like to go see some of the Smithsonian this afternoon?"

Amanda's sprightly eyes glimmered even brighter, "Yeah!"

Max turned to Mike, "Amanda, this is my friend Mr. Chandler. He's going with us. Can you say hello?"

He immediately saw the youngster's shoulders sag and her excitement diminish measurably. He put out his hand, "Why don't you call me Mike?"

"No," Max said. "I want her to learn to say 'mister' and 'miss' and 'Yes, ma'am' and 'No, ma'am'. Isn't that right?" she said glaring at her little girl who had her hands plastered down by her side twisting her whole body into one giant "NO" head shake.

"Well, why don't we just compromise. You can call me Mr. Mike. How's that?"

In typical five-year-old fashion, Amanda said nothing. She pulled open the back passenger door, flung her book bag inside, climbed in the seat, and buckled up. She searched the seat pocket in front of her, produced a lollypop, unwrapped it, and put it in her mouth with the satisfaction of an adult enjoying a beer after a hard day's work.

"Sorry, she's a little shy around people she doesn't know,"

Max explained.

"Don't worry," Mike said. "She'll warm up to me sooner or later."

Max started the engine, checked her side mirror, and pulled into traffic. Looking into the rearview mirror Max asked, "Do you have homework tonight?"

Amanda nodded her head "yes" with an exaggerated motion as she took a long, slow, refreshing drag on the cherry flavored lollypop.

Mike turned in his seat to face the young girl. "What are you studying in school?" he asked in another attempt to break the ice.

Amanda glared at him. "Do I *have* to talk to him, mommy?"

Mike's face turned bright red from embarrassment. He shifted back forward in his seat, watching the road.

Max shot her daughter a look that could have melted glass. "No, ma'am. You don't have to talk to him, even though that's extremely rude. As far as I'm concerned rude little girls don't deserve to go to museums, or to dinner. Maybe I should just call Adrienne to see if she can baby sit tonight and..."

Max's body stiffened as she locked up the Expedition's brakes, sliding and barely missing the back of a Toyota Camry. She had been so engaged in admonishing Amanda, she didn't see that the line of vehicles up ahead had come to a slow crawl. "Jeez," she yelled.

For a tense moment silence hung in the vehicle's interior. Then a small voice from the backseat said, "Is he one of those A-holes, Mommy?"

Mike roared with laughter and now Max's face turned bright red.

"What did I say that's so funny?" Amanda asked,

genuinely perplexed.

"Nothing honey," Max said, her whole body convulsing as she broke into snickers.

"I thought you didn't cuss in front of her," Mike said.

"I wouldn't know where she picked up something like that," she said, slightly regaining her composure.

"But you say it every *morning*," Amanda chimed in with a bemused tone as she joined in the fun.

Mike turned to the beautiful little girl and gave her a wink. "You're okay, kid. You know that? You're okay."

Not lucky enough to find parking near the Smithsonian, the trio pulled into a $35.00-per-day garage about two blocks away. As they walked toward the complex, Max took Amanda's hand and swung her arm to its full extension front and back.

"What are we going to see today, Mandy?" Max asked.

"*Amanda*...Mom," said the little girl with determined emphasis. "I want to see the dinosaur bones."

"We've seen the dinosaur bones before. Why don't we go check out the First Ladies' Inaugural gown display?"

"Aw...who cares about a bunch of yucky old dresses, anyway? Dinosaur bones...pleeease," Amanda said, her fingers laced in a praying position.

"How about it, Mike, you're our guest. What would you like to see?" Max asked, her eyebrows raised to suggest the answer she expected.

"Well, Doc, I hate to disappoint you but I agree with Amanda. I'll take cool dinosaur bones over yucky dresses any day."

"Yeah," exclaimed an excited Amanda as she reached up with her free hand to take hold of Mike's.

Max rolled her eyes, shook her head, and bit her bottom

lip as she smiled. It was two against one and the expression on her face indicated she realized she'd been had. Not only did Mike avoid going to the gown exhibit, he also scored some major league points with her daughter.

The Smithsonian displayed its dinosaur exhibit in the National Museum of Natural History, a three-story building featuring fossils, animals, birds, and gems. On the building's ground floor were an array of gift shops, restrooms, offices, and an auditorium.

The bones so precious to a five-year-old were not found among the first floor gift shops, restrooms, and offices of the National Museum of Natural History so Amanda bounded up the stairs to the museum's first floor with Mike and Max trailing behind.

She walked quickly past the "Native Cultures of the Americas" display, turned to the left, and stared in wonder at the 87-foot-long *Diplodocus longus,* the centerpiece of the dinosaur hall. The creature's bones had once been bleached white, but their antiquity and air pollution yellowed them over the past few years.

Amanda again took Mike's hand and led him over to her favorite display–the huge *Allosaurus*. "Read that to me, please," she said pointing to a placard beside the velour security ropes.

"The strong jaws and sharp teeth are giveaways that *Allosaurus* was a flesh eater. Its large head and jaws relative to its body indicate that *Allosaurus* was able to attack animals like the plant-eater *Stegosaurus* that rivaled it in size," Mike read. "Most of the fossils here are real, not casts, and seven were startling finds upon which new species were named."

Amanda nodded her head and soaked in the words as if she knew what every one meant. Mike smiled recognizing that

Dr. Max Sheldon had a budding scholar on her hands. Amanda slowly made her way from exhibit to exhibit, winding her small frame between other children and D.C. tourists snapping away with flash bulbs.

Mike looked toward Max, "Maybe we could convince her to go to the gown exhibit after we finish here."

"We'll see," she said, staring thoughtfully into his eyes. "You're just a sucker for kids, aren't you?"

"Well..." he said a broad smile crossing his lips, "I guess so, especially cute little girls who can wrap me around their fingers. Besides, I need an excuse for doing fun things like going to waterslides and playing miniature golf. It looks strange for a full-grown man to do those things by himself."

"Ah, so you're a user," she said, matching his smile.

"Okay, you've got me nailed. I was up to four kids a day, but I've cut my habit back to just one every now and then. I can stop anytime I want to, really," he kidded.

Through animated laughter that brightened her eyes, Max managed to say, "You're insane, you know it?"

"C'mon, Doc. Let's get your daughter and go see the dresses."

By the end of the afternoon, Amanda warmed up even more to Mike and the trio decided to dine at Fabrini's. The hostess seated Max, Mike, and Amanda at a round table. The place had the look and feel of an authentic Italian eatery. A red-and-white checkered cloth draped their table. An empty wine bottle whose bottom rested in wicker and whose sides were streaked with bubbly-wax from the candle that burned in its open neck served as a centerpiece.

All the waiters wore red waistcoats, black pants, and bow ties. And many of them spoke fluent Italian. In the background a CD played the lightly stringed tunes of the Mediterranean.

As a waiter stood over his shoulder, Mike looked over the menu and selected a large portion of twelve-layer lasagna. The entree came with a bottomless salad bowl and loaves of crusty bread.

"And for the ladies," the waiter asked.

"I'll have the pasta salad with clam sauce..."

"Oh no, not another one of those 'I'll just have a salad' women," Mike silently groaned.

"...and the veal parmigiana."

Thank God. A woman who knows how to eat.

Max ordered spaghetti for Amanda, one of only two Italian food groups, the other being pizza, known to exist in the realm of children under twelve.

Good to her word, Max didn't bring up work. No racists, no behavior modification, nothing. The closest they came to discussing her job came when Mike prodded her about her career.

"So, how did you wind up at the prestigious FBI?"

"My major course work as an undergrad was working with at-risk kids. You know, trying to get violent or crime prone kids to change their lives so they didn't wind up dead or in jail for life. That's where the behavior modification came in. I began working on my Ph.D. at Georgetown and I wrote my thesis on the FBI's profiling program. That was my connection with the Bureau. I worked in the profiling section until they shut it down and then I stayed with the Behavioral Science unit. It's more research than anything else, but then every once in a while a guinea pig like you wanders in," she said smiling and cocking her head to the side.

Max intrigued Mike. That someone could be so

remarkably intelligent and yet so down to earth amazed him. He didn't want to push his luck, and he especially didn't want to upset or embarrass Amanda, but he wondered what happened to Mr. Sheldon and what kind of man would leave such a beautiful little girl and such a bright, gorgeous wife.

He didn't have to ask. "I've been with the Bureau for nearly eight years now. The only time I thought about leaving was when my husband, Frank, died. He was killed in a car accident. I really didn't know how Amanda and I would make it, but..." She stared into the distance.

Max grew somber and she paled a bit. Mike could tell from the look on her face how deeply she must have loved Frank Sheldon. How lucky he felt that she trusted him enough to share her remembrance of him.

"But we're doing great. Aren't we Mommy?" Amanda asked through slurps of spaghetti noodles.

"Yes, we are, sweetheart." Max leaned over to stroke Amanda's hair, a genuine, yet tentative smile returning to her face.

They finished their meal and ordered dessert. Mike really wasn't hungry, but he thought by ordering the sweets, he could prolong his inevitable return to his hotel room and the departure of his dinner guests.

As Amanda licked the last remaining vestiges of chocolate from her fudge sundae off her spoon, Max tilted her head toward her daughter and said, "This has been so much fun, I hate to end it, but tomorrow is a school day."

"I understand," Mike said, hoping his voice conveyed the contentment he felt at that moment. "Maybe we can do it again sometime."

Almost immediately Max blurted out, "Maybe next week, huh?" Her cheeks turned crimson and she looked toward the table. Mike realized her words betrayed an eagerness she had not actually wanted to share just yet.

"Next week it is," Mike said as he stood to pull out the ladies' chairs.

Over the course of their many briefings, Mike and Jason Dilworth had developed a mutual respect that was slowly transforming into a friendship. Their backgrounds could not have been more dissimilar and they hadn't one shared experience between them. At the moment, they were kindred spirits with a common goal. But Mike knew the reality of such relationships was that they were fleeting.

The thought that, after their mission was complete, the two might never see each other again, was a recurrent, palpable, and sad one for him. A few weeks ago, he never would have assumed he would have been so profoundly disheartened at the prospect of missing Jason's companionship. But much had changed for Mike Chandler in the last few weeks, and for once in his life, he realized, most of the change was for the better.

Today Dilworth explained in further depth some of his genetic experimentation and the disastrous effects he expected it to have. It was not a pleasurable discussion for him. When it was over, he shook his head and breathed deeply. It seemed to Mike that he was deliberately trying to force the thought of his sins into the far reaches of his memory, to hide them among the physical folds of his brain, as if the mere recollection of them brought them to life again.

"Mike," he said after a long moment of quiet, "I want to say something to you, and I don't mean it as an insult to you or any of the agents working this case."

"Doc, say what you've got to say. The only way we're

going to make any progress is through honesty."

Dilworth thought for minute, as if trying to choose his words carefully. "I think the fundamental, and quite honestly, perhaps the fatal flaw in operations such as these is the tendency for law enforcement to severely underestimate who they are dealing with."

Mike furrowed his brow not fully understanding what Dilworth was trying to say to him and inviting him to continue.

"You see, my impression is that Donnelly and Tucker and the others, not you as much, but certainly the agents who have little street experience, think the members of the Board are as clownish as the rednecks who parade around in robes and hoods."

"And you're saying they're not cut from the same cloth?" Mike asked leaning toward the doctor.

"Ideologically, in some respects, yes. But the Board itself is comprised of people who are rich and well connected and they got that way because they are smart." Dilworth spoke faster now with a sense of urgency. He also leaned in as if doing so would cause Mike to better understand, or better hear, at least, what he tried to impart.

"When I was a member, we were working on a new constitution for the country after our takeover. The Board adheres to a strict Jeffersonian philosophy."

Mike sat back in his chair and chuckled a bit. "Well, Jason, I'm afraid you're going to have to explain that one. Us ignorant street cops didn't have a lot of reason to study up on, what did you just call it, Jeffersonian philosophy?"

Dilworth winced and Mike interjected, reaching to touch the doctor's forearm, "I'm kidding. Really, I was just kidding you to break the tension. Go on."

Dilworth smiled, slightly chagrined at taking Mike's poke

so seriously. He continued his explanation. "Thomas Jefferson believed in a true democracy, one in which the majority rules absolutely."

"Is that not what we have here?" Mike asked, his palms open and upward gesturing around the room.

"Actually no," Dilworth said. "We have a representative republic. Majority rules certainly, but with checks and balances in place to ensure minority interests are always considered and sometimes given precedence over the will of most of the people.

"Jefferson asserted that the national government existed solely for dealing with governments of foreign nations and that states and states alone should have sovereignty over what happens within their borders." Dilworth both spoke and gesticulated like a professor delivering a political science lecture.

"I'm afraid I'm still lost, here Jason," Mike said bewildered.

"The Board's constitution follows those guidelines. You see, the Board, should it ever come to national power, will decentralize the federal government leaving the broad powers to govern in the hands of individual states. If Idaho wants to make it illegal for black people and Indians to own property, the state would have that authority. By the same token, if California wanted to allow wholesale, unregulated abortion and permit homosexual or mixed-race marriages, it would, according to the Board's governing document, be quite acceptable."

"Oh come on Jason," Mike said, the disbelief showing on his face, "Abortion? Mixed marriages? The people I've been briefed on over the last few weeks seem like they would incinerate the whole population of any state that would allow that to happen. I know you've been around them and certainly you know them a hell of a lot better than I do, but I just don't see how they would allow it to happen. Besides, just because you have a governing document doesn't mean it's worth the paper it's written on if you don't have the power to enforce it."

"Again that's where you underestimate their intelligence, Mike." Dilworth's voice was louder now.

Mike and Dilworth pounded the table making their points and there couldn't have been more than twelve inches separating their noses. Mike mused that if anyone else were observing the two, surely he and Dilworth would look like two debaters locked in fierce verbal battle.

"Then explain it to me, Jason, in terms I can understand."

"The Board has a plan, Mike. Like Jefferson, they realize that in order to make certain you secure certain rights, you must give up other rights and move slowly. They are prepared to take years to implement their master plan."

Dilworth began counting his points off on his fingers as he made them. "For years they have silently but deliberately engaged in domestic terrorism, implementing strategies like the cancer genes I developed. They have systematically denied rights to minorities and coerced or methodically eliminated anyone who supported them." Jason stood and began pacing in front of his chair. "They have manipulated the legal system in every community they could. They have infiltrated the illegal narcotics market to keep drugs available to people of every race they consider weak minded. And I know of plans to poison supplies to eliminate those who are pathetic enough to become addicts. Over the last few years they have tried to demoralize and destroy education systems, employment opportunities, civil liberties efforts, anything that is designed to advance minorities in this country."

Mike sat mesmerized by Jason's passion. He didn't speak. He knew Dilworth had to get this off his chest. "And now I hear they are preparing for a race war. Oh no, but not any race war. *The* race war. For whatever reason, Truman and the others on the Board have decided now is the time. They've stockpiled weapons, recruited members, lined up followers all over the country."

Dilworth ran his hand through his thick brown hair. He looked tired and defeated after making his speech. He gazed, sadly, into some middle distance for a moment. He spoke again, but this time in a feeble, desperate voice. "And I helped them. I helped them." He grew silent again and contemplative.

Mike looked at the top of the conference table. He did not want to interfere with what was obviously a private moment of atonement for Jason Dilworth. He didn't want to muddy a sincere, heartfelt moment with a patronizing comment or disingenuous tone. So he sat in his chair mulling his own thoughts.

Finally he decided to speak. "Know anybody who's Catholic, Jason?"

Dilworth seemed perplexed by the question, but he answered it anyway, still casting his gaze into the nothingness on the other side of the room. "Yeah, a few. Why?"

"I have a Catholic friend who told me once that Catholics believe the way to salvation is not only through faith and repentance, but by those things combined with good deeds."

Dilworth turned to look at Mike. The two men's eyes bored into one another from across the room. "For what it's worth, Jason, this smart-mouth ex-cop forgives you. And if you'll let me, I'll help you bring these people down. For you, for me, for your grandson, for Bennigan and whoever else they've killed along the way."

Silence hung between the men, but it incubated a bond of trust, a new understanding. They nodded an affirmation to that bond, neither knowing what else to say. It was a tacit acknowledgement of agreement among two men, both star-crossed, but both resolute to change their fortunes, and along with them, the destiny of their times.

Jason resumed his place at the table and he and Mike began again developing a strategy to confront the Board.

Later that afternoon, Mike returned to his hotel room. He cranked up the air conditioning and positioned his chair between the vent and the television. Propping his feet on the edge of the bed, he mindlessly flipped through the channels with the remote control. He had become only mildly interested in a sitcom rerun when his phone rang.

"Mike? I need help. Can you come rescue me?" Max's voice was a mixture of frustration and mock pleading.

"Sure. What's the problem?"

"The Expedition has a flat. I'm on the interstate just outside the city with cars whooshing by. I've got Amanda and it's 110 degrees out here. I called Triple A over an hour ago and they said they were backed up even then." Over the phone Mike could hear the cars and trucks passing by. "I tried changing it myself, but Amanda keeps getting out of the car and with all this traffic.... Besides, I can't figure out how this jack works. You need a Ph.D."

Mike chuckled and said, "Hey, Doc...don't you have a Ph.D.?"

"Look you," she said, her voice forceful.

"I'm sorry. Couldn't resist that one. Tell me where you are and I'll get there as soon as I can," he said.

Max told him the interstate and mile marker numbers.

Mike wrote them down on a piece of hotel stationery and then called the desk to arrange for a cab. The ride out took twenty minutes, and as his taxi pulled in behind Max's Expedition, she got out.

"I feel so dumb. Right after we hung up, I told Amanda you were coming to help us and she asked me what kind of car you had. I didn't even think about you not having one until then. Here," she said reaching into her purse, "let me pay the fare."

Mike waved her off. "Ah, your money's no good here, Doc. You can make it up to me somehow." He raised his eyebrows and winked.

Max threw her head back and laughed. "You perv."

The heat of the late afternoon and the perspiration of her aborted effort at tire changing caused her blouse to stick to her back. She opened the rear hatch revealing the spare tire and a two-piece jack handle with a hexagonal design.

"Hi there, Mr. Mike," Amanda said with an exaggerated wave.

Mike winked at the little girl as he unscrewed the nut fastening the spare tire into its well and picked up the pieces of the jack. "Hey good looking. Are you tired of sitting here on the road?"

She sighed audibly and nodded her head. "Sure am."

"I'll get you going in a jiffy," he continued. Concentrating on the pieces of pressed metal in his hands, he said. "I think this fits in here like this."

He effortlessly put the jack handle together and looked at Max who plastered an exasperated smile on her lips. "I'll wait over here." She executed a quick about face and stood behind the Expedition as Mike placed the jack under the axle support.

It took him only about ten minutes to change the flat, but

in that time he became drenched with sweat. It saturated his shirt, flowed down in the delta beneath the small of his back, and dripped like a leaky faucet off his forehead and the tip of his nose. As he placed the jack and handle back in their place in the cargo area, he leaned his head to the side and wiped his forehead on the shoulder of his shirt. "Okay," he said. "You're all set. Can you take me back into the city or do you want to use your cell and call another cab for me?"

"Neither. You're coming home with us. I at least owe you dinner. We'll grill out."

"I can't do that. I'm filthy and soaking wet."

"There's a Wal-Mart a mile from our house. We can stop and buy you a pair of shorts and a tee shirt and I'll wash what you have on while we're eating. Does that sound good to you Amanda?"

"Sure. I got the new Maximo Playstation game. You could play that with me. We won't tell anybody you stink," the little girl said.

Max blushed as she laughed heartily. Mike threw his hands up and smiled. "Now, how in the world could I resist an invite as good as that? To Wal-Mart Dr. Sheldon," he said, taking his seat in the front of the Expedition.

At the Sheldon home, Mike went into the guest bath, showered, and changed. He brought out his pants and shirt, still damp with perspiration and whistled to himself as he deposited his clothes in the washer and added detergent.

Mike inhaled the distinct smell of sautéing garlic, hearing it sizzling in an unseen pan on the stovetop. "Hey, Doc," he called out. "Want to throw anything in with my stuff?"

Max, holding a half-peeled onion and a kitchen knife, peered around the doorjamb leading from the kitchen. "Well,"

Max said raising her eyebrows, "a man who can fix a tire and wash his own clothes. Do you cook too?"

"Why sho' nuff, honey," he teased in a falsetto drawl, "my Mama raised me to be an independent woman."

Max gave him a wide smile and cocked her head motioning him into the kitchen. "I think you've done enough manual labor for me today. Just come in the kitchen and fix yourself something to drink while Mandy and I finish up dinner."

Mike helped himself to a soft drink while Amanda pressed fresh ground round into hefty-sized patties for the grill and Max diced onions to add to the garlic mixture on the stove. He surveyed the Sheldon home, taking note of Amanda's refrigerator art and a stack of bills sitting beside a computer workstation in the far corner of the kitchen. He had wondered, ever since their "date" a few weeks back if he would ever have the privilege of visiting *casa* Sheldon.

He glanced over the bar countertop and into the den, a mix of comfortable seating, finely appointed antique tables, a grandfather clock whose mellow tones chimed each half-hour, and a scattering of dolls and games in front of the television set. He closed his eyes and drew a long, relaxing breath. Everything here–the sights, the smells, and the sounds–seemed relaxing and normal.

He accompanied Max onto the patio as she grilled the hamburgers while Amanda played her video game. He helped tear the lettuce and slice tomatoes while the burgers cooked. "You're slicing those tomatoes upside down, you know?" she said casting him a sideways glance.

"Excuse me?" Mike said halting his knife in mid-stroke.

"It's easier if you slice them from the bottom. You don't have to go to all the trouble of cutting out the stem. You throw the rest away when you cut down that far and then your slices don't have those huge holes in the middle."

"Well my heavens, Ms. Betty Crocker. I wasn't aware there was a right or wrong way to slice a tomato," Mike said without changing his method.

"You're still doing it wrong," Max said in a singsong tone.

"Yeah, well tell you what, you don't tell me how to slice 'maters and I won't tell you how to do electroshock therapy on your patients, how's that?" Mike smiled.

"Maters?"

"Maters," he said with finality.

They continued their banter over dinner, teasing with Amanda, all of them laughing and having a good, happy time. Mike helped clear the few serving dishes they used while Amanda discarded their paper plates and napkins. They retired to the den where Amanda proceeded to beat him without mercy in game after game of Maximo.

"I think you've trounced him enough," Max said finally. "Why don't you go get on your pajamas and maybe we can watch some TV before you go to sleep since tomorrow's Saturday."

Before Amanda replied, the loud ringing of the telephone intruded into the den. Max picked up the receiver on the portable phone by the couch. "Hello. Oh, hello...just a minute." Her voice sounded strained. She looked at Mike and mouthed a tacit, "Be right back," as she covered the mouthpiece and walked back to the kitchen.

"Guess that's Mr. Joe calling again," Amanda said without ungluing her eyes from the video screen.

"Who?" Mike's curiosity was piqued.

"Mr. Joe. He calls here a lot." Her fingers worked the game controls feverishly.

Mike stood up. "I need to go to the little boy's room." He walked gingerly toward the lavatory he used to change clothes earlier. The hairs in his ears stood on end, tuned for any hint of Max's conversation. He entered the bathroom and pushed the door almost closed. He tried to slow the heartbeats that were interfering with his ability to listen.

Max's voice, though low, sounded excited, almost agitated. He only heard snippets of her conversation. "...none of your business who I spend..." and then her voice lowered to inaudibility. "I know, I know..." Her voice sounded soft, almost placating and Mike immediately wondered if he was foolish to believe Max might find him attractive. He felt deflated.

He switched on the water for a few seconds as if he was washing his hands and then he opened the door, switching off the light as he departed the bathroom. As he turned the corner, Max nearly ran him over.

"Whoa, sorry." Startled, she backed away from him and Mike wondered whether she believed physical contact might belie some secret.

"Everything okay?" he asked.

"Yeah. Just business." Mike tried to penetrate her thoughts with his eyes. He knew that she spent much of her days training him, though certainly the Bureau wouldn't waste such a highly skilled resource like Dr. Maxine Sheldon just on him.

Still, her demeanor bothered him, but before he could ask anything else, she deflected him. "Amanda, honey, It's really time for you to got get on your pajamas. Quit stalling, now."

The little girl begrudgingly switched off the video game and dragged herself stoop shouldered up the stairs muttering the entire way. Max smiled at her, watching her climb the steps to her room while Mike observed how at home the two felt with each other. He let his suspicions subside momentarily.

Max reached for the remote control and flipped on the television set. "What's your pleasure, Mr. Chandler?"

He shrugged. "Anything but the news channels. Those talking heads irritate me. Sitcoms, game shows, sports, anything you want."

Amanda bounded back down the stairs dressed in a pair of footy pajama bottoms and an oversized nightshirt. She balled up in one corner of the couch and settled in. "Oh, this show. This show, please!" she asked as Max surfed through to a program on the Disney channel.

"Is it okay if we watch this for a few minutes? She'll drift off before long and we can switch it," Max said, beginning in a loud whisper and then slipping into a regular tone when she realized Amanda wasn't listening to her anyway.

"Anything's fine," Mike said, relaxed and comfortable, just happy to be sharing the time with Max and her daughter, and to be out of the confining walls of his hotel room. But most of all, he felt renewed and alive to be with them, to have something close to a "normal" Friday night with people who wanted him to be there and whose company he also enjoyed.

Before long, he heard Amanda's gentle breathing as she lay sleeping, still curled into a ball on the couch, only with her arms limp and her mouth hanging open, the sign of a contented, albeit exhausted, five-year-old hostess. Max pointed upstairs and mouthed something silently as she picked up her daughter to take her to her bed.

When she came back downstairs, she plopped down into a plush lounger and picked up the remote control. She flipped through the channels, but found nothing she wanted to see, though periodically she told Mike to stop her if he saw something he was interested in. She blew what seemed like an exasperated breath to remove her bangs out of her eyes. She surfed through the channels a third time. Then she switched the set off.

"A hundred stations with cable and there's never anything worth watching," she said.

Mike, listing heavily onto the full, rich leather cushions of the couch, remained silent. He looked at her intently, his forefinger curled up over his top lip.

"What are you staring at?" she asked a wide smile inching its way across her face.

"Just you." He smiled back. "This is so nice. Tonight has been great."

"Has been, huh? Does that mean you're getting ready to leave me?" she said winking and poking out her bottom lip.

Mike flushed, and squirmed in his chair. "I, ah...well, I don't have to leave, but I thought you might be ready to go to bed, and I still have to get a taxi into the city. But, ah...I'll stay if you want."

Now it was Max's turn to get embarrassed. "Oh, Mike, I didn't mean to make you uncomfortable. I was just teasing. To be honest, I'm a bit nervous. I haven't had a man over for dinner or anything like tonight since Frank died." She looked toward the floor and picked at her cuticle. "I mean, if it were up to me, you could just bunk up in our guestroom, but with Amanda and all..." She stammered her words.

"Oh, I know," he interrupted. "Nothing would make me happier than to wake up here in the morning. But I wouldn't put you in a bad position like that."

A blanket of tension hung in the room like the heavy humidity of earlier in the day.

Something screamed inside him. His ears were ringing. He wanted to kiss her, to hold her, to make love to her madly. He hoped she felt that way, too. But the phone call. This delicate dance around what each of them wanted to say but wouldn't commit to words. It was too much, too soon. So Mike did the only thing he knew to do. He left everything unsaid for the sake of decorum.

Max shifted from her chair onto the ottoman facing Mike. She sandwiched his hand in hers and softly rubbed the back of his hand. She tendered him a weak smile, the expression of a beleaguered compatriot, and he knew she felt the same way he did. But he also knew that relationships, such as the one he desperately wanted to cultivate with Max, advanced slowly, sometimes painfully slow. Tonight was one of those painful times.

"Maybe one day, huh?" Max said softly.

He pursed his lips and glanced down, breathing deeply, feeling every ounce of energy and expectation drain from his frame onto the floor. Then he raised his head and smiled at Max. "One day," he said. Then he added, "Why don't you call me that cab, Doc?"

Chapter Nine

Mike had just stepped out of the shower and was watching one of the morning news programs when the phone in his hotel room rang.

"Mike, David Donnelly here. Listen, change of plans for today. Rather than your usual meeting with Dilworth, how about meeting us in the conference room about 9:30?"

"Is something up?" Mike asked.

"We got word of some big meeting coming up in Tennessee. Looks like we're gonna need to kick things into high gear. We'll give you a full briefing when you get in."

Mike sat down on the edge of the bed after he hung up the receiver. His hair spiked out in all directions from where he had been toweling it dry. He stared blankly at the floor and had one of those weird out-of-body feelings as if he were watching himself from the ceiling.

He knew that one day he would have to put all this recent training to use, but he had so focused on absorbing information, he hadn't thought about the actual mission for quite some time. Now that was all about to change.

He tried to dress quickly, but no matter how fast he combed his hair or buttoned his shirt, it seemed as if he moved in slow motion. It was only seven forty-five. He had nearly two hours before his meeting with the agents, but he felt like he needed to get there as soon as he could. He had no idea why he felt such a sense of urgency.

He wanted to call Max but he decided against it. He thought she was probably rushing to get Amanda dressed and off to school if she hadn't left already. In the three weeks since their first night out together, he had seen her five other times. She had even been brave enough to have him over for a barbecue with friends, something, she told him, she hadn't done since becoming a young widow.

Their relationship grew in intensity and Mike found it hard to concentrate on behavioral or work matters when he was around Max. He simply wanted to look into her eyes and dream of what could be. This morning's phone call reminded him with cold, stark clarity that before he could make a future with Max, he had to make the Board a thing of the past.

Only four city blocks separated the hotel and the FBI building. Mike stopped in a small, bustling diner along the way and got a steaming, hot, black cup of coffee and a bagel. He walked quickly, taking long strides, and entered the FBI's main lobby at 8:20. Not even the receptionist was there yet.

Just after Mike finished reading the same article in the *Post* for the fourth time, Donnelly stuck his head through a secured, heavy door just beyond a metal detector.

"Mike, come on back."

Walking down the hallway to the conference room, he couldn't help but feel the corridor seemed narrower than it did the last time he came to this part of the building a few weeks ago.

As the pair entered the conference room, Mike saw Tucker and another agent he had never seen before.

"Mike, this is Russ Logan, from the electronic surveillance section," Tucker said. The men shook hands. Tucker continued, "As David told you on the phone, we've gotten word that the Board is putting together some massive meeting; what they're calling a worldwide convocation, at one of the Klan's paramilitary sites in Tennessee. Looks like they're setting it up for later this month, sometime around the 24th. We're going to brief you on what we know and then Russ is going to outfit you with some surveillance and tracking gear and give you a demo on how it works."

As in their previous meetings, Donnelly pressed a button to lower a slide screen and a second to dim the glare from the overhead fluorescent lights. Logan finished laying out his equipment and took a chair at the table to watch the presentation.

Rather than the faces Mike was used to seeing, photographs of the Tennessee camp appeared on the screen.

"This is an aerial view of the compound," Donnelly began. "As you can see it's isolated and geographically well protected. It sits on top of a rise and there's only one road in or out. The man who owns the compound also owns the acreage that surrounds it so, logistically speaking, setting up any kind of perimeter is out."

With a red laser pointer he circled a lake. "Should you encounter trouble, we could gain access from here, but it's a fair assumption that they patrol the shoreline and maybe even have it booby trapped."

Mike studied the photo. Donnelly was right. The camp itself appeared to be a bald, dusty spot among tall pine trees on a hilltop surrounded by dense underbrush. A small, tan ribbon of a road wound around the lake and up to the main entry gate, a large wooden stockade barrier.

Tucker brought the lights back up. "We've heard from five different informants over the past few weeks that the Board was putting this thing together. It's not your ordinary cross burning. Our intel has been pretty good on this group and they're gearing up for some kind of final holocaust."

Donnelly jumped in, "Our information is that there could be between 200 to 500 people there. Supposedly it's open to all Klan member groups, but for sure some muckety-mucks are coming to strategize with the Board."

"We're going to try to minimize the risks as much as possible. That's why we got Russ to come in with some of his toys," Tucker said.

Russ Logan stood up and spoke for the first time since Mike walked in the room. "Mike, from the looks of that photo, if things go to hell you should have plenty of avenues for concealment, but not for escape."

"I don't know," Mike replied, "Seems to me I could make a bee line for those woods. You know, the proverbial needle-in-a-haystack."

"Don't underestimate these guys. Out in the pine trees they could have stuff as sophisticated as electronic listening devices to weapons as crude as trip wires and tiger pits. Remember, there are a lot of ex-military and military wannabe's among these groups," Logan said.

Picking up a worn and tattered wallet, Logan tossed it across the table. "We've sewn a chip in the lining. That has your bogus driver's license and other paperwork in it, too, by the way. Using a global positioning satellite, we can locate you anywhere as long as you have it with you."

Logan then showed him his duffel bags and overnight cases each outfitted with similar locator chips. He gave Mike a pair of sunglasses rigged up with a micro-sized pinhole camera. "Everything I'm giving you operates on wireless technology. All of it is new, some even experimental. I don't want to blow smoke. I don't know how well these will work for intelligence gathering, but it should let the agents monitor your safety well enough to respond if they need to."

"So I really am a guinea pig," Mike said. He raised his eyebrows noting that no one responded.

"This is really cool," Logan continued as he smiled indulgently and handed Mike a shirt emblazoned with a familiar logo. The shirt depicted a Confederate battle flag carried by a frumpy, cartoonish Johnny Reb figure. The caption beneath it read, "Forget Hell!"

"What's so cool about this?" Mike asked. "I've seen them before."

"Yeah," Logan replied, "but this paint on the flag and in the wording is fluorescent. You get in trouble at night and you're wearing this shirt, any of our guys could pick you out of a thousand people using night vision goggles."

The agent continued his explanation of each of the wares he gave to Mike–all remotely accessible by the agents watching over him, all battery powered, light-weight, disguised, charged up, and ready to go.

Nodding toward Tucker, Logan said, "As he said, we can't be with you inside the compound, but we'll try to reduce the danger to you as much as possible. We'll have boaters in the lake pretending to be fishermen during the day. And we'll set up a perimeter and command post as close as we can without getting found out."

Mike thought for a moment, looking at his new equipment, staring through it, rather, trying to encompass every question he had into this one briefing, realizing he may not have another opportunity to ask. "What about something as simple as a cell phone?" he said looking at Tucker. "We could establish a regular time for me to call to check in. If I miss, you guys know to come running."

Tucker seemed to have anticipated the question. He didn't even glance at his fellow agents before answering. "Well, Mike, we don't know what kinds of things you'll be doing in the compound. You can't very well stop in the middle of a training exercise to call in."

"No," Tucker continued, straightening his papers on the conference table, "That would send up too much a red flag. Besides, from what we know about these guys, they're not the kind who are going to check in with their wives every night just to see how it's going. You can take a phone in and use it if necessary, but let's not set up any calls in advance." The other agents nodded in agreement.

Mike was trying to let all this information sink in. "What about satellite or infrared technology? I read where you guys can read the odometer off a jeep from a satellite 120 miles up."

The agents looked at each other as if to see who would answer, again apparently anticipating the question. Logan spoke up. "Mike, we could use that technology and not have to send you in at all. We could gather satellite photos of everyone there and compare them against driver's license databases to ID everyone we could. We could use the infrared to track movements in the camp, watch while people were training with weapons, building bombs...whatever." He held up his hands in exasperation.

"I hear a 'but' in there," Mike said.

Tucker picked up the conversation. "The 'but' is that federal judges have been suppressing evidence that we've gathered through these devices. Some lawyers have argued, and many judges apparently agree, that the technology gives us an unfair advantage; that it's an unreasonable invasion of privacy and, consequently, an illegal search."

Mike put his fingertips together and rested his chin on

them, mulling over this information.

Tucker continued, "That's not to say we're not going to use it."

Mike raised his eyebrows looking at the agent to imply he didn't understand.

"Mike, you're valuable to us. We're going to use the equipment to monitor you're safety. If things go to shit, then we're sending in the cavalry, to hell with the case. We'll just make the best of what we've got. We're not going to let anything happen to you."

"It's comforting to hear you say that," Mike said with much more seriousness than he had displayed to the agents before.

"You okay?" Logan asked.

"As okay as I'm going to get," Mike said.

Mike left the room and walked to Max's office. He had so many things to discuss with her. He peaked around her door and rapped his knuckles lightly on the doorframe.

"Anybody home?"

Her office was empty, her chair swung away from her desk as if she had just left. Her computer hummed on her desk. He walked around to the business side of her desk and glanced at her Daytimer trying to determine whether to wait or leave. She did not have an appointment noted, so Mike decided to hang around a bit.

He snickered to himself at the sight of her desk with scattered papers and notes scrawled hastily on Post-It notes she adhered to the side of her computer. On top of her terminal, she had arranged seven tiny model Volkswagen Beetles, each one no larger than a nickel.

"They're just so cute," she told him once. A red one stood out in the middle of the bumper-to-bumper line of toy cars.

Silver Beetles, three on each side, bounded it. Besides her books and a coffee mug emblazoned with a photo of Max and Amanda by the beach, the cars were the only personal collectibles to adorn her office.

Just as Mike turned to take a seat, Max's computer intoned a muted "ping" denoting an incoming e-mail. The noise caught his attention and as he looked at the screen, he felt his chest constrict as the small window in the corner of the screen popped up with the message, "Inbox: From joejens@freemail.com, Subject– 'Afternoon Gorgeous.'"

Mike furrowed his brow and felt jealousy flood over him. He could not resist the urge to pry. He felt proprietary and at the same time guilty for violating Max's privacy, but unbridled suspicion drove him. He had let down all his walls for Max. He did not want to fall victim to love unreturned measure for measure.

He maneuvered the mouse and clicked her Outlook Mail icon, he selected the button to view messages sorted by addresses. He had to brace himself as his eyes rested on a screen full of messages from "joejens" all with subject lines like "Hey beautiful," "Missing You," and "I love you, Sweetness."

Mike wanted to smash the screen. At that moment, he wanted to walk out on Max Sheldon and the FBI and never return. He wanted to die. How could he have been foolish enough to believe a woman like Max would want a man like him?

He crashed back into the present as he heard heels clicking on the polished floor getting closer, and Max's voice say hello to someone just down the hall. He hurriedly rearranged her view screen as she had had it before and moved around to the front of her desk.

Max smiled as she entered her office and saw him. She creased her eyes as she greeted him with a warm hand on his shoulder. "I was hoping you'd stop by today."

"I'm supposed to go in next week," he said, not even saying hello.

"Donnelly told me late last night. He called me at home to see if I thought we needed any more work. I told him I thought you were ready."

Max walked around and sat down behind her desk. Mike sat, doing his best not to explode. His heart and his head pounded. His cheeks felt hot and the blood pulsating through his veins made it feel as if his head was bobbing.

Max glanced at her computer screen. Mike studied her face for any reaction at all. He didn't have to wait long.

"Shit, shit, shit," she said.

"What is it?" Mike asked. He still wanted to be cautious and prepared for any deception.

Max leaned back in her chair, which squeaked in time with her exasperated exhaling. "Well, I haven't said anything, but," she breathed out heavily through her nose and stretched her lips into a tight expression of frustration.

"Yes," Mike said. He arched his eyebrows awaiting her answer.

"There's a field agent in Baltimore, named Joe Jensen."

"I see," Mike said. This time he exhaled a thick breath trying to purge the heaviness from his heart.

"He's been hitting on me for a year. The guy's a jerk. A decent agent, but still a jerk and he just won't take no for an answer."

Mike blew out a sigh of relief. "And you're not seeing him or interested in seeing him?"

"Hell no," Max said snorting out a contemptuous laugh at

the thought.

As angry as Mike had become before, he was twice as relieved now. "Well. You're a big girl. You don't need me to tell you how to handle it."

"Thanks, Mike. It's nothing you need to be concerned about. Really."

"Do I look concerned?"

She picked up the file folder with his name displayed on the tab. "Frankly, Subject: Chandler, Michael A., you looked as tight as a drum when I walked in here and now you're so happy, you could pee all over yourself, so you tell me." She began to putter on her desk, even-keeled, acting as if she didn't expect him to answer the question.

After a moment, he said, "Well. Donnelly thinks I'll be in briefings into the night. Could I call you tomorrow morning?"

Max stopped shuffling papers and looked directly at him. "Yes. Please do. I need you to call me."

Mike walked alone through the klan compound. Without warning, something seized him by the neck and swung him about. Rather than an enemy, he saw a faceless specter, sinister and insidious. His stomach clenched; his heart raced. Around him, he could hear Klansmen laughing, wickedly amused at the tormenting of his soul. No one came to his aid. No one stood or spoke in his defense. He faced death alone.

Mike, in the Devil's grasp, realized he had challenged evil and this was his punishment. He tried to scream, his throat tight in Lucifer's hold. He heard wind whistling and swirling, distant screams, and groans. Feeling himself slip into unconsciousness, and gasping for breath, he called on the only power supreme enough to fight this battle for him: God.

Blackness descended upon him.

Mike sprang bolt upright in bed, sweat streaming from his temples. The bed linens swirled around his feet as he kicked to free himself. Wide-eyed, he gazed around his darkened hotel room, trying to get his bearings. Heart pounding wildly, breath labored, he was not entirely sure whether it had been a dream or a warning.

"A nightmare," he muttered as he flopped back onto his pillow, covering his face with his hands.

Mike didn't normally have nightmares, especially ones this frightening. In fact, he hadn't had a dream this intense and unsettling since the days following Jarrod Payne's death. The irony did not escape him that that incident was what had led him to this moment in his life.

Mike sat back up, on the edge of the bed, gasping slightly, waiting for his heart to calm down. He felt so tense that the small of his back knotted into a hard ball. The only sound in the room came from a small noise machine on the nightstand beside his bed. Mike turned it off and listened, not sure what he was listening for. He was surrounded by the noise of nothingness. Ever since childhood, he hated the sound of silence. To him it was the sound of death and every pop of the floor or ping of the heat registers only signified the footsteps of death drawing ever closer.

Taking a last deep breath, Mike turned to check the clock beside his bed. It read 2:17 A.M. Looked like he had a long sleepless night yet to go.

Mike called Max at 8:30. He paused a while before saying, "Listen, I've got to spend the day getting some last minute things done. You think we could meet for dinner?"

"Better yet," Max said, "I'll arrange for a sitter and pick you up about 6:30. That way you won't have to rush for the

171

train in case we spend a lot of time talking. Ah...that is, if you want to talk," Max said stumbling over her words. She sounded as nervous about Mike's mission as he felt. He realized she violated her own rule and let him get too close– way too close–and her anxiety was the price she paid.

"Yeah, I think we need to. Talking is good," he offered just to break the tension. "I'll see you at 6:30."

Mike had an old will, but God only knew where the thing was. He thought about contacting a lawyer or maybe seeing if one of the Bureau's staff attorneys would help him draft a new one, but he knew he could hand write it on a napkin and, as long as it was witnessed and notarized, it would be valid. *Besides, I don't have much worth giving away.*

After he wrote out his new "Last Will and Testament," he made a list of things to buy: a gift for Amanda; clothes and toiletries for the trip; get a safety deposit box to keep his 'real' wallet and personal effects and the will after he had one of the hotel staff witness it for him.

Maybe I'll go sit on a bench by the Capitol just to think about what I'm about to do.

A few minutes before 6:30, Max's, by now familiar, Ford Expedition pulled up in front of Mike's hotel. He got in the passenger's seat and, other than choosing a restaurant, they said little. Max suggested Hilliard's, a cozy place that offered everything from nachos to steaks. Decorated in rich, dark mahogany with high-backed booths and burgundy velour bench seating, Hilliard's had an intimate, if not seductive atmosphere.

Mike felt like he had much to say and little time to say it. A lot had happened between them in such a short time, he jumped right into the conversation. "Look Doc, I know I ought to ease into this but...well, I've really enjoyed getting to know you and Amanda, If anything goes wrong I just want you to know..."

"Nothing's going to go wrong," Max said emphatically, reaching out to grab both his hands as if to physically restrain the thought of something happening to him. "You're a professional. You know what to do." Her edginess eased slightly, "But still you be careful, because, well Amanda has grown quite fond of you, enamored, actually. So if you get hurt, I'm sure...you know." She twisted a pack of sweetener as she talked.

"How about you Doc? How do you feel about me? About us?"

A strained silence settled between them. Then the dam broke. Max fixed her gaze directly into Mike's eyes. "You're a generous, caring, gentle man. You have a profane sense of humor, and you equate almost everything to something sexual. Still you're absolutely hilarious and it's impossible not to like you. I say like, because I'm trying very hard to keep my guard up to keep from falling in love. But, if you must know, it's not working.

"Don't get any ideas, though. I haven't even kissed you yet. I haven't felt this way since my husband died, much less said it to anybody. But you just watch your step mister, because if you break my heart, I'll hunt you down and kill you. There, I said it."

Mike said nothing at first. He was stunned, yet pleased at her words and at the depth of her emotion. A satisfied smiled crossed his lips as he eyed Max. She looked like a marathoner at the end of her race. The pent up emotion finally released. She resumed twisting the sweetener pack, which by this time had begun sprinkling white grains of its contents all over the table.

Red-faced, he looked at the table rather than Max as he reached into his lapel pocket and pulled an envelope from it. "I spent a lot of today writing." He lifted his eyes up to hers. "I'm not much of a writer, but when I have certain things to say, I'm much better writing them than speaking." Even now he fumbled his words. "I learned a long time ago not to leave things unsaid, even if it's not exactly what you want to hear. I had no real idea how or what you felt before just now. But I knew I had to take a chance and tell you this."

Mike slipped the envelope across the tabletop and as Max reached to receive it, their fingers touched ever so slightly. He felt the electricity, the excitement that just her touch brought and again he looked into her smiling eyes.

Max took the envelope and opened it slowly with first her fingernail and then one finger. She seemed eager to look at the contents, but almost afraid of what the note would say. She looked at it and appeared to read the first few lines. Her hands began trembling and her eyes glistened. She looked at Mike, deeply, lovingly.

"This is beautiful," she said. Her voice was wispy and emotional. Mike returned a plaintive smile and gently took the hand that held the note.

"Thank you," he said softly.

Max angled her head to one side as she continued to stare into Mike's eyes, beyond them, he felt, to the unfathomable depths of his being.

"Would you do me a favor?" she asked.

"Sure."

"These are beautiful words and I'd love to hear them. I want to hear your voice say them." She extended the note back toward him.

Mike felt no hesitation, no embarrassment, not one

moment's faltering as he took the note from Max. In a soothing, romantic tone just above a whisper, he began reading, "You probably notice I spend a lot of time looking into your eyes. What I see always warms my heart. When I look deeply into your eyes, I see kindness and compassion. I see a gentleness and contentment that I rarely see in anyone, man or woman. I see wisdom and intelligence and I see love. Whatever I am to you, I will always be your friend, your number one supporter, your partner, and your soulmate. I will never abandon you. One look into your eyes is all I need to confirm that all of this is true and real."

Max placed her hand over her lips and closed her eyes. A small tear worked its way out and she dabbed it with her napkin. Mike's heart sank, afraid he had upset her by being too forward. Before he lost himself in thought too deeply, Max reached over and clenched his hand. The force and intensity of her grasp let him know he had touched her soul. As quickly as his emotions dipped, they began to soar with a feeling of elation he had never felt before.

Max held his hand and his gaze as she reached into her purse at her feet to retrieve her own envelope. "You're not the only one who's been writing today," she said, handing Mike the card.

A single red rose decorated the outside of the note. He opened it carefully and read her words, his heart beating with anticipation of what this lovely woman might have to say.

So....Have I told you how I just love that little so—the drop in your inflection—the pause that follows? Have I told you how I just love your laugh? It brightens the moment and makes my heart swell and my belly smile back...Have I told you how I just love your

175

*voice–your words–running over and around and
down swirling inside of my head–lifting my spirits
and leaving me waiting for the next time? Have I
told you how I just love the touch of your hands–
those hands filled with strength yet so gentle? Have I
told you how I just love the mass of your being–of
feeling so small and protected by just being near
you? Of feeling vulnerable yet safe? Have I told you
how I just love you?–who you are, the way you are,
and who you were–how I'll love you, always...*

She looked at him. "What are you staring at?"

"Just the most beautiful woman on the face of the earth."

Max and Mike finished their meal, laughing and talking
about ordinary things. They didn't consciously avoid the topic
of Mike's mission, but after relieving the tension that hung
between them at the beginning of dinner, it simply never came
up.

During dessert, Max, with the toe of her shoe, played with
the cuff of his pants, and he, occasionally, would brush against
her shoulder while extending his arm across the back of her
chair. They exchanged jokes and laughed wildly.

The waiter took their check and Mike noticed that Max
cast a melancholy look across the crowded restaurant.
"Something wrong?"

"Just a little self-pity, I suppose," she said. "None of the
other people here realize or care that, for the first time in years,
I'm enjoying the company of a man I truly feel for deeply, and
now you're leaving for an assignment that might cost you your
life."

For a moment, both of them sat in silence, Max cupping
her chin in her palm while Mike stared down and fiddled with

the lone remaining spoon on their table.

"I guess we'd better head back," she said.

"Guess so," he repeated. Their eyes met, and for one incredible second, he knew in his heart there were a million more things to say, but with all his human frailties, not one single way to put them into words.

Just like the drive to the restaurant, Max and Mike rode back to his hotel without speaking, though this time, theirs was the silence of contentment. Max pulled to the curb and parked.

"Why don't you come in," Mike said smiling. "You've never seen my beautiful Washington townhouse."

Max turned off the engine and opened the door. Still silent, the couple entered the hotel and walked to the elevator. Waiting, their gazes drifted upward to the digital display watching the recorded descent of the elevator car.

A soft, dulcet ping sounded and the shimmering brass-plated doors parted revealing a mirrored compartment with a handrail and gold toned carpet. The coupled stepped into the elevator alone, turned, and faced front.

A thousand thoughts coursed through Mike's brain, but, as the doors shut, his thinking stopped, and action took over. He pinned Max against the corner of the car and tilted his head to kiss her.

Max dropped her purse, clasped her hands behind his neck and pulled him in tight. Their lips met and parted and their tongues caressed each other. Mike's heart beat with a passion he hadn't felt in years.

As the doors opened, Max reached to pick up her purse. They giggled as Mike, trying to keep their lips touching, bent down with her. He took her hand and they walked briskly to his room.

He opened the door, but he stopped short of crossing into

his room. He turned to Max and said playfully, "But doctor, we've only just met. I don't want to appear forward."

She stepped passed him, tugged him into the room by his necktie and pushed the door closed with her foot. Still kissing him, Max led him to the bed, kicking off her shoes as she went.

She broke away, walked over to the bed, and pulled back the covers. Mike stood motionless unswervingly aroused, but at the same time, disbelieving that he was about to make love to the most beautiful woman he had ever seen.

Mike thought she looked sexy, lying across the bed. She had a long, beautiful neck that was extremely kissable, and he had noticed the arch of her back as she undressed silhouetted in the dim light of his room. She exuded sexiness and innocence at the same time, and that combination stirred him incredibly.

Mike felt overcome by the moment, the battle between lust and love raging inside him, yet somehow both driving him in the same direction. Still it was their first time and the desire to make it both loving and hotly sensuous made him nervous.

Max seemed to feel the same. Though she lay undressed on the bed, her bottom lip quivered with what was, Mike thought, nervous tension. The curves of her body and the glint in her eyes exuded an intense longing, revealing an unequivocal desire to be held, to be loved, to be kissed, to feel his flesh against hers.

Yet like a shy little girl, she blinked her eyes repeatedly and gently pulled the sheet up, tucking it just under her chin hiding her beautiful body. She rolled slightly onto her side facing partly away from Mike. As she did he noticed the roundness of her firm bottom. Her pose seemed both an invitation and a barrier, two disparate thoughts that coursed through Mike's brain simultaneously, but such was the irony of this corporeal fantasy-come-true playing out in his head.

Mike sensed she was anxious.

So was he.

He was unbelievably aroused. He felt a nearly overwhelming urge to take her, but he fought it. This would not be a taking. It would be a sharing, the sharing between two people who had found love, genuine and sincere, and who would consummate it enraptured in the only moment in time that mattered–right now.

After their lovemaking, Mike and Max lay intertwined amid pillows and the few rumpled covers that hadn't been kicked to the floor. Both were silent, seemingly lost in their thoughts. Mike propped himself on the headboard, staring across the room at nothing in particular. Max lay with her head against his chest. Her arm draped across his waist and she breathed softly.

Mike stroked her hair, "You okay?" he asked

Max moved her hand up to his chest, looked at him, and smiled. "*Umm, hmm*."

"No regrets?"

"None at all," Max said as she leaned up to kiss him. "I just want you to be careful in Tennessee, because I could get used to this."

"When I get back from Tennessee, you'll have a lot of this to get used to," he said, crooking his head to kiss her. She met his lips and they kissed passionately.

When they released, Mike closed his eyes and rested his head on the pillow. Max again laid her head on his chest and tightened her arms around his body. They held each other close and drifted off to sleep.

Chapter Ten

Mike departed Dulles at 11:56 a.m. He had a brief layover in Cincinnati and then caught a puddle jumper to the Knoxville airport where the FBI parked a beat up Chevrolet truck. It was registered in his assumed name: Chandler Marks, the only delegate from the newly formed N.B. Forrest Klavern 16 in Kinston, North Carolina. His agent friends had placed a loaded .38 caliber snub-nosed revolver in the truck's glove box. They asked him to refrain from using it unless he had to. But, they said, no self-respecting Klansman would be caught without a firearm of some sort.

In selecting Chandler's alias, Donnelly and his fellow agents thought that preserving one of his names would be easier for him to remember–too many opportunities for slip-ups if he had to memorize a whole new identity.

Two FBI advance teams had been in place for a week–one in Knoxville and one in Tullahoma, the site of the big meeting. As an added security measure, Mike wouldn't have contact with any of them.

At 3:00 o'clock in the afternoon, he and his decrepit Chevrolet started toward the dusty hills of Tullahoma. He had a long ride ahead, one that afforded nagging doubts and fears to creep in. Mike's thoughts returned to Jarrod Payne and Parris Bennigan, two men who, had it not been for their encounters with him, might still be among the living.

Mike turned on the truck's radio and surfed through the channels, but none of the music distracted him from the images attacking his conscience, so he turned it off in disgust.

His thoughts wandered to his own ruined career and the devastating effects his decisions had had on the career of Ken McMaster, his partner. He thought about his failed romance with Jennifer and he mused about the wisdom of beginning a new relationship just before such an intense and danger-fraught assignment. *I'm setting myself up for heartbreak at best or tragedy for Max and Amanda at worst.*

Then an ice-cold chill gripped him as he faced the reality of his mission. He realized that even the best-trained federal agents with the latest equipment could not keep him under surveillance twenty-four hours a day. What if someone had tipped off the Board? What if someone shivved him in the john or the shower? What if this was all one big set-up, a trap?

Mike's thoughts began to run wild, but he decided to let his imagination loose. He couldn't contain thoughts any more than he could trap air in his hands and hold it captive. He silently wondered if Donnelly was on the up-and-up. While his restrictions in Washington had been few, the agents made sure he did not contact anyone in Columbia, not his partner, not any of his friends. He essentially had contact only with Jason, Donnelly, and Max.

Max, oh God what if she's... Mike literally and mentally stepped on the brakes. He immediately berated himself for thinking that Max could somehow be connected to the Board, that his work with her had been fake or that her feelings for him had been insincere.

If there was one thing he was absolutely sure of in this whole sorry episode, it was the depth of her feelings for him and his for her. He was both ashamed of his thought and glad for it at the same time. It was cathartic, a precious moment that broke his fever of paranoia. The mere notion that Max would betray him that way was so far out of bounds, so inconceivable that it brought everything back into perspective. He accelerated again and with a light and uplifted heart, he switched the radio back on. Darius Rucker's soulful voice singing, "Only Want to Be With You" poured loud and strong through the speakers. Mike smiled.

By 6:30 he began his ascent of the logging road that led to the compound. After a mile of twists and turns, he finally arrived at the 10-foot-tall stockade-gate entrance.

Above the gate flew the Confederate Stars and Bars and two large men stood guard outside. One wore blue jean overalls, the other a paramilitary camouflage jumpsuit. Both carried shotguns and the camouflaged man wore a sidearm, too. They eyed Mike and approached his car suspiciously. His palms dripped sweat and his heart beat wildly.

"Can I help you?" asked the man in overalls.

Mike handed over his Klan membership card and said, "I'm here for the meeting."

The man dressed in military garb said nothing, though he circled the Chevrolet as if inspecting it.

The man in overalls returned the card and asked, "What's the password?"

Mike smiled wide and winked at the man as he said, "Apocalypse."

"Let him through." With that, the gate swung open wide. Mike steered into a large grass lot with all the other cars and trucks. He noticed that not one of the vehicles bore a license plate, so he removed his and locked it in the glove box.

He walked to a makeshift registration desk set up near a

fire pit over which three hogs roasted. The aroma of the smoked pork made Mike realize he hadn't eaten all day. Several men stood in line to pick at the pig and dollop oversize spoonfuls of baked beans and slaw onto their plates.

"Could I get your name?" asked the woman at the registration table.

"Chandler Marks," he replied with confidence.

"Okay, Mr. Marks, you're assigned to bunk house number six. I see you're in a new chapter."

"Yes ma'am. Didn't seem to be anybody looking out for our rights around where I live."

"So you formed your own klavern. Well, good for you," she said patting him on the hand. "Now go stow your gear and come on back out for supper. They just started serving and after dessert, they got some guy in black face all made up like a nigger and they gonna do a comedy routine. It's a hoot."

The woman handed Chandler a grainy, mimeographed map of the compound and pocket folder with a schedule of events and assorted literature. The folder was white and nondescript. The printing quality of its contents was poor–a copy of a copy of a copy. Yet one glance at the words on the page showed him the depths of his new colleague's inbred hate and the conviviality with which they embraced it.

- *Thursday–10:00. Computer hacking. How to screw up credit reports for mud people, the white trash that love them, and anybody else you hate.*
- *Saturday–2:00. Survivalist training (Classroom). You've burned their churches. Now you have to hide out in the woods from agents of the Zionist Occupational Government. How to choose a lair and lay in supplies for the long haul.*

- *Sunday–7:30 P.M. Fellowship. Guest speaker: Rev. Phillip Deneuse. Sermon--"Master Plan for the Master Race"*

Interspersed among the scheduled items were times for marksmanship training, manual combat training, and personal and property target selection.

Chandler held the book open with one hand while he walked slowly to his bunkhouse. He reached the creaky screen door whose hinges were badly in need of oil and whose spring was so devoid of tension that the door double popped, loud and then soft, as it bounced against the wooden doorframe. Motionless and mesmerized by the booklet as if he'd just discovered an unholy text, he stood by the cabin door with his jaw dropped open.

"Look like some good shit in there don't it?" asked a scraggly-haired boy who had just come out of the bunkhouse. He stood stoop-shouldered, wearing a black Harley-Davidson tee shirt. He had his hands in his pockets but took his right hand out long enough to extend it to shake. His fingertips, yellowed with nicotine; thick, uneven, and grimy fingernails; and ragged rotten-black teeth showed fifty years of bad hygiene in a boy who couldn't have been more than eighteen years old.

Chandler took his hand and shook it. "Yeah," was all he could say.

"Name's Johnny. Johnny Filbert, from Klavern 678 down in Greenview, Tennessee."

"My name's Chandler Marks from Kinston, North Carolina. This your first convocation like this?"

"Yeah. I'm up here with my daddy. He runs a garage back home. Use to be in a good section, he says, till all the niggers moved in. Says he remembers when they knew their place. Wants me to learn how to treat 'em.

"He says the only good nigger is a dead nigger. I've heard that a lot the last couple of days. You reckon they'll teach us how to kill 'em up here?"

Chandler didn't know what to say. The young man was talkative and seemed naïve. But he spouted ferocious racial vitriol with the ease of talking about his high school football team.

"I don't know if they will or not, Johnny. It'd suit me fine if they just show us how to run 'em out of town. Live separate, you know. The blacks have their towns, we have ours," Chandler said.

"Seems to me you could be right," the boy replied, "but my daddy says we got to git rid of 'em. How 'bout go stow your bag and let's go get something to eat. I'm starvin'."

Chandler ducked into the cabin. A damp, musty scent hung in the air and mildew crept up the walls from the bottom boards. He found an empty bunk with a lumpy, thin mattress covered by a coarse woolen army blanket. He heaved his bag onto the bed and left the cabin heading for the mess tent.

Chandler picked up a set of plastic utensils and a paper plate, filling it with barbecue, slaw, and baked beans. He overheard snippets of conversation about fishing, about how good the barbecue tasted, about how long it took to drive here from Akron. From the sounds of the varied discussions, this convocation could have been a church picnic, a family reunion, or any one of a thousand gatherings.

To Mike it all felt surreal. The blood coursing through his veins at racetrack pace and the thumping of his heart against his chest wall reminded him that if he were found out, he'd be dead before the next plate of barbecue got served.

He ate alone, choosing the far seat on a stretch of

weathered wooden picnic tables set up on a concrete slab beneath a canvas canopy. He didn't want to stare at anyone enough to arouse suspicion, but he just couldn't take his eyes off of Johnny Filbert. He was young. He was a boy. Yet his mind seemed poisoned beyond redemption.

At the far end of the tent near the food tables, a balding, older man stood up and called for everyone's attention.

"Folks, if I could get everybody to listen up a minute." The crowd noise diminished to silence. "Everybody, my name's Don Rayfield and I'm the Klokard of Klavern number 667 in Detroit, responsible for setting up the convocation this year." His statement was met with sparse applause.

Chandler remembered the term Klokard meant "enforcer." If Klan members needed discipline, the Klokard handed out fines or punishment. And, in extreme cases, if a member changed his hateful ways and ever cooperated with authorities in any way, the enforcer was generally the last person he saw before he was executed.

"If you need anything while you're here, let me know."

"My bunk's too damn hard," shouted a heavyset man, causing Rayfield to smile and the rest of the crowd to crow in laughter.

"With all the padding on your ass, John, I'm surprised you noticed," the Klokard replied. The crowd roared. "Seriously, now I'm going to turn it over to Bill Rickman."

Chandler recognized Rickman from the many slides he'd seen in the FBI briefing room. A banker, he was the vice-chairman of the Board. Rickman rose before the assembly with the distinguished air of a businessman. He wore khaki pants and a short-sleeved blue button down shirt. His trimmed hair, silver around his temples, wisped in the cool of the evening breeze.

He addressed the men as if he were a general about to go into battle. "Men, I'm proud to stand before you now. This country is in a crisis. White men–the people who made this country great, who made it what it is today–are losing out to minority interests in every town in every state in the Union."

He looked into the eyes of several people in the audience as he spoke. Chandler realized the man was an accomplished and persuasive speaker.

"We've tried to live apart and we've tried to live together. What we should have done is tried to live by the Bible. The Bible says that white men and niggers can't coexist. The Bible says that we have domain over niggers, like the beasts in the fields. If you have a nigger living beside you, it's your fault. Run him out. Burn down his house. Kill his children, but get him out!"

A smattering of "hell yeahs" emanated from the audience as Rickman worked himself into a lather.

"And if they don't like it, pack up the whole damn bunch of them on a rowboat and send 'em back to Africa. Let 'em swing from coconut trees and eat each other, but get 'em the hell out of here."

The crowd erupted with cheers. Chandler stood up and clapped. He let out a rebel yell and fell in with the audience shouting "*Sieg Heil*" in unison. Rickman raised his hands to settle the crowd down.

"The time has come. A race war of an untold magnitude is upon us. People will call us all sorts of names. Even our families and so-called friends will hate us and like Peter denied Jesus, they will disown us. This is the test of our mettle, of your loyalty to your race. What we do here today will affect the next hundred years in this country."

The speaker grew quiet and with an intentional pause he

let the audience await his next words. "Men who think like us often quote Thomas Jefferson. I even see the phrase on a few shirts in the audience tonight. 'Sometimes the tree of liberty must be refreshed with the blood of patriots and tyrants.' We never question spilling the blood of the tyrants who drive us down. We don't like killing innocent white people, especially children, but when we find it necessary to bomb government buildings, sometimes they're in the wrong place at the wrong time. We have to consider them martyrs in the good fight. The question for you tonight is are you willing to spill your own blood for the future of your children and theirs."

Rickman trailed his voice off to a near whisper and walked back into the crowd to take his place. For a moment the assembly was quiet, letting the vitriol sink in. But as Rickman took his first step toward the audience, the men stood and shouted their approval, war whoops and all.

Then Rayfield, acting as emcee, took the floor again. "Folks I'm gonna turn the floor over to Reverend Deneuse for the evening prayer and I know some of you have been trickling in over the last day or so, but since this is our first official day here, we'll adjourn after that to let everybody get set up for the night. Remember, we'll start early in the morning with a flag raising ceremony followed by breakfast. Reverend Deneuse…"

Mike watched as the cragged old man shuffled to the front of the picnic shelter. He bore the title of reverend and he wore a small brass cross on the lapel of his jacket, but years of hatred, it seemed, had wrinkled Deneuse's face. His nose was pointed and he appeared to seethe with abhorrence and disgust.

He spoke. "Let us pray." He had a gravely voice backed by a hissing delivery. He was like no other preacher Chandler had ever seen. The crowd assembled under the shelter

189

collectively took off their caps and bowed in reverence.

"Almighty God, creator of the universe, please bless the people here. Let them train safely. Let us all enjoy the fellowship with those who were indeed created in your image.

"Help us eradicate the mud people and the Jews, Catholics and Muslims–all the spawn of Satan. Lord, it's hard to do battle with the forces of evil, but ours is the good fight. The white race is your race. We are the lost tribe of Zion born again as the Aryan people, your chosen ones." His voice rose and fell like the swells of the sea. "Please hear our prayer. We ask this and all our blessings in your name."

The crowd spoke a muffled amen and one of the teenage skinheads started chanting "White Power" at the top of his lungs. Soon the whole group had joined in and Chandler imagined that anyone hearing them at the foot of the compound might mistake the noise for the growl of some ferocious animal. He thought how ironic it was that they would be right.

He walked back to his bunkhouse among a group of his compatriots. Although he had participated with zeal in the night's speeches and discussions, Chandler couldn't help but feel alone. He climbed onto his bunk, fluffed the rock hard pillow, folding it under his head for support and lay there, unable to make his mind stop working. *It's like being by yourself on an empty street with only the sound of your own footfalls on the pavement.*

He thought of Max and Amanda; of what they were doing and whether they were thinking about him. With them fresh in his mind, he finally drifted off to sleep.

A garish blast of a bugle ripped Mike from a comfortable sleep. He had been pleasantly dreaming of walking hand-in-hand with Max down a deserted stretch of beach while Amanda darted before them, plundering a treasure trove of seashells from the white, foamy surf. But it had only been a dream.

Even in the heartbeat between sweet slumber and brash awakening, he flooded his brain with the feel of Max's touch. He drank in her aroma and imagined he felt the soft coolness of her skin touching his, the gentle touch of her hair as it covered his face as they lay locked in intimate coupling, caressing and kissing each other. But it had only been a thought.

He awoke with a white, pasty smack of his lips and with disdain at his surroundings–a weathered plank bunkhouse in the Tennessee mountains. He shared accommodations with a half-dozen other men whose musky earth odors, groans, and stretches made Chandler imagine a thousand other places he wished he could be. How did I get myself into this, he thought, as the cold, steel rod of reality struck him between the eyes.

He plodded from the bunkhouse toward the mess tent where a slight, white column of smoke spiraled into a cloudless sky the color of blue crystal. His legs made a begrudged march to the tent as the last few of his ligaments stretched into full consciousness. Whatever resistance he had left hypnotically gave way to the pungent perfume of smoked sausage, bacon, and eggs plucked fresh from the hen house.

Mike filled his tray and poured a steaming stream of coffee into a large Styrofoam cup. He took his place at a table beside Johnny Filbert, his bunkmate, who had just taken a large bite of a country ham biscuit. Several other men filled the mess tent, most of them feeling their way as groggily as Chandler, but there were a few animated old men who had risen before dawn and seemed to find humor in the mental states of the "late sleepers." It was 6:15 in the morning.

"What do you reckon they'll have us doin' this morning?" Johnny asked, white crumbs of biscuit dropping off his lips.

Chandler took a tentative sip of hot coffee. It burned his tongue, but still the infusion of caffeine perked him up immediately. "If we follow the schedule I saw yesterday, we'll have a class this morning on how to do things like planting dope on coworkers or getting the police to help set up blacks for crimes like robbery or break-ins." He reached for a peppershaker and spiced up his scrambled eggs. "Then this afternoon, we do some hand-to-hand combat tactics."

Johnny turned up his cup, draining the last bit of orange juice. "I wonder if we'll have any free time today," he said, as he reached underneath his seat to retrieve a woodcarving and a pocketknife. He held in his hands, in amazing artistic detail, a small Indian chief in full headdress with his arms folded. The figure had a rugged but dignified face. Not satisfied with the crease of the chief's pants, Johnny smoothed a new crease in the soft wood with the delicate touch of his blade.

It encouraged and at the same time bewildered Chandler that the young man seemed to have no interest in what this gathering was all about. "Did you do that?" he asked, amazed.

"Yeah. My grandpa taught me how to whittle. Pa don't much like it. Thinks it's a waste of time. So I only do it on my work breaks or when I'm away from the garage."

"That looks a great deal better than just whittling," Mike said. "You could make a living doing carvings like that."

Johnny, looking gratified, but slightly embarrassed, shrugged off the idea.

Chandler silently admired the boy's craftsmanship when Johnny's father appeared noisily with a full tray of food. "Put that shit away, boy. We've got things to do." Johnny closed the knife, pressing it into his palm and shoved it and the figure into his pocket. Chandler noticed he immediately looked dejected and a dreary, black change of mood seemed to sweep over his entire body.

"Johnny does some good work, Mr. Filbert," Chandler said in the boy's defense. "You ought to encourage him."

Filbert glared at Chandler. "You reckon the niggers and the Jews will let him sell that stuff in stores? Hell no. They too busy sellin' their Afrosheen and matzo balls. You think they want to buy that shit? Put it in a museum maybe?"

"Hell no, Johnny's better off learnin' to work on cars. Even if we lose the race war, which we won't by God, if we have some good, dedicated soldiers," he loudly directed the comment toward Johnny who hung his head, "niggers and kykes still drive cars so at least he can make a livin'."

All that over a simple comment, Chandler thought. He was glad he didn't ask the boy's father how his day was going. "You have a point," was all he said. He shared a bemused glance with Johnny outside the father's view. He realized that he and Johnny had more in common than he first thought. Not only did neither of them want to be in this place, but they both also thought Mr. Filbert was a buffoon–but a buffoon who was big, scary, and dangerous.

Chapter Eleven

After breakfast, Mike disposed of his paper plate and coffee cup. He felt as if he'd intruded enough on Johnny and Mr. Filbert. *No use making the old guy mad or suspicious.* Before the morning speaker, Tom Windsor, took the podium, Chandler selected a seat as far away from the Filberts as possible.

As the assortment of Klansmen and Skinheads settled down, Rayfield rose to introduce the speaker. "Gentlemen, and ladies, of course," he chortled, "the man about to address us this morning needs no introduction. Tom is the chairman of the United Klans of Indiana and has served in more leadership positions in our movement than I can name. I hope you enjoy his message. Please give a warm welcome to Mr. Tom Windsor." The introduction produced only a smattering of applause from the groggy assemblage.

Windsor looked over the crowd without speaking until everyone grew quiet and gave him their attention. When at last he spoke, he said, "I want to begin the morning with a quote from our leader, Adolf Hitler." He slipped on a pair of reading glasses and lifted a sheet of paper in front of his face. "'The man who is not opposed and vilified and slandered in the Jewish press is not a true National Socialist. If a comrade opens a Jewish newspaper in the morning and does not find himself vilified there, then he has spent yesterday to no account.' *Sieg Heil*." Windsor raised his arm in a Nazi salute and received a raucous "*Sieg Heil*!" in return with the Skinheads standing as if in a religious service.

"What I want to speak to you about today is the ultimate act of courage–revealing yourselves to the world as united Aryan people. The time to sit back and let other people do the work for you is over. The press has interviewed many movement leaders, myself included. We've identified ourselves with the cause.

"We've taken abuse. We've been spit on and cursed at by niggers, Jews, and nigger-loving white trash of all description." Windsor's voice grew into a trembling crescendo, "We've done our part; upheld our end of the bargain. We've come forward for *you*, not for us."

Windsor swept his hands across the crowd and looked several people squarely in the eye. Chandler could see that he was an intelligent man, a communicator of the first degree. He held the crowd's rapt attention.

"To stay clear of the federal government that whores itself to the Israeli State, our policy up to now has been one of leaderless resistance. But everywhere you turn in this country, our elected officials pass new laws about hate crimes and special interests for minorities. Maybe they're smarter than we are. Maybe they *know* that we don't just want to deport niggers and kykes and spics, we want to exterminate them. Kill them all! Kill them now. Just get rid of them!"

Windsor worked himself into a fiery, podium-pounding fury, met by the shouts and whoops of the crowd screaming, "Kill, kill, kill," in unison. Chandler stood and cast his gaze across the tent at Johnny who sat unmoved by the speech. Mr. Filbert emitted a raucous two-fingered whistle, clapped his hands, and slapped his neighbor's back. He was too caught up to notice that Johnny was just fidgeting, making shapes in the dirt with the toes of his shoes.

Windsor waited until the crowd calmed, easing the tenor by motioning them to sit. "This leaderless resistance shit is just that–*shit*. If you're proud to be white, by God, then get out in the streets and tell it to anybody who'll listen. Pass out pamphlets, make speeches, hold rallies, but quit waiting on every-damn-body in the world to do your work for you. If you piss off a nigger or a Jew, who the hell cares? They're just niggers and Jews. Tell all your like-minded friends to get off their asses, too. If they whine about getting caught, or being seen, maybe losing their jobs, you give 'em a good swift kick. All the jobs and money and savings and 401(K) retirement plans ain't gonna mean nothing in this world as long as the Jew boys in Washington continue to hand it out to free-loading, no account niggers! I started this speech with a quote from one famous leader. I'd like to end it by paraphrasing another." He clutched the lectern with both hands and scanned the crowd. He looked as if he wanted to make eye contact with everyone in the tent just to make sure they heard his final words.

"I have a dream today..."

A collective groan grew within the crowd and mingled with breathy snickers as a few people anticipated the parody about to ensue. Chandler, nearly breaking his cover, leaned back in his bench, rolled his eyes, and muttered, "Jesus Christ." He had had just about all he could take. He regained his composure and again looked over toward Johnny. Johnny had wandered off and his daddy looked like he could blow up at any moment.

Windsor so enjoyed his brand of humor, he grew a wide enough smile that he could hardly continue to speak. But continue he did. "I have a dream that one day in the red hills of

Georgia, the sons of slaves and the sons of slave owners will come together at the table of brotherhood. And that the sons of the slave owners will come to their senses, rip out the planks of the table, and beat the hell out of every mud person in sight!" He slapped the podium and the effect was a feverish wave of hate-filled voices carried on the wind into the hills of Tennessee.

"Ours is the blade of honor! Ours is the sword of truth. Ours is the cause of righteousness! *Sieg Heil*!"

Mike realized there was little time and he needed to get on with the business the FBI sent him to the compound to do. He recalled agent Donnelly's words with vivid detail, "When you're talking about bombing a building full of people during working hours or killing a bunch of kids, there aren't too many people seriously psychopathic enough to do it. So when a volunteer comes along who seems determined to follow through, the Board usually jumps all over 'em."

The words, the thought of that kind of action, the scenes of TV images of Oklahoma City, scenes of mangled bodies and limp, lifeless children combined in Chandler's mind. He shivered and shook his head with his eyes closed to block out the pictures and to clear away his nervousness. He couldn't appear tense or uneasy before the Board. He had to be resolute.

He chose his moment carefully when Rickman appeared to be alone in the mess hut, reading a novel and taking slow luxurious sips from a cup of coffee as if this encampment substituted for a relaxing summer vacation. Rickman looked up at Chandler as he approached.

"Enjoyed your speech yesterday," Mike said, his jaw set and tone confident.

"Thanks," Rickman replied, glancing at Mike over the top of his gold-framed, half lens reading glasses.

The two men continued to look at each other as a mild, curious silence hung between them. Chandler did not want to seem overly anxious, but he did not get the impression that Rickman was about to engage in idle conversation either.

"I'll get right to the point, Mr. Rickman," Chandler said. "Every word you said in that speech and every word of every speech that has followed is true. If white people don't take action and do it now, we're going to lose the race war."

Rickman set his book on the table face down, keeping his place. He looked around as if to ensure their privacy and gestured to the bench opposite him on the other side of the picnic table. "Sit down son. You sound like you have something on your mind."

Placing his palms on the tabletop and sliding into his seat, Mike also looked to his left and right, not to check for others, but to add to the illusion of gravity. "I want to take action. I want to do something big. Something the news will report on for weeks."

As Mike spoke, Rickman fiddled with the wooden stirrer in his coffee looking as if he was about to dismiss him and put an end to the audience.

"Of course, I would first resign from the Klan and prepare myself for disavowal," he said arching his eyebrows and tilting his head, giving Rickman a knowing glance.

At the mention of the word 'disavowal,' Rickman stopped playing with his coffee. He slightly, but visibly, rocked back and immediately met Chandler's gaze. He quickly regained his measured composure. "Almost everyone at this encampment is willing to take action of some sort."

"Oh, hell," Chandler said. "You and I are smart enough to

know that for most of these people, their idea of taking action is burning a cross in a cornfield at midnight or holding a rally in some piss-ant little town in Ohio or somewhere. Ten times as many nigger lovers than klansmen show up and out shout us. Then we go on some talk show and claim that was a victory for the white race. All that is, is petty bullshit." Chandler spoke with what he believed to be the appropriate amount of contempt for the lackluster efforts of the so-called white power leadership.

Rickman placed his elbows on the table, laced his fingers, and placed his chin on his knuckles, apparently considering Chandler's words. He looked at Chandler almost like a business manager coaching an underling. He pursed his lips and said, "What sort of *action* do you propose to take?"

Chandler took a deep breath. Before he spoke, he slumped his shoulders as if he were about to unleash a terrible burden. "Next Veteran's Day, the President is supposed to make a speech at the National Holocaust Museum." He curled his lip and nearly spat out the words. "I have access to some pretty high grade weaponry–grenade launchers, shoulder mounted rocket launchers, stuff like that. I say it's time for an all out assault on the Zionists in Washington. I may not eliminate the President, but I'll bring the roof and a few walls down and take out somebody high up in the government and probably a good number of kykes with 'em."

Rickman appeared interested and agitated at the same time. Again he surveyed the dining hut for eavesdroppers and passersby. Seeing none, he turned back to Chandler and said in a low tone, "Who else have you told about this plan?"

"Nobody. Not even the guy who has the weapons."

Rickman leaned back a bit, crossing him arms trying to again display a guarded posture. "Why are you telling me? If you're so determined to carry it out, why not just get on with it?"

Chandler momentarily considered making an impassioned speech about preserving the white race and sacrificing for the cause, but he felt like he had Rickman interested enough in the idea that such a tactic would lose him ground. No, Rickman was too smart to blow smoke at him at this point in the conversation, he surmised, so he opted for a more pragmatic approach. "I need financing," he said in an even, matter-of-fact tone. "The weaponry will cost plenty and I need to start identifying good locations as firing points. When I pick the best vantage point, I'll need to buy or lease space early to avoid suspicion. To do that, I'll need false identification. All that takes cash and lots of it."

Rickman listened intently, but neither his face nor his body language betrayed his thoughts. After a brief moment, he said, "I'll take this up with my colleagues, Mr. Marks. I'll get back to you with our decision. Either way, you understand, this conversation never took place."

"That's what I was hoping."

Over the last two days, Mike had gotten fairly friendly with Johnny Filbert. He learned that Johnny worked in an auto garage with his daddy. Chandler was a bit shocked to learn, given their surroundings, that one of Johnny's closest friends was a young black man with whom he played high school baseball.

"Bernard is different. Daddy don't think so. Says he's just as worthless as any nigger, but Bernard an' me is tight," Johnny told Chandler.

"You better be careful how loud you say that around this place," Mike said. "You could get your ass beat."

"Aw, I'm about tired of this bullshit anyway. Bunch of guys playing like the whole world depends on 'em. I'm just doing it to please my daddy. I'll go along with it and when we get back to Greenview, me an' Bernard'll get us a pint an' go fishin'." The boy seemed to have more going for him than Mike first thought.

"Well," Chandler said, not wanting to dwell on this subject too long and give anything away himself, "I'm going to go to the hand-to-hand combat session. Want to go?"

"Might as well," Johnny said. "Might be fun."

The two made their way to a clearing in the compound set aside for the training. It was obviously a popular course. By the time he and Johnny arrived, both sets of gray, weatherworn wooden bleachers were full and men were standing along either side of them waiting on the session to begin.

A tall, extremely fit man soon took his position in front of the bleachers. Mike thought the man was probably six-foot-four and maybe two hundred eighty pounds. He looked like a pro football tight end, with blond hair cropped in a military high-and-tight haircut. His muscles stretched the sleeves of his T-shirt and he didn't have an ounce of body fat anywhere.

"Gentlemen," the man said, ending the muted rumblings of conversation in the crowd, "I'm Staff Sergeant Lawrence and today I'm going to instruct you in the art of manual combat. I, with a demonstrator, will show you some of the basic techniques of self defense and how, when necessary, to inflict mortal injuries."

Chandler could see the sergeant had a no-nonsense style. His delivery revealed no bias or hatred. It appeared as if he was simply there to teach. Still, Chandler was wary. Appearances always seemed to deceive these days.

"After the demonstrations," the sergeant continued

motioning to stacks of padding, helmets, and other assorted gear, "we'll suit up and let you try some of the techniques on each other."

The men in the bleachers turned their heads, looking at each other and snickering like schoolboys on a field trip.

"Let me say a word about what you're about to learn. This is serious business." He had the group's attention. "I can show you how to perform these techniques. I can show you how to inflict so much pain that your enemy begs for you to finish the job and kill him. I can show you how to kill your enemy instantly without forewarning." The sergeant looked intently through the crowd making eye contact with as many people as he could. His tone was powerful and passionate to the point that Chandler grew tense and on guard.

"Make no mistake," the sergeant carried on, "the person with whom you employ these techniques must be an enemy. This is not for fun and games. This is life and death. This is for the struggle. These techniques are designed to harm, maim, and kill. Either be prepared to use them for that purpose, or pledge to yourself right now to forget everything you learn here today."

The men in the bleachers almost all collectively leaned forward enraptured by the sergeant's speech. They even seemed to breathe as one. They were obviously impressed by the seriousness with which he took his craft.

Since he now had their full attention, he decided to proceed quickly. "All right, who wants to be the first volunteer?"

A man who had been sitting in the middle of the bleachers stood to offer himself as the guinea pig. He was every bit as tall as the sergeant, but with a paunch in his middle. He looked as if he were a member of a motorcycle gang, bare-chested except for his black leather vest emblazoned with the Harley Davidson logo, blue jeans, and wallet held in place with a chain.

Mike surmised the man had seen quite a few fights in his time. He looked rough, and his offer to be first met with a few hoots of encouragement from his friends in the bleachers.

"Now," the sergeant said as he centered his volunteer in full view of the spectators and placed himself to the side and slightly behind the big man, "these tactics I'm about to demonstrate are all based on pressure-point control."

He lifted his hand up to the volunteer's upper lip, making sort of a mustache with the index finger. "Between the bottom of your nose and the top of your dental plate is one of these points." Without fanfare, he held the back of the volunteer's head steady while he pressed his index finger firmly into the soft tissue under his nose.

The big man's eyes teared up immediately and his body seemed to convulse as he tried to fight the enormous pain. The spectators drew a collective breath as the man faltered and finally fell to his knees yelling, "That's enough."

Chandler wondered whether the biker's pride might be hurt enough to try some sort of revenge on the sergeant. He hoped he would be smarter since the instructor probably knew a hundred ways to strike the guy so that he would be dead before he hit the ground. But Chandler also knew that intelligence was not the hallmark of this breed of racists.

The man surprised him though, patting the sergeant's shoulder and saying, "Damn, that's some good stuff," before retaking his seat in the bleachers. His face was pale except for a mean-looking red mark below his nose, a classic inflammatory response where the blood rushed at the brain's instruction to the point of injury.

In the next series of volunteers, the sergeant demonstrated several other pressure points, bending thumbs backward and bending finger joints, striking the common peroneal nerve along the outside of the upper thigh to disable a person's leg, and pressing his thumbnail into the soft spot just behind and under the ear. Each man fell quickly to his knees, dust swirling up amid their kicking legs and faces contorted with pain, some uttering surreal laughter seemingly to keep from breaking down in tears of agony. Jesus' name was spoken loudly and with some frequency.

Mike observed that Johnny took this show in with some bemused amazement. Even Chandler himself found himself engaged in the demonstrations thinking the techniques might come in handy, maybe sooner than he wanted to believe.

As the last of the demonstrators hobbled back to the bleachers, the sergeant addressed the assembly. "One of the problems that we as American men have to overcome in fighting is that we fight too clean. We're macho. We stand toe-to-toe and try to slug it out." He paced methodically in front of the bleachers, again trying to look each of them in the eye.

"That's great if you're in a boxing match; we ain't talking about boxing." The sergeant placed his hands on a man seated in the front row of the bleachers and guided him into the demonstrator's position as he kept addressing the crowd. "This is war and war ain't fair. So don't fight fair. Aim your hits to the groin, and don't just pop it, put some force behind your punch. Drop that bastard to his knees and then drive your kneecap right into his nose." He imitated executing these moves on the volunteer in slow motion as he spoke, gently pushing the demonstrator to the ground and carefully moving his knee toward the man's face.

"He won't get up. If he does, slice him across the throat with your hand and crush his windpipe," he said as he slowly drew the blade edge of his hand across the volunteer's throat. The more the sergeant talked the more animated he became.

In the two hours before lunch, the sergeant suited up in an overly large outfit stuffed with padding. He let each of the men take turns attacking him. He was relentless. The first few men were tentative. The sergeant cured their hesitation by pushing them or tackling them to the ground.   He taunted them, shouting, "Come on! Attack! Don't be a pussy! Attack me, or I'm going to attack you. Come on!"

Johnny had taken his shot at the instructor and had done an adequate job. When it was Chandler's turn, he had become so entranced with the instruction, he almost forgot why he was at the camp. When he was at the police department, he always loved these kinds of training sessions. They were fun and this one, despite his surroundings, was no different. He grabbed a pugil stick and approached the instructor as if they were two gladiators in the Coliseum. When the sergeant nodded that he was prepared to be engaged, Chandler didn't hesitate. He immediately struck toward the sergeant's head.

"Good," growled the sergeant moving sideways trying to anticipate the next blow, his arms up in a defensive posture. "Betcha' can't do that again, pussyboy. I'll whip your ass."

Chandler struck again, but this time the sergeant deflected the stick and charged him. The padded suit slowed him down considerably and Chandler was able to sidestep him. As the sergeant hurtled past, Chandler used the man's momentum against him. He rushed onto the sergeant's back, pushing him to the ground. Reflexively, the sergeant turned onto his back trying to recover and regain his standing position, but as he did, Chandler laid all of his weight on top of him and put the end of the pugil stick at his throat. Chandler smiled a bit, pleased with himself.

"Good job," the sergeant roared as he held out his hand for Chandler to help him up off the ground. "Where did you get your training?"

Chandler froze. He got so caught up in the competition he showed every man at the session he was a veteran of hand-to-hand combat. He felt a frisson of ice slide down his spine and he imagined every man there looked at him with suspicion. He tried to recover. "Army," he said. The word buzzed out of his mouth. He felt his temples pound and his muscles tighten. He waited for the sergeant to catch him in his lie.

"Well ooh rah, Mr. Army," the sergeant yelled. "Which one of you is next?" he said turning his attention away from Chandler and toward the dusty assembly of men.

Chandler's shoulders slumped in relief and he felt his heart slow from it's breakneck pace as he rounded on his heel and headed for the showers. *Close.* Much *too close.*

Chapter Twelve

After the manual combat instruction, Mike decided to forego some of the afternoon sessions. They weren't mandatory, he discovered. And many of the other men had decided to fish in the lake or try to get some relief from the relentless midday Tennessee sun by taking a swim in the cool mountain water. He wanted to take a closer look at the perimeter of the encampment to get to know his avenues of escape or places where he might hide until help arrived.

He had seen members of the Board sporadically during meals or group meetings. But their mere presence at the encampment wasn't what the FBI needed to bring them down. They had to have hard evidence of complicity.

As Mike neared the mess hut, he saw Rickman standing near one of its support posts motioning him over. He drew Chandler close and whispered to him.

"I've discussed your proposal with my colleagues," he said. "We're a bit concerned about this weapons provider. How do we know he won't cooperate with the authorities if he's caught? What if he tries to tie us or your Klan organization in with the attack?" Rickman spoke in low, breathy tones and he talked quickly.

"I can only give you my word," Chandler said.

"We need more than a *word*. We need a name."

"Look, I'll give you the name I have, but," Chandler said,

as in his previous conversation, with what he felt to be an appropriate amount of cynicism, "you know as well as I that people who agree to sell you enough grenades and C4 to blow up half of Washington ain't gonna meet you at the Lincoln Memorial to exchange pleasantries."

"Give me the name anyway," Rickman said. "I understand your argument. Some of our members, you understand, are very cautious. I'll explain it to them further and get back to you tonight."

"The name is 'Sergei'," he told him.

"That's not much for me to tell them," Rickman said arching his eyebrows as if doing so would coax a last name or a description.

Mike decided to play his hand, "Look, if the Board is more interested in making fundraising speeches than taking action, I'll go to somebody else to–"

"No, no," Rickman said in an excited tone. He furrowed his brow and put his hands up, palms forward as if to explain to Chandler that his questions were merely formalities the Board felt compelled to address. "Give me until this afternoon," he said with a businesslike smile of assurance. He came along side Mike, reaching around behind him and clasping his shoulder. "I think I'll get you the answer you're looking for."

After his assignation with Rickman, Mike felt the adrenaline leave him as quickly as it rushed in. His heart slowed back to normal and he felt spent. He had scouted avenues of escape and places where he thought he might hide if the need arose, but more than anything he wanted to go out to check on the truck he'd driven to the encampment. It was, in a sense, his only connection with the world outside this smoldering, hate filled hellish place.

He returned to his cabin to retrieve a pile of dirty clothes, a prop to have as an excuse for leaving the compound and walking into the parking area, which sat about seventy-five yards from the front gate. "Getting these nasty smelling things away from my bunk," he imagined he would say if confronted, but nobody stood guard by the gate and he breathed easily as he passed through it.

He took a deep breath of fresh Tennessee air and though he was only one step and less than one second outside the perimeter fence of the compound, Mike felt relief and freedom. He kicked up dust as he walked down the earthen road, red with subterranean iron and gouged with deep trenches on either side and irregular shaped ruts carved by heavy rains weeks before. He felt the heat of the late afternoon as it beat down on his neck and arms and his mouth felt dry and pasty after his encounter with Rickman. He smacked his lips and drew his tongue across his teeth trying to work up enough moisture for a good swallow.

Chandler approached his truck. It radiated the heat it had absorbed over the last two days sitting unprotected in the sun. He unlocked and opened the passenger door and dumped his dirty clothes into the seat. Half of them rolled in a limp pile onto the floorboard.

Though he tried to resist the temptation, he opened the glove box and eyed the cell phone that he had placed there before entering the compound. Again he felt his heart quicken. He wanted to call Max just to hear her voice; just to let her know he was almost home. He knew better. His palms sweated and he looked around for anyone who might be lurking near. The beads of perspiration that had formed on his brow now rolled down his sideburns and converged just below his chin and dripped onto the truck seat. Was it the heat? Was it nervousness? He could not distinguish that for himself.

At last he decided to take the chance. He pressed the phone's power button and dialed the area code and first six numbers of Max's home phone. He could feel the pulse beat in his temples, and realizing this could be a fatal mistake, he pressed the power switch again and the LED readout went black.

He sighed deeply and stared at the phone. "Just make the damn call and get it over with," he told himself. He pressed the power button again, dialed in the number and waited...one ring, then two, then the phone beeped and went dead. The "low battery" indicator light shown in the corner of the read out screen. "Dammit," he said aloud, rummaging through the glove box for the power cord.

He found it and plugged in the connector to the phone and then shoved the business end of the cord into the cigarette lighter. Nothing. "Shit," Chandler whispered to himself, "this must be one of those where the ignition has to be on for the lighter to work."

He again shot a nerve-wracked glance around the parking area. He saw nothing but two dragonflies chasing each other end to end through the hay-colored scrub brush that ringed the lot. He inserted the key into the ignition and turned it to the ready position. Immediately hot air blasted from the air conditioning vents and the truck hummed the incessant buzz of the open-door alert.

Mike quickly shut the door and moved the air conditioning lever to the "off" position. The cell phone toned indicating full power, so he pressed the redial button and listened for the ring. "Come on, come on," he said aloud, drumming the dashboard with his middle three fingers.

Max's answering machine clicked on, "Hi you've reached

Max, and Amanda." The five-year-old had added her own name with an enthusiasm possessed only by children. "We're unable to take your call so please leave a message."

Chandler cleared his throat and tried to assume a normal, businesslike voice. "Hi, Max. This is Mike. Listen, I should be finished and back in town early next week. I'll touch base with you when I get in. Take care, now."

He pressed the power button to the phone and turned off the ignition. He replaced the phone and cord into the glove box and slid out of the truck. Maybe the message will give her some reassurance that I'm all right, he mused. At any rate it made Chandler feel much better, just for having made the connection. Even if it was only with an answering machine, it was indeed Max's and Amanda's voices.

As he made his way back to the compound he reached behind him. The back of his shirt and seat of his pants were drenched with perspiration. His nervousness, he realized, showed in a quite tangible way. I need to work on that, he thought.

Dusk was approaching as was the dinner hour, and several people had already gathered at the picnic tables in the mess hut. Nothing could have prepared Chandler for what happened next.

As the large group grew larger, the men wondered at the strange wooden crate sitting at the front of the mess hut and the desperate cries emanating from within it. All of them knew someone was definitely encased in the box, but who were they and what had they done?

Rayfield took the floor. "Ladies and gentlemen, we've got a unique opportunity tonight to witness the power of the Klan. I'd like to call on Johnny Filbert to come forward."

Mike's heart froze. He didn't know what was about to

happen. And from the look on Johnny's face, neither did he. All the blood had drained from his cheeks and he walked forward haltingly, seemingly unsure of his feet.

His father appeared from the darkness behind the box. "Come here, Johnny. Son, it's time to prove to me and all these people that you're the kind of man the white race can count on for our future." Johnny's gaze shifted between the box, his father, and the crowd. He appeared dazed, as if struck by a heavy blow.

Then two men unlatched the front of the crate. It fell to the concrete floor with a deafening pop, billowing up dust into the air. Inside the box, tied by his hands to its top and leaning forward at a painful angle was a tall, broad-shouldered black man, cut and blood-soaked, beaten almost unconscious.

Johnny let out a barely audible gasp. "Bernard?" he said. He looked up at his father. The tears forming in Johnny's eyes betrayed him.

"Stop that sniveling," his father ordered. "It's time for you to become a man." Holding out a pistol to his son, the father said, "Now finish the job we started. Prove to everybody here you're not the whining coward your Mama raised you to be."

"I can't," Johnny yelled, covering his face.

His father thrust the gun in his hands. "You kill him and kill him now, or else we'll all go to prison over this stupid little nigger."

Johnny took the gun. He deeply into Bernard's eyes. Bernard answered his gaze with an intense, silent plea for his life. Johnny brought the gun up. He fidgeted with in his hand. The sweat on Johnny's palms prevented him form gripping the gun tightly.

Mike swallowed hard. His heart beat at a pace he couldn't measure and couldn't slow down. He knew he was one trigger pull away from witnessing a cold-blooded murder. The sweat, more from fear than from the heat of the evening, trickled down Chandler's back. *Put the gun down.* He tried to force the young man, through sheer willpower, to do the right thing.

"Do it son," his father said. "Show me you're a man," he seethed with hate and measured fury.

The crowd remained mesmerized, so quiet that even the breeze seemed frozen in place, afraid to blow.

Johnny brought the gun up, steadying his shaking right hand with his left. He closed one eye as if to take aim, then both eyes as he resolved not to watch the death he was about to cause. Then he took a slow deep breath as a precursor to pulling the trigger.

Donnelly, I hope you're listening and ready to send in the cavalry. "No, Johnny! Stop! Put the gun down." Mike couldn't stand it anymore. Better to blow his cover than not stopping this heinous death.

Johnny lowered the gun and, surprised, snapped his head to stare at Chandler. All eyes turned to his direction. Angry rumblings permeated the mob and a couple of skinheads took a step toward him, fists balled and jaws set in anger.

"Well it looks like we've revealed two Judases in our midst," said Denny Rayfield who took his place at the head of the mess hut. Rayfield smiled a knowing smile, an unholy mix of vitriol and bemusement. "I wondered how long it would take you to reveal yourself, Mike Chandler."

Mike braced at hearing his real name.

"Gentlemen," Rayfield continued, "Mr. Chandler here is a former cop turned private detective who tried to steal more than a million dollars worth of our money."

Mike looked from side to side. Men armed with guns, pipes, and boards surrounded him, boring holes in him with steely glares and hate fueled by betrayal. There was no escape.

"Why are you here, Mr. Chandler? You wouldn't be trying to infiltrate this group of God-fearing white Americans, would you?"

The men who comprised the Board worked their way to the front of the crowd and stood in a half circle around him. "Still want to volunteer to blow up the kyke museum, Chandler?" Rickman asked with an expression on his face that looked like it was half disgust and half high humor. The other members of the Board laughed heartily and slapped each other on the shoulders.

"Up your ass," Chandler said. It wasn't an effective retort, but the only one he could think of at the moment.

A lean, blue-jean clad man with a Stars and Bars T-shirt spoke up, "Mr. Rayfield—Charlie Hudson of the Rutherford, North Carolina Klavern 336. Since this nigger lovin' piece of trash claims to be from my home state, our chapter asks to have the honor of...dealin' with him, the boy, and the nigger."

Rayfield thought for a moment. It was apparent to Chandler that as wonderful as Rayfield thought it would be to have the entire convocation witness the loyalty and dedication required to be a member of the supreme race, he didn't want them to be just that—witnesses. If these men took the three away, how was he or anyone else in the camp to know they simply didn't eject them from the compound?

He looked at the boy and then at Chandler, completely ignoring Bernard. He conferred with a group of other men congregated at the front of the mess hut, each nodding his head in agreement with something Rayfield said. "Take them away," he said. Two armed men, Hudson and an accomplice, approached. They cut Bernard loose from his bindings and, with pointed gun barrels, urged Chandler and the young Filbert boy toward the woods.

Johnny began to scream. "No! Daddy, help me. Don't let them take me away!" His father turned his back and walked toward his bunkhouse.

About fifty yards into the woods, the second Klansman pulled a compact radio from his front pocket. "KB-65 to KB Base. We have an extraction. Meet us at the dock."

Smart, take us off the compound to kill us, so no one would find the bodies on this property. He had to think of a way out.

Johnny continued to scream, and sobbed wildly. "Shut his ass up," Hudson barked. The other man took the butt of a rifle and slammed it into the base of Johnny's skull, rendering him unconscious. He grabbed Johnny back the nap of his shirt and dragged him. Now the only noise was the group's traversing through rustled leaves and underbrush.

As they neared the water, Mike's mind moved swiftly. *Where the fuck is my backup?* He nearly said it out loud. Mike thought he could probably make a move and get away, but that still left Johnny and Bernard facing death. He thought it might be better to have one person left alive to tell this story than three people no one ever saw again. He started to make his move, but before he could execute, Hudson grabbed him around the neck from behind and threw him to the ground.

Lying on top of Chandler, his weight pinning him to the ground, Hudson covered Mike's mouth. "Mr. Chandler, I don't have the time to explain this fully, but both of us," he said cranking his head in his partner's direction, "are federal agents with the ATF. Now when I fire the first shot from this rifle, you scream like a motherfucker. After the second shot, all I want is dead silence. Understand?"

Mike was still confused, his adrenaline still pumping at

full force, but he relaxed his guard somewhat at the agent's words. Hudson raised up on his knees, removing his weight from Chandler's chest. He raised his gun in the air to fire the fake shots when Mike heard the rifle crack. But Hudson hadn't fired.

At the same second, he saw an explosion of bone and flesh and blood spraying toward his face. Then he heard two more quick shots. Hudson slumped forward unblocking Mike's view. He saw the other federal agent, smoking pistol still in hand and the bodies of Johnny and Bernard lying lifeless in the leaves and dirt.

"Hudson was only half right," the agent said. "He was a federal agent. I'm a federal agent turned white patriot. Looks like you're not going to have to fake that scream after all, you piece of trash."

The agent drew closer, taking aim on Mike's head and was only about three feet away when Chandler reached for Hudson's rifle laying in the leaves beside him. He moved with the swiftness and determination of a caged animal. Before the agent knew it, Mike swatted the pistol out of his hand with the butt end of the rifle and then used the same end to smash most of the agent's teeth out. As the agent lay in the dirt, writhing in pain, his mouth bleeding horribly, Mike gathered up both weapons and ran toward the lake's shoreline.

Hearing the muted buzz of a trolling motor headed his way, he almost jumped into the water to swim to his rescuers. But in an instant, he thought better of it. *Are they here to save me or kill me?* He crouched in the high foliage near the bank, cool water gently slapping against his shoes.

The boat carried two men. They cut the motor and drifted silently apparently listening for any movement in their direction. When no one came, one of the men whispered,

"Hudson? Hudson?" Hearing no reply, the other man in the bow used hand signals to tell the motor operator to silently paddle the boat ashore.

The men gently slid out of the boat into the lake and pushed the craft into soft, sandy soil at the water's edge to anchor it until their return. When the men disappeared into the wood line, Mike made his move. He ran quickly, but he felt as if he were trudging through mud. Slinging the weapons into the boat, he reached beyond the trolling motor and tried to crank the Evinrude 350 bolted to the stern.

The engine choked without catching, but it made enough noise that Mike could hear shouting and the men running through the brush back to the boat.

Although the boat was drifting, he was still only about four yards from the shoreline, a long dive and two swimming strokes for any well-trained law enforcement officer. He pulled the rope again–still no power. The two men hit the water running and screaming for him to stop. Instead of swimming, they took long, goosestep strides into the waist-deep lake, reaching for the aluminum boat. One grasped the lip of the outer hull just as Mike pulled the rope a third time with blind fury. The engine caught and he bounded away like a projectile across the lake leaving them behind. He didn't look back until he reached the opposite shoreline.

Sam Morton

Chapter Thirteen

"Tucker, if I get my hands around your neck, I'm gonna choke the fuckin' life outta you." Mike's voice in the telephone receiver was ice cold and white-hot at the same time.

He had ditched the johnboat and weapons on the far side of the lake across from the compound. Not knowing whom he could trust, he headed for the interstate and hitched a ride with a trucker all the way to Pigeon Forge. On the road, he hit up a cash machine. It only allowed him three hundred dollars, but he could make due until he was safe.

After leaving the trucker and giving him fifty dollars for his trouble, Mike checked into an inexpensive motel deposited among the town's outlet malls. Across the street from his room, he could see the orange colored roof of one of the most frequented malls, and he heard the constant flutter of rotors as two blocks down, an industrious pilot offered tourists helicopter rides for ten dollars.

He wanted to call Max. He knew someone from the Bureau would tell her about the incident at the camp. He knew, or hoped at least, she would be worried. But he had to call the Bureau first. He had to find out why they almost got him killed and what kind of incompetents he was dealing with. Once he settled in, he decided to call Tucker.

"I swear to God, Tucker you guys could screw up a wet dream," Mike screamed into the phone. " You sent me into a camp full of gun-toting idiots. You sent in a group of people ostensibly to watch my back, which, by the way, you neglected to tell me, so I assume they were there to spy on me as well. Then, at least one member of that group turns out to be a card-carrying, cold-blooded member of the unit you wanted me to infiltrate. So what the hell is your problem?"

"Calm down, Mike," Tucker intoned with a vocal balm.

"Calm," he yelled. "This is calm, you double-breasted government asshole. If I hadn't calmed down before I called you, the freakin' phone would be melting in your hand about now."

Mike could hear himself panting with deep breaths of anger. His cheeks were hot, flushed with blood and adrenaline.

"Mike we need you to come in–back to D.C.," Tucker said.

"Not on your life, pal. No way!"

"Mike it's not safe out there. These guys have better equipment than we do. They probably found out before we did that you used your card at an ATM in Jacksonborough at 3:58 this morning."

Tucker continued methodically, "They may even know that you're calling from the motel Mas El Grande in Pigeon Forge. And with the contacts they have, you might be dead before this phone call is over."

"You may be right," Mike said. His voice was defensive, "But I'll get out of here and take my own chances before I put my life in the hands of a bunch of dumb shits like you."

There was a long pause as if Tucker was measuring what to say next. "Hold on a minute, Mike," he finally said. He heard Tucker's hand go over the mouthpiece of the phone and then a muted, nearly inaudible conversation. From the voice inflections and volume he could manage to hear, it sounded like Tucker was asking someone questions. In more muffled tones farther away he could hear a response. Chandler waited him out for what seemed like an eternity. He was almost ready to hang up the receiver when Tucker finally spoke.

"Mike, I didn't want to tell you this over the phone, but they've got Max."

Mike felt his head swim. He flexed his arm to catch himself, preventing his sideways fall onto the bed. His stomach tightened immediately and a bitter metallic taste formed in his mouth.

"What happened?" he asked with a tired and defeated voice

"We got an e-mail from someone calling himself the Prince of Light. He said he had the doc and if we wanted to see her alive, we had to turn you over to them."

"Have you had any contact with them?" Chandler asked, squeezing his temples with the thumb and forefinger of his right hand. He tried to keep from vomiting. He closed his eyes but he only saw a searing white light.

Mike's mind immediately went to the cell phone call and message he left from the compound. If the Klan security people there had any sort of tracing technology, he could've led them right to Max's doorstep. He felt the bile rise in his throat.

"We checked the lab and Amanda's school. Neither one showed up today. Max hasn't answered any of our beeps. We sent a couple of agents to her house and found Amanda just coming to. Looks like they used chloroform."

Oh God! Mike felt his throat close.

"We canvassed her neighbors," Tucker said. "One old guy said he saw a white exterminating van backed up to her garage about 6:20 this morning when he was getting his paper. He gave us what he thought the name was on the truck. But it doesn't exist and we can't find anything close to it, so we're assuming that's how they got her."

Mike tried to think, tried to let it all sink in. Max and Amanda weren't part of this equation. They weren't supposed to get hurt. Inside himself he could smell Max's hair and a hint of perfume she wore. He felt little Amanda's innocent, trusting hand in his as he imagined them walking in the Smithsonian. Then he shuddered as a curtain of black descended on his vision.

It didn't make sense, but it made *perfect* sense. *I have information that could put this whole organization away. And the only way to stop me from conveying that information is to catch me and kill me.*

Mike not only knew their secret about the silver, but about how they had arranged for Bennigan's murder. He'd been to their secret training camp and learned first hand about their strategies for what they believed to be an impending race war. He had witnessed what had happened to Bernard and Johnny. Even if the testimony he could offer was only circumstantial, the media would play this story out to the hilt and that would expose, and therefore destroy, the organization. They could not afford to have that happen.

"I'm coming in," Mike finally said.

"We'll send a car to take you to the airport and fly you straight here on a bureau plane. Then–"

"I want to be part of this solution, Tucker," Mike interrupted. "Don't even think about any of that house arrest, witness protection bullshit. You meet with anybody, and I'm included. Understand?"

"I understand," Tucker replied. "We've got to hurry. The e-mail said we had only seventy-two hours to respond to them with you in our hands and we've already burned twenty-six.

I'm afraid if we don't do as they say..." His voice trailed off. He knew Mike understood the implication.

"Tell whoever you're sending to step on it. I'll be outside in the parking lot."

Mike walked into the conference room, his deliberate strides indicating his readiness for action. Tucker and the other agents were waiting stone-faced, thick portfolios perched in front of them. All of them looked as if they'd slept in their clothes and had been up most of the night strategizing. Mike realized that, although they might not have the emotional investment he did with Max and Amanda, Max was still a fellow agent and they'd do anything to get her out alive.

"They want us to turn you over to them," Tucker said.

The bold statement struck Mike right between the eyes, not because he was unwilling to give his life for Max's, but because it was so direct. The meeting began with no preliminaries, no announcements, no agenda; just Tucker's direct, stark declaratory sentence. "Fine with me. Anything to get Max out."

"Obviously we're not going to just hand you over. They'd kill both of you," Tucker said.

"I agree." Mike said, outwardly calm, a circumstance he felt was as remarkable as rewarding. *Max would be proud of me.* "So what's your plan?"

"Before we proceed with that, we need to get some information from you regarding your relationship with Dr. Sheldon," piped in an agent Mike had never seen before. He let the word "relationship" drip off his lips with contempt. The agent was a honey-tongued Southerner with a politically correct drawl, soft but educated and businesslike. Tufts of gray hair at his temples accented his well-tanned face. He looked as if he spent his weekends sailing out of Baltimore Harbor entertaining friends from inside the beltway.

"Perhaps, you're aware that Dr. Sheldon's relationship with you was a direct violation of Bureau policy. And should she make it out of this situation intact, she may still face disciplinary action–severe disciplinary action," he added, leaning forward and placing his forearms on the conference room table, for extra emphasis.

The agent sat back in his chair, crossed his legs, and wrapped his entwined fingers around his kneecap as he continued with his elaborate dressing down of Mike. "Be that as it may, because we weren't aware of your, ah...friendship," he said gesturing to the agents assembled around the table, "we've been flyin' a little blind. We don't know the extent of your relationship. We don't know what the kidnappers know of it beyond the fact that it exists. And without that knowledge, we don't know how that impacts the dynamics of the situation."

Mike wanted to grab the pompous bastard around the throat and rip his windpipe out. He fought terribly to remain in control of his anger. Max was in real mortal danger, and this guy wanted to dock her pay for going out on a dinner date.

The other agents around the table appeared tense. From their previous prep work with Mike, they knew how sharp-tongued and abrasive he could be. But Mike, realizing the task at hand, neither wanted to disappoint the agents nor further delay getting Max out of danger, and decided a battle of wits with someone who obviously enjoyed control and the sound of his own voice was not in order.

"Sir, I realize our relationship was an error in judgment, given the circumstances. But the responsibility for it is mine." The man started to protest, but Mike threw up his hand and cut him off still wanting to deflate the man's ego. "And even if you don't agree, whatever authority you wish to exert at this point is moot if we don't get her out. I'm sure you'll agree that there will be plenty of time to discuss punishments and responsibilities after we get Max out alive." Mike then proceeded to give the agents the information they needed.

Chapter Fourteen

After he finished his debriefing with the agents, Mike asked to see Amanda. Donnelly offered him an agency car, but Mike declined opting for a taxi instead of having to maneuver the D.C. traffic and the unfamiliar rural roads to the Sheldon household in Falls Church.

As he got out of the cab and paid the fare, he was impressed with the security around the house. He also felt angry that the Bureau hadn't provided them this same protection from the beginning of the operation. But they couldn't have predicted this, he thought.

He showed his identification to the agent at the end of the driveway and again to the agent at the door. Donnelly called ahead to clear the visit with them. A female officer greeted Mike as he entered the house.

"Hello, Mr. Chandler. I'm Beth Campbell, one of the victim's advocates with the sheriff's office here."

He shook the officer's hand weakly and, releasing his grip, asked, "How's Amanda holding up?"

"She's a brave little girl," Campbell said. "Personally I think she's terrified, as anyone would be in a situation like this, but she's trying to be strong."

"Is there anyone with her?"

"A colleague of mine right now. Her Aunt Sally, Dr. Sheldon's sister, flew in from Chicago a few hours after the

Bureau called her, but she's been up about 40 hours straight now, so my partner and I made her get some sleep. I think she finally passed out from exhaustion about an hour ago."

"Can I see Amanda?" Mike asked peering around the officer's shoulder toward the den.

"Sure. She's asked for you. I wish I could give you some advice on what to say or not to say. Just be gentle."

Mike walked into the den. Amanda sat on the couch by the fireplace, a long tee shirt pulled down over her knees and ankles, her knees tucked under her chin. She was rocking slowly back and forth, as if trying to exorcise the pain of her mother's kidnapping, looking as if she were playing the scene over and over in her head. Her eyes were rimmed with red and her mouth slightly swollen, her lips a deep berry color, a reaction, Mike surmised, to the chloroform.

She looked up, apparently sensing someone's presence in the room. When she saw that someone was Mike, she got up from the couch and melted into his arms sobbing. "Please save her Mr. Mike. Please..." she begged.

"This is the first time I've seen her cry," Campbell mouthed silently behind Amanda's back.

He felt the little girl's tears moisten his shirt. Around his neck he felt her grip, a desperate grasp at the only connection she had, at this moment, to the mother she loved so much.

Mike wedged his face against Amanda's neck and he sobbed, too. Their tears mingled. He took her face in the palms of his hands. He placed his forehead against hers. Both still crying, both snuffling and heaving with despair, Mike choked out his words, a simple pledge. "I'll bring her back to you Amanda. I swear."

They spoke not another word. He held Amanda tightly, attempting through his embrace alone to tell her how much he loved Max, how he wanted nothing more than to bring her mother home and whisk them both away to safety. Amanda loosened her grasp and her limbs went limp, but she alternately snuffled and heaved as she held on to him. He could only imagine the horrific images that swept through her five-year-old mind.

"*Shhh*...baby," he said in a low voice that he hoped comforted her. "Everything's going to be fine."

He held her for almost an hour, rocking her in his arms and brushing her long straight locks away from her face. Twice she jerked, and Mike knew she must have been fading toward sleep, only to be snatched back awake by nightmare figures that, unfortunately, were all too real. At last she fell asleep in his arms.

He held Amanda long enough for her to go into a deep sleep before he laid her in her bed under the careful watch of Beth Campbell. He pulled a soft cool sheet up to her chin and she rolled to her side grasping the silky band of cloth that outlined her comforter. Mike looked at her lovingly and swept her hair back, away from her forehead and behind her ear, stroking her as if the tender touch of his hand would soothe her fears. But he knew it would not.

"I've got to go," he told Campbell, making a quick turn on his heels.

"What if she wakes up asking for you?" Campbell asked nodding her head toward Amanda's bed.

"Tell her I've gone to get her mommy and I won't come back without her."

Chapter Fifteen

Mike didn't need the FBI to tell him that it was he, not Max, the Brotherhood wanted. He also realized that if they were smart enough to kidnap her, they would be thorough enough to find a way to contact him. He decided to return to his hotel room and wait. It was not a long one.

The envelope was left lying on the front desk, the clerk said. Awfully lucky someone found it; could've gotten lost; could've been thrown away, lying there with just the name "Mike Chandler" scribbled on it, barely legible. No room number, just the name, the clerk said with slightest hint of expecting a tip.

Mike tore into the envelope and peeled out its contents. The note was to the point. "Be waiting near the dumpster behind the hotel restaurant at 3:00 a.m. Wear black shirt and jeans. Anyone else besides you there and she's dead."

Mike stood in the lobby and read the note again and again. He was oblivious to the comings and goings of the people around him. All motion and sound stopped, and his ears rang with the incessant white noise of disbelief.

He tried to imagine the hands that typed the note. He tried hard to put a face with the image in his mind, someone visible, someone tangible, someone on whom he could focus his hate and anger, but he couldn't do it.

For hours he walked the streets around D.C., trying to

figure out a plan in his mind. In the span of a minute he conjured up scenes of a daring rescue in which he saved Max and then swung to the opposite scenario in which he failed miserably. He replayed the scene in his head, pacing the sidewalks while the stinging bile rose and fell in his throat and the acrid odor of revenge burned his nostrils.

Mike knew if he returned to his hotel room, he wouldn't be able to resist answering his telephone, jumping with a start each time it rang, hoping it would be the kidnappers with other instructions. His logic told him they wouldn't call. They gave him clear instructions. There would be no phone call or other communication from them. But logic didn't rule him just now, and he realized it.

He knew the FBI would call. Agents were probably falling all over themselves trying to find him now. He couldn't risk contacting them either. They'd want the note and the envelope to fingerprint it. They'd insist on having a man take his place at the dumpster or at least wiring Mike up with electronics to trace his movements or transmit his conversations. *No, the FBI screwed this up to the point it is now. No more. I'm on my own.*

Mike returned to his hotel room around 10:00 p.m. He decided a preemptive strike was in order to keep the feds at bay. He called Tucker at home. "David, this is Mike Chandler."

"Mike, where've you been all day? We've been trying to find you since lunch."

"I know. I'm sorry. I've been walking the streets thinking about this whole thing. I think I have a plan figured out," he lied. "Could we all get back together in your conference room at 7:00 sharp tomorrow morning?"

"Why so early?"

"Shit, David, I got a personal stake in this. I can come down right now if you want to round everybody up..."

"No, no. I'll call everybody who's looking for your ass and tell them to go home and get some sleep."

Any other time Mike would have cracked at least a small smile of satisfaction at his own craftiness, but not today, not under these circumstances. "You do that. I'll see you at 7:00."

He placed another call to Jason Dilworth. He had waited intentionally to call this late. While he no longer questioned Dilworth's motives in providing information to the FBI, he wondered whether the man was truly prepared to take action, to live up to his vow to bring down the Board. The men spoke.

"Oh my God, Mike. No, I hadn't heard," Dilworth said, his voice almost inaudible with concern. "What do we need to do?" It did not escape Mike's attention that he had said *we*.

"Do you have any idea where they might have taken her?"

"I remember a house in rural Virginia where we met often. It's a fair assumption that's where they're holding her."

"I'll need weapons. I'm short on time. There's no way I…" Mike let his voice trail off.

"Don't worry. I'll take care of that. It's a certainty we'll need them."

"Look, Jason. I can't ask you–" Dilworth cut him off.

"Save the sentimentality for later. Time's of the essence."

Mike hoped his silence conveyed his gratitude. They made the necessary arrangements. And now all that was left to do was to wait.

When Mike hung up the phone, he turned off its ringer and headed straight for the shower. His every move seemed robotic, in slow motion. He shaved without turning his face. He showered without moving, simply letting hot water stream over his muscles taut with nerves and fear and rage.

Mike sat naked in his room with the lights off. He tried to fine-tune his primal senses. Where he was going, he couldn't afford to be less than full on. He needed every survival instinct at top dead center. He tried to control his breathing and thus focus his anger.

At 2:30, he dressed. Then he paced.

At 2:45, he left his room, walked with deliberation down the corridor, and entered the stairwell. He barely noticed that it smelled of concrete and stale cleaning solvents. He concentrated more on the weight of his feet, which at the moment and with each step downward, felt immense.

Outside the hotel, a warm breeze washed over him. Distant traffic noise barely registered. As he walked toward the dumpster, he was hit with the stench of rotting, discarded food and soured wine, the residue of fine dining. He noticed the streetlight above had been shattered. He stood awash in the shadows.

From behind the dumpster, a silhouette emerged, arm outstretched, gun in hand. Mike started and then saw it was Dilworth. "Know how to use a 9mm?" Dilworth asked.

"Yes," Mike said while pulling back the automatic weapon's slide, tilting the gun, and using what light was available to make sure he had a round chambered.

Dilworth handed him two extra clips and a handful of loose bullets. "These clips only hold ten rounds each, and I've divided a box of ammo between us so you have twenty-five rounds and I have twenty-five. Think that'll do?"

"I hope so," Mike said, breathing slowly and looking directly into Dilworth's eyes. "But if not, we'll use the guns to shoot our way in and I'll kill the bastards with my bare hands if I have to."

"Mike, I know getting Dr. Sheldon out is your primary

objective, but this could actually yield bigger results than you can imagine."

Mike was confused. He had been, and remained, so focused on rescuing Max that he hadn't thought of anything else. His was a narrow strategy, a surgical strike to get in, get Max, and get out. "What do you mean?"

"If I'm right, they are holding Max at Preston House, an estate belonging to Truman Wise. That's where the Board meets and determines its strategy. That's where it selects its targets and debates the merits of pursuing different projects that impact minorities." Dilworth stopped waiting for some of his information to sink in. Then he continued. "It's also where Truman keeps all the Board's records. No duplicates are allowed. Everything original is there and he keeps it locked away."

Mike rocked back on his heels and whistled a long, single descending tone, stunned by the implications of this new information. "Do you know where they are? Have you seen them?"

"Yes," Dilworth said. "He keeps everything in a room in his basement right off the main room where we used to meet. It's all there–membership records; financial records; lists of judges, political officials, cops, and anybody else on their payroll; minutes of our meetings; planning documents for riots, assaults, or even murders the Board orchestrated. It's all there."

"This could sink this whole organization. It would break everything wide open. Do Donnelly and the other agents know about this?"

"Yes, they know. If they didn't mention it to you, I'm sure it's because they never thought you'd have reason or opportunity to go to Truman's house."

"True," Mike said, his thoughts racing. He was

readjusting his strategy as fast as he processed the information Dilworth just delivered. Dilworth apparently sensed that.

"Why don't you concentrate on getting us in and getting Max out safely? I'll handle getting what evidence we need. I know where to look and how it's arranged. It's a logical plan."

"Oh, I know it is," Mike said, "but I can't ask you to go in there and risk your life." Mike winced straining to find the right words. "I know we have to bring these people to justice, but I made a decision and a promise to a little girl to bring her mother home. That's my objective and that's what I have to do. If I get the chance to get to the room, I will."

"I'm going with you, Mike," Dilworth said with finality.

In the back of Mike's mind, a tornado of memories whirled, laying waste to his focus and determination. His thoughts were of Jarrod Payne, Professor Bennigan, Captain Perotti, and the other people his brash and thoughtless actions always seemed to hurt.

"Look," Mike finally said, "this isn't your fight. I really just needed the gun. I can't ask you to go in there and take a chance on getting hurt, or worse, for Max. All I ask is that you give me until tomorrow morning until you tell the FBI where I've…"

Dilworth cut him off. Reaching out with his hand to touch Mike's arm, he reassured him, "Mike, this is very much my fight. Quite frankly, you and I both know my actions on the Board have been responsible for many people dying." Dilworth looked down, seemingly ashamed.

Then he raised his head, resolute, and locked onto Mike's gaze. "Maybe you and I don't fully understand the implications of it, but this is a war, a very real race war. And in wars people have to die. That may be you and it may be me, but one way or another we're going to end this tonight."

The profundity of what Jason just said settled on Mike like a heavy weight. He knew his friend was right and he also realized from a tactical standpoint, the scope of his mission had just intensified beyond measure. He started to reply when both men heard the approach of a slow moving car. Dilworth stepped back into the shadows.

His captors were punctual. They arrived in a black four-door sedan in a city full of black four-door sedans. "Get in," said a disembodied voice from somewhere within the car's dark interior. Mike didn't move.

"Godammit, I said get in," the voice said. Mike stood fast. The man belonging to the voice, he assumed, started sliding across the back seat. From the way the car's shocks reacted, he knew the man was going to be the size of a linebacker.

The man emerged from the back seat. Mike was right. He had to be 6'5 and close to 300 pounds. The sleeves of his dark blue suit jacket were tight and too short for the man's massive arms. He pointed a fleshy finger in Mike's face and said, "Now you're going to get in that car right there or..."

As the man turned to point to the car, Mike pointed the nose of the 9mm to the arch of his foot and pulled the trigger. A garnet gush of blood accentuated by white flashes of shattered bone spattered against the pavement. The man collapsed immediately, screaming in pain, his face turning white in disbelief. "Franklin, shit! Franklin, help me!"

Mike caught a glimpse of a dark figure rushing past him and knew it was Dilworth, running to head off the other man. As the driver thrust open the door, Dilworth was there to meet him with another 9mm pointed at his head. "Stay right where you are or you'll be worse off than your friend. Now reach in slowly and hand me your weapon," Dilworth said.

Mike leaned down to the injured man, took the man's

pistol from a shoulder holster beneath his jacket and pointed the gun at his face, "Now you're going to take me to wherever you're holding Dr. Sheldon or the next bullet's going in your head, understand?"

The man panted heavily and jerked in spasms as he lay in pain. "Okay, okay. Just get me some help for my leg. Oh Jesus, you've gotta get me some help. I feel like I'm dying."

Franklin, the driver, standing in the crook of the door and looking warily at Dilworth's gun still pointed at him yelled over the top of the car. "We're not taking you anywhere, you son-of-a-bitch. You've just cost that woman her life." He tried to stare down Dilworth.

"Jason," Mike said in an even, calm tone, his gaze still directed at the man writhing at his feet, "take his wallet and toss it over here."

"What? So, now you're going to rob me, asshole?" Franklin said with a half-bemused, half-exasperated sneer as he reached slowly into his back pocket.

"Just throw me the goddamn wallet," Mike yelled.

Franklin complied and Mike rifled through its contents until he found the man's driver's license. Standing, he stared at the license and then back at the driver. Finally Mike said, "We've wasted too much time here Jason. Somebody's going to show up pretty soon." He looked at the license again. "So we're just going to waste this fat pig bleeding all over the street right here and go to Franklin's house at...let's see 4820 Palm Harbor Terrace."

The driver threw a terrified look at him as Mike glared fiercely, letting him know just how serious Mike's words were. "You got family at that address there, Franklin? Wife? Kids, maybe?" The man blinked, but remained silent. "Well, here's your option. You can take me to Dr. Sheldon or I'm going to take you to your house and make you watch while I eliminate every motherfucker in there."

Mike walked around the front of the still-running sedan and placed his nose against the driver's nose and glared into the driver's eyes. He felt the rage rise in his chest. His breathing was becoming more and more difficult to control. He uttered his words through clenched teeth, "You want to take what's important to me Franklin. Well, it's a two-way street, motherfucker. I'll even kill your mangy-ass dog in front of you before I give you the pleasure of dying, you son-of-a-bitch. So what's it going to be?"

The man hesitated for only a second before he looked away from Mike's stare, and broke down. "I'll show you where she is, man. Please, just forget you ever saw my address. Please!"

Mike regained some of his composure and backed a step away from the man. "Go drag your buddy into the back seat and let's get going then."

Franklin reached the man who was beginning to lose consciousness. "What about him," he said standing and pointing down. "He looks pretty bad."

Mike walked with deliberation around to the passenger side of the car. His sense of mission was clear. "He should have thought about that before he fucked with me. Now get him in the car."

When all four men were in the car, Dilworth said, "Preston House is about seventy-five miles outside the beltway in Virginia on the banks of the James River. It's surrounded by a lot of acreage. It's quite secure with a perimeter fence and cameras and sensors everywhere."

One of things that stuck in Mike's mind from his sessions with Max is that Americans are particularly susceptible to patterned behaviors. He took a chance that Franklin might be one such person and checked the gas gauge and tripometer on the car's dash. The gauge measured slightly less than full and the tripometer read 63 miles.

Mike glared at Franklin and said, "Drive us to where you're holding the doctor. And don't do anything stupid. My friend here knows the way. If we're not there in an hour, you and your buddy here will be rotting in a ditch on the side of the road. Got me?"

Franklin, taking steady, shallow breaths to control his panic, nodded a slow acknowledgement. He placed the car in drive, and carefully pulled back onto the road.

Chapter Sixteen

Preston House. Mike thought that even its name breathed class warfare. The main house stood framed amidst towering magnolias that bowed with the wind like a butler greeting houseguests. The house, white clapboard with glossy shutters that shimmered iridescent in the moonlight, sat against the backdrop of the levee that held the James River at bay.

Ornate wrought iron gates hinged against tall brick columns blocked off a long, crushed gravel drive on either side of which alternating juniper and red cedar trees stood like sentries. Since the property did not appear fenced in otherwise, the gate only ceremoniously kept out the unwanted and the unwashed. Mike surmised that, from Truman's perspective, the milieu of arrogance stood as sufficient warning to keep people in their places, which meant away from Preston House.

Still shielded from view by a line of trees, Franklin pulled the car within yards of the gate. Mike ordered him to stop. As an incentive for complicity, he kept the muzzle of the 9mm pressed against Franklin's temple. "How are you supposed to bring me into the house?"

Franklin nodded slightly toward the driver's side visor. "Those two remotes. The left one opens the gate up ahead. The other one works the garage door on the right side of the mansion near the carriage house."

"Put the car in park and hand me the keys. Dilworth will

243

make sure you get out nice and slow." As Mike opened the trunk, he removed the lug wrench. He instructed Franklin to drag his semi-conscious and moaning colleague to the rear of the car and place him next to the spare tire. As Franklin struggled to lift the man, Mike began a wide-arching baseball swing and caught him in the base of the skull knocking him unconscious.

Both men fell like limp sacks of flour into the trunk well. Mike and Dilworth lifted their legs over. Mike tore off part of Franklin's shirt and ripped it in half. Then he closed the trunk lid.

"What's that for?" Dilworth asked with a curious glance at the torn shirt.

"We'll wrap them around our guns," he said, handing a piece of the torn fabric over to Dilworth. "It'll suppress the flash and the sound if we have to shoot. We'll need to keep the element of surprise as long as possible."

With the keys dangling from the lock, Mike kicked the ring breaking off the trunk key. "That way no one can get them out in a hurry," he told Dilworth.

Mike got in the driver's seat and pulled forward to the electronic gate. He pressed the button on the device above the visor and the black iron gate began its slow, melodramatic swing open. Easing his foot off the brake, he let the car roll through. "Here we go," he said to Dilworth keeping his eyes focused on the winding drive. Dilworth did not reply.

As he approached the garage, he again slowed the car and glanced at his partner. Hands shaking, Dilworth remained silent, but he nodded, acknowledging his readiness. Mike pressed the garage door opener and the door lifted with a mechanical jerk before it settled into a smooth, steady ascension.

He pulled inside, parked, and switched off the car's engine. Light flooded the garage and, except for spare auto parts, hoses and belts, it was empty. Nothingness was the one eventuality Mike had not prepared for. He was primed for an all-out assault, fisticuffs, and gun battles. The men sat in the car for a full minute and nothing happened.

Sliding the lug wrench across the seat to Dilworth, Mike said, "Take this. I'll open whatever doors we come to. You whack the hell out of whatever is on the other side of them. We'll try to save our bullets and our element of surprise as long as we can."

"All right, but be prepared to abandon that pretty quick," Dilworth advised. "I haven't been here in quite a while, but I'm sure he's got security cameras all over the place."

The men slid out of their seats, gingerly clicking the doors shut with the heel of their hands to avoid making noise. They didn't have to wait long for the initial encounter. They heard steps, and Mike motioned to Dilworth to take up his position beside the door that led from the house to the garage.

The door swung open. A large man dressed in Khaki slacks and a V-necked Hawaiian shirt stopped in his tracks. Seeing Mike standing alone on the other side of the doorway, he said, "What the hell," and turned as if to call for reinforcements. Just as he did, Dilworth swung from the side of the doorframe using his momentum to strike the man. His skull audibly cracked and he fell, face down on the floor.

The men could see a flash of bright white bone through the gash in his head that pumped scarlet fluid onto the doormat. They dragged him feet first into the garage behind the car and bound him, feet and hands, with large plastic ties they found on a shelf.

Jason and Mike re-entered the door into a laundry room.

Mike went first, gun drawn and quick-peeking around corners and walls just as he had been taught at the police academy. They made their way slowly into a kitchen lit only by a dim bulb on the range hood that cast an amber hue throughout the room. The pair stood still listening to the silence.

"Where do you think she'd be?" Mike whispered, staying alert for slight noises and shadowy movement.

Dilworth came along side him and pointed. "On the other side of the den is a staircase that leads to a basement/game room kind of area. That's where we used to meet. Off to each side there are a couple of rooms where she could be. The stairs are the only way in or out, so it's probably safe to assume she's down there, if she's here."

The pair inched through the darkened den, careful not to make noise or otherwise make their presence known. Mike could see light through the opening at the top of the staircase. He stopped and turned toward Dilworth, placing his index finger over his lips and pointing to his ear to indicate he wanted to listen first before they descended the steps. Dilworth nodded his understanding.

After a minute with no sound except that of their own measured breathing, Mike took the first step. He ducked to get his body beneath the top of the stairs as quickly as possible to properly survey the room. A small lamp provided the only light, but it was enough for Mike to see that no one was in the room. His heart pounded even louder and he worried about how many more guards they might have to overcome.

Dilworth came down the staircase right behind him, noting the pictures on the wall, a veritable human genome of Virginia aristocracy, with all the birthrights of white supremacy appertaining thereto.

"If she was here, wouldn't they leave a guard or

something?" Mike asked in a voice just above a whisper.

"Not if she's locked in, or maybe handcuffed to something in the room."

"Or if maybe somebody's got a gun to her head just itching to blow her brains out," said a third, disembodied voice from a far darkened corner of the room. Drawing their weapons at the same time, both Mike and Dilworth swung in the direction of the voice. Emerging from the shadow, Rickman walked with a slow and awkward gate, pushing in front of him a terrified Max Sheldon, her chaffed wrists secured in front of her by rough, abrasive rope and duct tape placed over her mouth.

Mike could see her chest heaving almost as if she were about to hyperventilate. A few thin strands of her hair were caught in the tape over her mouth and tugged painfully. From behind her right shoulder, Rickman pressed his chin snuggly against her neck. He held his pistol just below her right ear. It dangled at a precarious, but still very deadly angle. A man stood behind them in the shadows.

Dilworth leaned back toward Mike from behind. "That's Truman," he whispered.

"Put your guns down," Rickman said.

Nobody moved. Everything in the room from the men to the guns to the dust particles in the air remained still and silent.

"I said, put the guns down," Rickman repeated.

Mike's eyes met with Max's and he seemed to detect in them relief, pleading, and terror in equal measure. "Let her go and I'll put down my gun," Mike said trying to stare down Rickman.

The man brought his gun up perpendicular with Max's temple, its barrel flush with her skin. He cocked the hammer, two clicks of evil intent. He sneered and with his mouth bent and cruel said, "I'm going to fire if you don't–"

Immediately Mike thrust his weapon onto the chair in front of him. He threw his hands in the air, palms facing outward. "Okay, okay," he said, his voice pitched a half-octave higher, urgent and tense.

Dilworth followed suit. He tossed his weapon aside. His shoulders shrugged and his back looked bent in the manner of someone desperate and defeated.

Truman stepped out of the shadows and retrieved both guns. He was a thin man with a pointed nose and a strong jaw, the picture of landed gentry. His khaki pants and blue shirt with its French cuffs were pressed and creased. With the impression he made with his appearance, he could easily have been a corporate CEO. But his eyes and the hateful tone of his voice betrayed the monster inside him.

"Well, if it isn't our old chum Jason Dilworth," Truman said as he placed both pistols in the front waistband of his pants. The grips protruded out and he looked like a ridiculous parody of a Wild West cowboy. "I suppose we should thank you, Doctor, for bringing Mr. Chandler to us. You've furthered your service to the Cause."

For an instant, Mike felt his face flush with anger. His muscles, already taunt, tightened even further. Had he been betrayed? Had Dilworth delivered him and Max to their deaths? Dilworth turned his head over his shoulder and shook it slowly as if he had anticipated Mike's uncertainty. With one glimpse, Mike knew the doctor had not sold him out. He saw it in Dilworth's eyes. He felt it deep within him, and somewhere in the back of his brain, even amid everything happening in this confusing, tense, surreal, mess of reality, he felt remorse for doubting this man.

Dilworth turned his head back to look at Truman. With almost imperceptible motion, he craned his wrist behind his back. He extended his index finger and caught Mike's attention. Mike looked and saw the lug wrench cinched snugly under Dilworth's belt in the small of his back.

Truman had a conceited, gratuitous grin on his face. It was a cocky little smile that emoted his tainted, sinister sense of victory. He turned to say something to Rickman and Rickman angled his head slightly to receive the message. It was the opening Dilworth had waited for.

Mike watched the scene play out in slow motion before him. As the two men's eyes turned from him, Dilworth's frame exploded with motion. He pulled the lug wrench from his belt, stepped forward with one foot like a batter at home plate, and, with all his might, he drove the broad end of the wrench into Truman's skull.

Mike winced as the solid, wet crack of bone reached his ears. Truman never knew what hit him. The musculature in his face seemed to collapse, and what had been a nose and lips and eyelids, imploded into a hanging mass of barely distinguishable flesh with no life, no feeling. Truman hung motionless, bent over for the slightest moment before he fell, dead, in a heap on the floor.

The move most definitely took Rickman by surprise if Mike could gauge by the look on his face. His eyes grew wide and his attention diverted from Max to watch the horror in front of him, a mistake while trying to hold a trained FBI agent hostage. Max's survival instincts and training kicked in. She used the point of her elbow to deliver a rib-crunching blow to Rickman's midsection. When he bent at the waist gasping for air, she turned slightly and drove her kneecap into his nose.

She broke free and ran toward Mike who had already begun running toward her, his arms open, ready to embrace her and literally pull her from Rickman's grip.

"Get her out of here," screamed Dilworth as he pivoted on his heel to face Rickman who, while still writhing on the floor with blood flowing freely from his nose onto his shirt, still held the pistol in his right hand.

Dilworth raised the lug wrench above his head, clutching it with both hands, resolute in his decision to deliver the same deathblow to Rickman that he did to Truman. But Rickman was too quick. He rolled to his left and brought his pistol up. Without hesitating, he fired.

The shot caught Dilworth directly in the middle of his chest.

Chapter Seventeen

Mike nearly lifted Max off the ground as he pushed her up the stairs out of danger. She reached for his arm and called after him as he turned and ran back down the staircase. He could see Dilworth lying face down on the carpeted floor, choking shallow, but heaving, breaths. He started toward him intending to pick him up and get him up the stairs and back out to the car, but he stopped short as he saw Rickman pulling himself up from the floor.

"You might as well get down there with him, you nigger lovin' piece of trash," Rickman said, his voice strained and labored from the force of the blows Max dealt him. Rickman pointed the gun at Mike's head, but the gun rose and fell with each breath Rickman drew.

"Your hand's shaking, Rickman," Mike said defying the order to get on the ground.

Rickman sneered. "It's still steady enough to kill you."

"Are you sure of that?" Mike was afraid, but enraged. He knew Dilworth was either dead or would be soon. The man now threatening him had all intentions of killing Max. The time for reason and negotiation was over. One of them had to die. Mike, determined that it would not be his day to meet death, took a step toward Rickman.

"I said, are you sure? What I mean is, if you're not sure," eyes wide, Mike gestured, both hands outspread and his bottom lip stuck out as if in mock thoughtful consideration, "then you better not pull that trigger."

Rickman pulled the gun up and tried to steady his aim. Mike stopped and held his ground. "There's enough distance between you and me to crack off one shot, Rickman, so you better make it count. I swear to you, I'll get to you before you get off another round and you'll be dead before you know it."

Rickman took a breath and held it. Mike saw his finger tightening around the trigger and braced himself. But before Rickman pulled the trigger, Max screamed from the top of the stairs, "Mike, duck!"

Mike whirled around to see Max armed and crouched in a three-point shooter's stance, her wrist, now devoid of its rope binding, braced against the handrail on the stairs. But Rickman was a millisecond swifter. He moved his gun barrel a half-inch to the left and fired over Mike's shoulder. Max rebounded against the wall, a flow of crimson blossoming against her sweatshirt just below her right collarbone. She collapsed in a heap on the stairs.

Mike bellowed a low and guttural, "No!" as he leaped at Rickman. He felt as if reaching him took forever. Rickman didn't see the attack until it was too late and he had no time to recover.

Mike dropped his upper body. Like a linebacker, he drove the crown of his head into Rickman's sternum.

Rickman dropped the pistol.

Mike rolled off and prepared to tackle the man again.

Rickman scrambled to find his lost gun. Confused, he searched the floor.

Mike drove his knee into the side of his head.

Rickman lay dazed, momentarily.

Mike sensed the kill. He felt like an animal and the

wounded, immobilized heap of flesh at his feet became his prey. He knew he must finish this job quickly. The woman he loved and the man he had befriended were lying wounded, possibly dead.

Suddenly, Rickman raised up on all fours, feebly trying to get to his feet.

Mike drew back his leg and punted through the man's ribs, flipping him onto his back and causing him to gasp for breath like a landed fish. He straddled Rickman's chest. No weapon would cheapen his triumph by taking his enemy in ambush. He would beat Rickman to death looking the man in the eyes as he passed from this world into hell.

With his right hand he clasped Rickman's throat until the man's face turned purplish-red. He drew back his left fist and, like a piston, delivered one cartilage-crushing blow after the next to Rickman's face until he fell fully unconscious.

Mike raised his hand again, his fist still clenched in white rage. He prepared to strike the man one last time when he felt gentle pressure on his shoulder.

"Mike. That's enough...Mike. Mike!"

He turned to look over his shoulder. Max stood behind him, her shirt crimson-stained and her face pale, but otherwise all right. Mike stood, releasing Rickman's head and allowing it to fall limp against the carpeted floor. He embraced Max.

"I thought Rickman had killed you," he said, trying to stop the tears running down his cheeks. He buried his face in the crook of her neck. Max held him tightly against her breast as wet teardrops coursed in small rivulets mingling with the blood on the front of her shirt.

"It's okay," she said. "He just grazed my shoulder." Then Mike felt her shudder as if she had jolted back to reality.

"We have to get Dilworth and get out of here," she said,

her voice tense and near panic and she released her hold on Mike. They both leaned down where Jason Dilworth lay on the carpet, his breaths coming in shallow and rapid puffs.

Mike put his hand on his friend's shoulder. "Jason. Do you think you can walk? We need to get you out of here."

Dilworth kept his eyes closed, reaching up a bloodstained hand and touching Mike on the forearm. He said something barely audible, his voice weak. Mike leaned in closer.

"What? What did you say, Jason?"

"The room, the one I told you about. It's there behind the stairwell," Dilworth said in a raspy whisper.

Mike could see the color drain from his friend's face and he knew his life was slipping away. "Help me, Max. We've got to get him to a hospital." He again felt hot tears welling up in his eyes and his vision blurred as he tried to blink them away.

Max slid her arms beneath Dilworth's shoulders. His head rolled to one side and his eyes transfixed on Mike's. In his gaze Mike sensed a mixture of emotions–remorse for Dilworth's racist past, the feeling of grace that accompanies sins forgiven, and well-earned pride in his last few hours of heroism.

"Get them. Don't let them win," he said. He swallowed and blinked, fighting death for one more moment of lucidity. He looked at Max, "Please, Max. Tell my grandson...tell him I love him." Jason Dilworth shut his eyes, inhaled deeply, and let go of the last breath he would ever take.

Mike let Jason's body descend slowly back onto the carpet. For a few moments, neither he nor Max said anything. Silence draped the room, the only noise a buzz from one of the fluorescent lights overhead. The entire basement smelled of gunpowder, sweat, blood, and death. Mike was physically and emotionally exhausted and his thoughts seemed to be seized and suspended for the moment.

Finally, Max placed a tender hand on his shoulder as he hung his head. "Why don't I call Donnelly and get some people over here, Mike. I need to get this shoulder wound looked at, but we can take a look at that room while we're waiting on help to arrive," she said in a gentle, low voice. She seemed to realize his fatigue and confusion.

Mike nodded his head and rose in slow motion from one knee to make his way over to the room behind the stairwell. The door was shut, and given the room's purported contents, Mike believed he might have to force it open, but it was unlocked.

He swung open the door and felt along the inside wall for a light switch. Not knowing what the light might reveal, he halfway expected to see something magnificent, a shrine, the holy of holies for the white supremacist movement.

Mike found the switch about and flicked it on. The light revealed no shrine. It was utilitarian—four walls lined with lateral files. He walked in, taking slow, tentative steps. Not quite sure where to begin, or even what he was looking for, he selected a middle drawer of a cabinet to his right. It contained neat rows of hanging files as if it were in any other office file room.

But the labels on the folders were intriguing. He saw alphabetical listings, by state, of klan membership rosters. In each folder sat a floppy disk and a printout of each klavern's most up-to-date rolls.

Max came in the room behind him. "I got Donnelly on his cell phone. He wanted me to give him a full briefing, I think, but I told him just to get somebody here and we'd explain it all." She had tucked the pistol she had aimed at Rickman in the waistband of her pants. With that, her tousled hair, the smell of sweat, and the crimson bloodstain that adorned her shirt, Mike thought she looked like a grizzled police veteran rather than a FBI-trained psychologist.

Mike nodded his head at the open file drawer. "Looks like Jason was right," he said. Max's eyes grew wide as she looked over his shoulder at the file in his hand. He opened another drawer and then another, methodically picking his way through, but as a former policeman, he knew he was tampering with evidence, and he didn't want to disturb it. He and Max saw labels that read "Oklahoma City" and "Alan Berg." There were dossiers on almost every leader of note who identified himself with the Aryan movement. But Mike's eyes, and heart, stopped when he spotted a file labeled "Parris Bennigan."

His eyes shifted toward Max's as he gingerly, almost reverently, plucked it from the drawer. In it he found a summary of who had contacted the professor about finding the lost silver and how they had accomplished that. The Board had documented its efforts to locate Bennigan after he disappeared, and a reference to Henry Stearns that identified him as a member of a South Carolina Klan organization stood out in the summary. Mike spied his own name a few sentences later.

After scanning the summary, he and Max saw what appeared to be an old letter in the file. It had been placed in a protective jacket, one like state archives offices use. The writing on the letter was visible through the jacket.

Max gasped. "My God, Mike. Do you realize what that is?" she said.

Mike knew. "Yes. It's the letter from that Union soldier Stearns told me about," he said flatly. His mouth was dry as he pulled the letter and its jacket from the file.

* * *

March 11, 1864

My dearest Sarah,

It is my fondest hope that you and our lovely daughters are doing well and find yourselves in good health. I write to you today with a heart made heavy by guilt and remorse. I have suffered a grievous injury in battle and I fear, my love, that time on this earth for me is short.

I must confess to you, as rest assured I have to our blessed savior Jesus Christ, that I engaged in a massacre so that my compatriots and I could steal rebel silver bound for the Carolinas. I tremble at the memory of it, of causing such death without honor.

After our crimes, we stored the silver and made our way back to our encampment. That was nine days ago. Friday last, we were met in ambush along the road to the state capital. Though it was rebel guns that killed us, I am convinced their aim was guided by the Almighty as retribution for our acts.

I am the single survivor of that battle. I have deferred on all medication the doctors here have ordered so that I might, my dearest wife, confess to you and make bare my soul. Please pray for my forgiveness, and when this disastrous war is done, please notify anyone with the authority of government, whom you judge to be a disciplined and Godly man, of the whereabouts of the silver I am about to reveal.

In an opening beneath a shallow falls on the southeastern bank of Turkey Creek, one mile due west of the town of Ware Shoals, So. Carolina, my fellows and I secreted away a wagonload of silver. We dismantled and sank the wagon in the Broad River several miles north.

I beseech you, Sarah, do not contract for the recovery of the silver yourself. We have cursed it by our cowardly acts of murder and I will not further extend the sin or its consequences to you, my beloved wife, or my family. Please see to it my wishes are carried out and pray for me, my sweet.

Your loving husband,
Chas. A. Chapman

Mike held the letter in hands that trembled. Silence held still in the air while he and Max read and re-read the letter. It was, Mike thought, a love letter, a confession, and an evil text all in one.

They were so engrossed in the find that Mike almost did not notice the barely perceptible motion near the doorway. He had no time to react. Rickman had somehow regained consciousness and dragged himself, limp-footed, to the room, blocking any avenue of escape. He huffed ragged breaths and braced himself on the doorframe. Without a word or warning, he leveled his handgun at Mike's chest and fired a single round.

In slow motion, Mike saw the blue smoke coil from the gun barrel. He smelled its acrid, numbing odor as the sound of the shot deafened him to any other noise in the room. He fell to his knees and felt his chest burn and tighten. He dropped his head to see a black-tinged hole in the front of his shirt, just under the pocket that covered his heart.

Somewhere in the far reaches of his consciousness, Mike

thought he heard Max's voice. She was screaming, it seemed, but the voice sounded miles away. He felt her hand land heavy on his shoulder as she pushed him to the floor. He blinked and tried to comprehend why her arm extended beyond his face with a gun in its hand.

Then a second, even more deafening shot rang out and Rickman convulsed against the doorframe, his body braced upright and rigid by the impact of Max's deadly aimed gunfire. Mike lay face down on the floor now, his cheek flattened against the tile. The dust accumulated on the floor tickled his nostrils as he breathed in. He wanted to say something to Max, to turn his head and look at her, but his body would not cooperate and he could not understand why.

Again he thought he heard her voice, but even in its shrillness, it remained muffled and incomprehensible to him. She was crying, that much he knew. Then he heard more muted voices and the shuffling of feet. A uniformed police officer knelt and checked Mike's pulse. Another tried to gently usher Max out of the room, but she resisted. Mike could see her holding her ground. She bent down to him and stroked his hair.

It was then, when she drew close that he finally made out her words. "Don't leave me, Mike. God, please don't leave me." She sobbed and tears poured down her reddened cheeks. She squeezed his hand and, with her other hand, she stroked his hair. Then a black curtain fell over Mike's eyes.

Chapter Eighteen

Mike's return to consciousness was like a slow sun peeking over a cloudy horizon. He lay flat on a bed not much wider than his frame, a tube that felt as big as a drainpipe lodged in his throat helping him breathe. He fought the reflex to gag as he tried to remove the offensive tube, but his hands wouldn't obey his brain. He had no sense of time, of whether it was day or night, and he drifted aimlessly between a semblance of lucidity and complete unconsciousness.

When he tried to open his eyes, his eyelids flitted like moth wings, feeling weighted by pasty, half-encrusted goo. For the few seconds he was able to keep his eyes open, Mike spied through milky vision a tangle of wires and tubes and instruments that *whirred*, *hummed*, and *beeped* at regular intervals.

His chest felt on fire, his lungs full of fluid, and his throat dry and scratchy. When he tried to move, his entire frame seemed bolted to the bed. Every hair on his body ached and underscoring it all, the putrid cocktail odor of sweat, blood, antiseptic, urine, and iodine invaded his nostrils.

He continued on his anesthesia induced, soundless flight through the great expanse of nothingness when one sentence from a sweet voice speaking softly jarred his brain. "Mrs. Chandler, I'm afraid visiting hours are over. You'll have to come back tomorrow."

"Thank you," said a familiar voice in response. He knew the woman's voice, but he couldn't place it. The woman's spoke in soft, delicate tones, but her words were tinged with concern, doubt, and sadness.

Mike felt his senses awaken. He discerned the swish of her clothing as she rose to leave. He felt a gentle, loving hand brush through his hair and soft lips barely touch his forehead.

Mrs. Chandler? Who are you? I'm not married and my mother died years ago. Who are you? Mike fought to open his eyes, to make a sound, to reach out to this person, so kind, so close, and yet unknown. But in an instant she departed, his body again having failed his mind's instructions. He calmed himself and tried to think, but his synapses revolted and once again fell comatose.

When Mike next awoke, he had been moved to a private room, a bright one with a window, a television, and several arrangements of cut flowers. His breathing tube had been removed, though many of the wires and intravenous tubes remained connected.

He blinked, though this time his eyes opened fully. He began to scan the room and stretch his muscles as best he could while lying propped in a hospital bed. When his gaze reached the guest chair in the corner of the room, Mike felt a wide smile begin to grow across his lips. There, peeking at him above the folds of a newspaper sat his old friend and former partner, Ken McMaster.

"It's about time your lazy ass woke up," Ken said as he laid the paper on the floor beside his chair and stood up. His deep voice and strong grip were welcome and comforting for Mike as he shook his friend's hand.

"Good to see you, partner," Mike said, surprised at the sound of his own voice, raspy from the effects of the breathing tube. "How long have I been out?"

"About six days. Long enough for the accountants in this place to start worrying about how you were going to pay your bill," Ken said, laughing and jerking his thumb over his shoulder toward the nurses station outside the door.

Mike crinkled his brow, confused.

"You got no job, no insurance," Ken explained. "It was looking like somebody was gonna get screwed, you or the hospital."

"Damn, that's right," Mike said, concern showing on his face as some of the cobwebs in his brain began to clear.

Ken waved him off, lowered his resonant voice, and looked round as if hatching a conspiracy. "Don't worry about it, man. I got the number for the deputy commissioner of the FBI from Chuck Meredith. That's who called me and told me about you getting shot and what all you've been up to the last few months, by the way. Anyhow, I call the guy's office, right," Ken began to snicker, "and I told him I was the chief of staff for the general counsel of the NAACP." He began to have difficulty speaking he was laughing so hard. He put his hand up to his mouth and looked away from Mike–who was also getting amused–to regain his composure. "I told him that after all you had done to infiltrate and break up this racist organization, the NAACP would find it extremely objectionable if the FBI didn't pick up your medical bills." Ken's laugh turned to a guffaw. He bent over double and slapped the bed rails. "He just said, 'Yes, sir. We'll take care of it,' and hung up."

Mike's body was shaking. "Oh, God. Don't make me laugh. It hurts!" he said grimacing and holding his chest.

Ken blew out a breath and wiped tears from the corners of his eyes as the pair finally calmed down. "Want me to call the nurse and get you some pain killers?" he asked.

Mike shook his head and again began to drift to sleep.

He slept for another two hours before he began to stir again. "You back with me, partner?" Ken asked.

Mike cleared his throat and tried to shift his body. He had been sleeping with his head and chest raised and all of his weight and most of the blood in his body felt like it had accumulated in his lap. "I guess," he said, still groggy. "But I can't say for how long. Whatever they're giving me makes me have weird dreams," Mike said as he told Ken about the mysterious "Mrs. Chandler" incident.

"That wasn't a dream," Ken said. "That was just your friend, Max."

Mike's eyes widened and he made a weak attempt to sit upright in the bed. Pain shot through his torso and he rocked back onto the mattress, but he still strained to reach the phone. "Max! I've got to call her," he exclaimed as he pulled the handset toward him and hurriedly punched in her number. His fingers felt heavy and awkward to control. He winced and grunted as he budged his rear end closer to the edge of the bed closest to the phone.

"Uh, Mike–" Ken tried to interrupt.

Mike put up his hand and raised his finger, "Just a minute. It's ringing." His tongued thickened and slowed his speech.

After two rings, he heard a signal followed by, "We're sorry. The number you have reached has been disconnected or is no longer in service."

A confused look appeared on Mike's face. "*Hmm,*" he said more to himself than Ken, "I'll try the work number."

Ken walked back over to the side of the bed and placed his hand on Mike's forearm. "Mike. Hang up. Max isn't going to answer. She's gone."

Mike's heart skipped a beat and the hairs on his neck stood at full attention. He felt his blood pressure rise and panic begin to build. "What do you mean she's gone?"

Ken instantly reassured his friend. "She's okay. The people in charge over at the FBI just thought she should go into protective custody."

Mike felt the tension spill out of him in a rush.

"As a matter of fact, there's a guard outside your door, now," Ken continued. His voice was low and soothing now. "Max stayed with you as long as the docs would let her after you got out of surgery. She just told them she was Mrs. Chandler as a cover in case somebody tried to run her out of the room."

"So did something happen? Why has she gone into hiding now?" Mike asked. His eyes pleaded with Ken for answers.

"It took a couple of days for the FBI to comb through all the stuff you guys found. Plus, they had to draw arrest and search warrants, and that took time. But when they started rounding people up, they just wanted to be real cautious about anybody trying to get to the two of you," Ken said.

Mike became dizzy. He wanted to know more, wanted to ask Ken to tell him everything, but his energy drained and he sank back into his bed. He blinked, expending all his efforts at staying awake, but he couldn't make his eyes stay open or his brain alert.

Again he went down fighting as the warm, black curtain fell.

When Mike awoke again, Ken was gone. His eyes welled with tears as anger and frustration rose in his chest. *Was he really here or did I imagine that, too?* Mike felt like he was having a mental breakdown. He couldn't move, couldn't think, and he couldn't remember what was real and what was not.

He reached for the nurse call button and punched it repeatedly. In short order an orderly knocked as he opened and came through the door. "Can I get you something, Mr. Chandler?"

Mike didn't know exactly where to begin. His mind remained fuzzy and he couldn't decide whether he wanted more drugs to force him from consciousness or someone to help him out of his prone position so he could take some action, no matter what it was.

"Could you help me wash up? Maybe get out of the bed for just a minute?" He didn't look at the orderly as he placed his request. Depression gripped him.

"Sure I will," the orderly said in a peppy voice. "Just let me go get some towels and fresh linens. We'll change your bed for you while you're up." Mike continued to avoid the orderly's look.

The orderly pushed the door back open and called out over his shoulder as he left, "Oh, and your friend said he'd be back in a few minutes. He went to get some breakfast."

Mike raised his head, hope elusive, but now glimmering somewhere on a far horizon. "My friend?" he asked.

"Yeah, heavyset black guy."

Mike closed his eyes again, though this time with a sense of genuine relief.

"Thanks," he said as the orderly disappeared down the hall.

Ken returned just as Mike gingerly leaned over so the orderly could snap on a fresh hospital gown. He carried a coffee cup in one hand and had a thick paperback book wedged in his armpit. "Well, you sure look a lot better," he said. "You even got some color back in your face."

Mike smiled at his friend. "So do you know where Max is?" He wasted no time in returning to the last, and most important conversation he had before losing consciousness.

Ken shook his head, signaling he would respond, but he cut a glance out of the corner of his eyes toward the orderly, indicating he wanted to wait until the man finished gathering the soiled linen, wash rags, and towels and left with them first.

After the door had swung shut, Ken spoke. "No, I don't know. I'm sure she's okay, but I don't think even she saw this protective custody thing coming," he said as he set down his coffee and book on Mike's tray table. "She was real worried about you. When the ICU nurse told her to leave the other night, she came out into the waiting room. An agent was waiting on her and told her she had to go with him." Ken took a sip of his coffee and shook his head as he swallowed before continuing with his story. "She was pissed. She called him all sorts of names. It was kind of funny, actually," Ken smiled as he recounted the incident, trying to ease Mike's mind. "She went, but she made me promise I'd be here with you every day."

Mike considered this information for a moment. He was glad she was safe and touched at the news that she spent so much time at the hospital just to be near him, but he wanted to be with her. He needed to be with her. His relationship with Max was the one gem forged from this whole nightmare, and Mike did not intend to let her slip away from him.

"Think she'll call?" he finally asked Ken after a few silent moments.

"I call Meredith every day, sometimes twice if you pee or grunt or something," Ken said winking and nodding affirmatively. "I'm told he relays it to somebody else who gets the message to Max. You know these government boys, Mike. It's very CIA-ish."

Mike relaxed back into his bed. For the first time in several days, he felt something close to comfort. He had gotten cleaned up and shaved, so he felt refreshed. Ken had set his mind at ease about Max. Now he wanted to sleep. He relished it as if it were a reward for days and nights filled with nightmares and worry.

"I hate to make you watch me sleep," Mike said, his voice low and content, "but I think I'm gonna rest some."

"Fine by me. That's why I brought this," Ken said holding his book aloft so Mike could see it. "All those damn soap operas on TV make me tense. Who's pregnant with whose baby? Those people get laid way to much for those shows to be realistic," he said.

Mike smiled, adjusted his pillow, and shut his eyes.

When Mike stirred next, Ken was asleep in the chair beside the bed, his book propped open across his wide chest. *Wonder when he drifted off.* Mike shifted in the bed again, grunting at the pain that seared through his chest. The noise roused his friend.

"Hey," Ken said through a yawn. He stretched his arms, arched his back, and contorted his face trying to wake up. "Have a nice nap?"

"Yeah, I did."

For the next two hours, Ken got Mike water and snacks when he felt like eating. Caught him up on the gossip around his old office–who had been promoted or fired, who had left the department for better jobs, and who of that group couldn't handle the lack of adrenaline rushes in the "real world" and returned to police work.

"It was hard on a lot of us when the news got back about what happened in The Bahamas," Ken said.

"Really?" Mike asked, genuinely baffled. "I didn't think anybody would even care."

"Shee-it," Ken said, leaning back in his chair. "It was all anybody talked about for a solid month. There were a few of us who knew something had to be up, but most of the young guys, especially the ones who came on after you left, bought into that bullshit they put out about you when you resigned, and they thought you were guilty."

Ken looked down. "They tried to make any of us who defended you feel like we were idiots. It was all I could do some days not to punch some of them out," he said, his voice low and expression somber.

Mike waited a moment while Ken sorted through the memory. When Ken looked up, Mike said, "There's something I need to tell you about my resignation."

Mike adjusted himself in the bed, again grimacing at the pain that, at the slightest movement, shot through his torso like shards of glass. He propped the pillow behind him, settling in to tell his story. "Larry Davis called me over to the courthouse. He locked us away in one of the conference rooms. He told me we'd never find Amber."

Ken's eyes grew wide. "What? He lied to your ass, partner. She did disappear for a while, but she was back in town by the next September."

Mike's face suddenly sagged as he felt the full force of the betrayal. "Well, damn. That makes what I have to tell you even harder to say since I was such a fool."

"What is it? Just get it off your chest."

Mike took a deep breath and let out a long resigned sigh. "Davis showed me two pieces of paper. One had all of us sharing the fall. You would've been fired, Perotti reassigned, and some of the other boys demoted back into marked cars doing traffic patrol."

"And you took the other choice, then? The one where you took the heat for everybody?"

Mike nodded his head almost imperceptibly.

When Mike finished, Ken said, "And that SOB Davis just got promoted to lieutenant about three months ago. When I get back, I'm going to bust his ass, if I have to call every newspaper and television station in town."

Mike shrugged. "It's not worth it, man. You get rid of him and another jerk will just take his place. It'll be the same as when the Bahamas thing went down. Some people will believe you and some people will call you a liar and think you're crazy. Just leave him alone and maybe somebody on the street will shoot his ass one day and we'll be rid of him."

Ken didn't reply. He merely gave his friend a bemused look. "What?" Mike asked.

"You don't have any idea, do you?"

"Any idea about what?" Mike threw his hands up, palms open.

"You're a national hero, my friend. You're ugly mug has been all over the TV since last week. You've got stacks of mail from school kids, get-well cards from every ghost town and ghetto between here and Los Angeles."

"What are you *talking* about?"

Ken shook his head in exasperation like he was having to explain to a child for the hundredth time why you close a refrigerator door or turn out a light. "Maybe it's the drugs."

"Tell me!"

"Okay, see if you can follow what I'm saying here. You and Max and this Dilworth guy are responsible for breaking up the largest group of white supremacists in the world. The FBI has exhausted almost all its manpower, and damn near every police and sheriff's department who will lend them anybody, arresting people and gathering evidence. They've got over a hundred people in custody now and got warrants on at least a hundred more on everything from murder to driving with a suspended license."

Mike drew in a deep breath and whistled it out as he tried to imagine it while Ken continued with more patience.

"There have been reporters and producers talking to every last girl you ever kissed and trying to buy stories from anybody who ever talked to you. Hell, the tabloid TV people have even interviewed a couple of guys on parole you arrested, who talk about you like a guardian angel who saved them from death and destruction."

Mike raised his eyebrows. "And Max, too. They're profiling her on television?"

"Man, whatcha talkin' about? They've spotlighted her books, which are flying off the shelves, by the way; they've interviewed her neighbors and college classmates. And whew, you should've seen that ugly ass picture they found of her from high school, braces and all." Ken winced like he just drank sour milk while Mike laughed out loud while holding his side. "Seriously, Mike. The press has told the whole story–or as much of it as the FBI will carefully leak–about her kidnapping and how you and Dilworth went in to save her. They've almost given Dilworth sainthood and you and Max are hotter than any Hollywood romance."

Mike grew somber at the memory of his dead comrade. "I wish Jason hadn't died. It took a while to, you know, warm up to him," he said trying to explain to Ken exactly why he should honor the memory of an ex-Klansman, but he couldn't seem to find the words. "In the end, he was a good man."

Ken again touched his friend's arm. "I learned a long time ago that humans are complicated animals. The news magazine shows have done a good job of telling his story, even the down side."

Of all that had happened, Mike felt that Jason's story was the far more compelling one. Jason had had a sincere change of heart. Mike merely wanted to exact revenge and straighten out his life. The Board hated and killed Jason for his thoughts, his philosophy on life. They wanted Mike dead as a matter of self-preservation because he held the key to hurt them. Jason was fighting for his honor and while Mike felt honored himself to be a part of Jason's battle, he felt his own motives to be far less sacrosanct.

Jason deserved the same accolades, the same attention. The thought that he could not share in it made him sad.

Mike breathed deeply, trying to take in everything Ken had just told him. After a few moments of thought, he said, "Do you think they'll take me into protective custody, too? When I get out of here, I mean."

"I don't think there's any doubt about it. At least until after all the arrests are made and probably through the majority of the high-level trials," Ken said.

Mike sighed heavily again, looking his old partner in the eye and patting the back of his hand. "I'd just like to get on with things. You know, try to get something firm going with Max and finding a good, steady, safe job. I'd just like to start things over fresh."

"That's good, because Mike, my friend, I don't think your life will ever be the same again."

Epilogue

The double-decker tourist boat belched black smoke from its engine and the captain gave a loud blast from his horn as he backed away from the dock, the boat screws churning the tea-black waters of the sound to a muddy milk chocolate brown. Nesting cranes standing one-footed in the tidal marsh gave the captain a tired, annoyed glance as if they were all too used to the boat's intrusion.

Some of the tourists returning to Bluffton waved as Amanda rushed to the end of the dock trying to spot the dolphins arching their way up the sound behind the boat. Sometimes there were three or four that raced along beside it, their fins and backs undulating and breaking the surface to the delight of the passengers. Sometimes a single dolphin escorted the boat, a lone sentry, but a good omen for its safe return.

Max held a mug full of tea and Mike interlaced his arm in hers as they walked the beach at the end of the dock. They watched Amanda shield her eyes against the late afternoon sun in her attempt to find her marine friends.

Their fellow Daufuskie Islanders knew them as Mr. and Mrs. Steven Conrad. Officially they listed Amanda and a non-existent child as living in their household, a further ruse to thwart anyone–reporter, snoop, or foe–who might be looking for two adults and a single child who might be Mike, Max, and Amanda.

Every few weekends they even brought over a young girl from the mainland, an FBI agent's daughter who posed as "Steven Conrad's" daughter from a previous marriage. She and Amanda had grown to be friends. The girls were happy and the ruse worked, so they gladly continued the charade.

The protective arrangement had a few genuine aspects Mike relished. The "Mr. and Mrs." were real, the result of a hastily set wedding prearranged by FBI agents Mike had pestered daily. The feelings he had for Max and Amanda were not only sincere, but growing deeper every day. Given all they had been through, Mike was grateful to be with them, to love them, and protect them in his own way.

Max nuzzled her head next to Mike's shoulder and Amanda joined them on the beach. The three of them, Mike in the center, walked ankle deep in the surf. Amanda ran ahead to gather up a shell she spied tumbling in the foam before it returned to the ocean.

"This is heavenly," Max said, as she craned her neck and kissed Mike softly on the lips.

"Yeah, the way life should be," Mike said.

Most of the people arrested in the aftermath of the investigation had pleaded guilty to some charge or other. Many of the others, those with enough money to hire high-powered attorneys, had had their trials delayed. Some of the agents involved speculated one or two of the older defendants might even die before they ever saw the inside of a courtroom. But certainly the Board and its followers had been crippled. For every hundred people who expressed their gratitude to the couple, there were a distinct few who would rather see them dead.

"Mike, do you ever think things will get back to the way they were? Back to normal?"

"I hope not Doc," he said, and she gave him a curious look. "Oh, I think things will settle down, if that's what you mean. We'll be able to have regular lives. We won't have to look over our shoulders or worry about Amanda being out of our sight."

Mike stopped and grasped both her hands in his. "But you have to remember, the 'way things were' for me means I didn't have you or Amanda and I'll never, ever let that happen again." He smiled and tilted his head and began giving his wife a long, slow deep kiss.

"Oh, yuck not that again," Amanda said, rolling her eyes, yelled over the crashing waves. "Would you two, puhhleeze stop it?"

Mike pulled away from Max, grabbed Amanda, and threw her over his shoulders. She screamed in delight at the top of her lungs, competing with the sounds of the gulls screeching overhead.

The three of them were a family at last.

Meet the Author:

A Rock Hill, S.C. native and 1985 graduate of The Citadel, Sam Morton is co-author of five fiction anthologies. He is a member of The Inkplots, a group of published writers and authors active in South Carolina's vibrant literary experience.

His past occupations include a twelve-year stint as a robbery/homicide detective for the Richland County Sheriff's Department in Columbia, S.C., a ten-year career as a professional wrestler, and one long week as the blade changer on the potato cutting machine at the Frito Lay plant in Charlotte, N.C.

He is a freelance writer for a host of periodicals and an editorial consultant to a political marketing and strategy firm. He resides in Columbia with his wife, Myra, and two children, Alexey and Nikki.

Echelon Press

Publishing

Echelon Press Publishing

Celebrating Five Years of

Unique Stories

For

Exceptional Readers

2001 -2006

WWW.ECHELONPRESS.COM

Also available from Echelon Press Publishing

While the Daffodils Danced (Women's Fiction)
Cathi LaMarche

Pregnant by a married man, Cara faces the devastation of offering her child up for adoption. Having made the ultimate sacrifice, she seeks solace in her field of daffodils. But in the shadow of her pain, Cara finds a kindred spirit, forging an unbreakable friendship that sustains her through lost love and the betrayal by those she loves the most.

$15.99   ISBN 1-59080-402-3

Justice Incarnate (Women's Adventure)
Regan Black

Whoever said, "you only live once" didn't know Jaden Michaels. Attacked by an evil nobleman in 1066, her life took a dramatic detour. In the following millennium, she's lived repeatedly with one goal: eliminate the demon that preys on women and children. Now, in 2096, Jaden must fight to find the one weapon that will banish him forever.

$13.99   ISBN 1-59080-386-8

Laura's Secret (Romantic Suspense)
Shannon Greenland

Mysterious Laura Genny knows how to hide her dark past. Always wary and on the move, she accepts a lifelong dream position as a sound engineer with an international rock group. But when lead guitarist Will Burns gets too close, she must decide if love is worth the price of exposure.

$13.99   ISBN 1-59080-415-5

Operation: Stiletto (Romantic Suspense)
T.A. Ridgell

Teamed with Python, an ex-wrestler struggling to slay a multitude of inner demons, Special Agent Kendal Smart will do anything to infiltrate the wrestling culture and eradicate a deadly crime ring. Even if it means wearing skintight clothes, stilettos, and immersing herself in a bizarre, sexually overt world.

$14.49   ISBN 1-59080-393-0